{23:59}

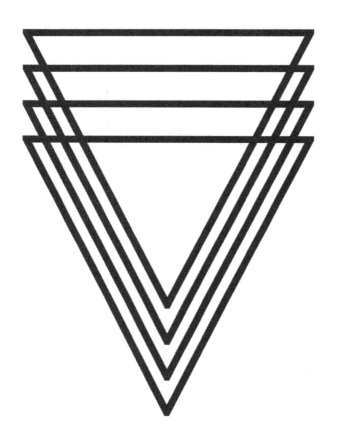

{23:59}

D. I. Richardson

ISBN: 1514294893
ISBN-13: 978-1514294895

Dedications

Dedicated to:
The monster under my bed for keeping me up at night.

"That's part of what I like about the book in some ways.
It portrays death truthfully.
You die in the middle of your life,
in the middle of a sentence."

— John Green, The Fault in Our Stars

{Chapter: **One**}

I hate Christmas. Not the holiday itself, just the confusion and frantic shopping that goes along with it. Going shopping last minute is the worst, and that's the exact kind I have to do today, Christmas Eve, which doesn't leave me a whole lot of time to shop. And the fact that I'm going with friends probably doesn't help the whole time issue either. All well, it'll get done. I'm good at getting things done in a short amount of time, ergo why I'm a straight-A student.

But I don't think it helped that a storm was supposed to be rolling in tonight. I better hope we all get home before that crap starts.

I got up from my twin-sized bed and stretched out my back, my small back. I say small because I am a pretty short teenage girl. Only a mere five-foot-one, barely five-foot-one though. But what I lack in size I make up for in brain.

I took a seat at the chair by my wooden desk and began digging in my laundry basket for a good pair of socks. I can never seem to have any good pairs just lying around my room. I always have to make things more difficult for myself by putting things away. Pfft.

"Spencer, you getting ready? Your friends are gonna be here any minute now. The mall's probably gonna close soon," my younger sister, Jordan, said from my door.

I turned and saw her poking her freckled face through the door. We all had freckled faces in this family, just more so Jordan though.

"Yeah. I'll be down in a minute. I gotta find socks," I told her, wiggling my bare foot at her.

"Okay. Well, hurry up. Taylor's coming over and she wants to see you. She misses you," Jordan stated.

I let out a small groan. "I know, I know. I don't wanna be at the mall all day either."

Jordan turned and walked back off down the hallway and down the stairs. Taylor, she's my older sister. She's 22 and lives five hours away for schooling and whatnot.

It's been a while since I saw her last since she had missed Thanksgiving with us this year. And then there's Jordan, who is only 14 years old. And then there's me. I'm in the middle at 18. I'm in college too, freshman year for me, but I stayed at home and went to a college closer to here than Taylor did.

My parents named us all unisex names so that they wouldn't have to think of a boy and a girl name for each pregnancy, but we all came out girls. Must have been a fun time for Dad when we all started puberty, poor guy.

"Your squad is here," my mom yelled to me.

"One second!" I called back.

I gotta find these stupid socks. I dug around and started to toss a fair bit of clothes out of the basket until I found a pair of clean socks that matched. I quickly stuffed my feet into them and took off towards downstairs, double-checking that I had my phone and purse with me as I went.

"There she is," a voice said as I came down the stairs.

I looked over to see my friend, Mindy, standing there. She, like me, was a very small girl. She was a half-Asian girl with black-to-blond ombré hair framing her face.

This was kinda like a goodbye shopping trip for her. She's been long-distance dating some girl from somewhere around Toronto lately. They're so cute together though. I think her name was Haley or Emily or something.

All I really know is that she has colourful hair.

My other friend that was coming with us today was Charlotte. She's a monster compared to Mindy and I, but she's actually only five-foot-seven.

She came all the way from California for college. So, naturally, she's got a nice tan. And she's also got a pretty nice head of golden hair, stereotypical of a Cali girl. Not trying to say all of them are like that, but just think Hollywood California babe from the '80s.

"Here I am," I said as I outstretched my arms for a hug.

Mindy rushed up to me and threw her arms around me. "We gotta make today good, okay?"

"I know. You have to be home for six or whatever. I got it," I said, letting go of her.

"So if you get lost or something, I have to steal Charlotte from you so she can drive me home. No hard feelings though," Mindy stated.

"I can always call Timmy to come and pick me up. I mean, he lives outta town and all, but he'd come to pick me up."

"Only 'cause he's got a crush on you," Charlotte chimed in.

I turned and smirked at her. "You know it." But not really. Boys I've met never seemed to like me. Maybe it's because I'm too pretty, too smart, and way too busy for them.

"We gonna get ready to go, then?" Charlotte asked, probably getting annoyed that we were even taking this long. She's pretty impatient.

"You guys better be careful out there," my mom said, walking over to us with a big plate of cookies, warm and fresh homemade ones too.

"Will do, Miss Everett," Mindy said, grabbing a cookie and then taking a bite of it.

"Don't eat my cookies," I snapped at Mindy.

"They're not yours. They're for Santa," my mom sassed me.

"I'm the chubbiest and jolliest here, so..." Charlotte said, also taking a cookie from the plate in my mom's hands.

"Yeah, that's the truth," I joked to her as I passed by her and walked towards my living room. I found my sister plopped out on the couch, watching some cartoon show.

"What do *you* want?" she asked as she saw me walking over.

3

"For you to let me use the TV a sec, ya brat," I said to her, sitting just in front of her on the couch.

"Fine," she groaned, handing the remote to me. "Make it quick though."

I took the remote from her. "I just need to check the weather," I told her, punching in the channel number for the weather channel.

"It's the middle of winter. What other weather would we have other than cold and snow and more cold?" Jordan said, scoffing slightly.

"We might have cold and wind and snow, silly." I said as I turned up the TV. "Now, shh."

"Record-breaking amounts of snow have fallen all along the east coast and in the American Midwest as a part of these 'super' blizzards that have been making the steady trek towards the Maritimes," the lady on the TV stated.

"Yeah. The storm swooped down and avoided Chicago and came back up and hit Ohio, New York, and the rest of New England," my mom said from behind the couch.

"The best advice anyone can be given over the next three to five days is to just stay indoors and stay safe. Power companies are warning customers of likely power outages that will accompany the heavy blanketing of snow expected for us in the later evening," the weather lady rambled on.

"Well, shit," I muttered.

"Stay tuned for more information on what many are calling the Blizzard of the Century," the lady said, and then it cut away to commercials, so I turned the volume down.

"Blizzard of the Century, eh?" Charlotte said from behind the couch. She scoffed. "It probably isn't gonna be *that* bad."

I glanced over to see that my mom and Mindy had both joined Charlotte in standing behind the couch to watch the brief weather news.

"Better get going. I don't wanna get caught out in that shit," Mindy stated.

"Relax. It's only two o'clock. We still have lots of time," I said to her as I reached back and grabbed a cookie from the plate of cookies that my mom was still carrying in her hands for some reason.

4

"But… you heard the news, it's the *Blizzard* of the *Century*," Mindy whined.

"For someone who isn't very timid, you're being a little whiner about this," I sassed to her.

"I also have deadlines to meet, trains to catch, things to pack, goodbyes to say, and flights to board. I'm allowed to be timid and/or impatient," Mindy snapped.

"Oh, my God, shut up."

"I don't want to."

"Shut up, Mindy. I'll make sure I get you home. We can leave the mall at five and let Tim come and pick Spencer up," Charlotte butted in.

"Boom. See, everyone can be happy this way," I said.

Mindy pouted a little. "Fine."

"Don't be such a baby," I said to her.

She smiled widely and gave me the finger, such a classy lady.

"You girls are always bickering," my mom said as she walked over and placed the plate of cookies onto the table. "Play nicely."

"I don't think she wants to," I said.

"I'll play nicely… I just won't like it," Mindy chimed in.

"You're such a loser," Charlotte teased her.

"Stop ganging up on me, or my girlfriend will come and beat y'all up," Mindy said with a stern tone and a pout to match it.

"She isn't that scary though," I teased.

"You 'on't know that," Mindy snapped.

"Stop bickering," Charlotte said, taking a seat beside me on the couch. "I'm getting a headache."

"Okay, Jordan, scram," I said, turning to my sister.

"Mom, she's being a jerk again," Jordan whined.

"Sorry, Jordan. I'm with Spencer on this one. You have to go clean up the basement anyway," my mom said to Jordan.

I smirked at her as she got up and sulked off to the basement to clean up a mess, which there was always a mess wherever she went, so she should be constantly cleaning things up.

"Finally," Mindy shouted, proceeding to jump onto the couch, she managed to squeeze in just behind Charlotte and I.

"Really, dude?" Charlotte asked, turning back to face her.

Mindy was on her stomach, so she turned her face up and smiled. "Yes, really. It's warm back here behind your fat ass," she chirped at Charlotte.

"You're just mad 'cause I actually have an ass, and not one of them long backs like you two," Charlotte sassed back.

"Eh, don't bring me into this," I stated.

"I like her butt," Mindy said.

"Both of you, hush," I demanded, turning the TV up again.

The weather lady rambled some jargon about weather and she used a lot of weather terms that I don't care about, but I did get the gist of the fact that the raging blizzard was moving in faster than expected, with a foot of snow supposed to fall before seven o'clock tonight. So we'd basically be snowed in, and that's just for the before night falls too. It's just gonna keep snowing throughout the night and the next few days, which would essentially bury us in snow.

"We about ready to go, then?" Charlotte asked after a few minutes of our eyes being glued towards the television screen.

"Mm, yeah. Lemme just go run and get my sweater," I said, standing up from the couch.

Charlotte stood up and stretched a little and yawned. "I hope I don't fall asleep while driving. That'd suck so bad."

"Please don't. I don't wanna die," Mindy said, rolling over and spreading out on the couch.

"You wont die, you little sissy."

"Spencer, she's being mean," Mindy whined at me.

"What's gotten you so emotionally sensitive today?" I asked with a slight laugh.

"I dunno. I blame love. I used to be a badass," Mindy said, flexing her biceps.

Charlotte and I exchanged a quick glance and then laughed.

"What?!" Mindy shouted at us, pouting slightly as she stopped flexing.

"You're the tiniest girl in the world, and that's coming from me," I said with a laugh. "And now I am off to get my sweater so we can get going."

Mindy kept pouting. "Whatever."

I walked off and up to my room and grabbed my sweater. I

grabbed it and then decided to check my phone to see how much battery I had left. I only had, like, 24% left. That should last until I get home later. I hope. Now, time to go back and get Mindy off my couch, that lazy bugger.

"I'm all good to go," I yelled down, closing the door to my room.

"I don't know if Mindy is gonna be good to go, she looks pretty comfy right now," Charlotte said as I walked into the living room.

"I don't wanna move," Mindy groaned from the couch.

I turned and looked over to the couch and saw Mindy curled up in the corner with one of the couch pillows.

"She's such a baby," Jordan said, walking past me.

"Am not. Babies don't know what comfortable things even are," Mindy snapped.

"How would you know?" I asked.

"I was a baby once."

"Yeah, and you still are," Jordan chimed in.

"Jordan, butt out," I said to her.

"Get up if you wanna get going," Charlotte said to her.

"I don't wanna go though," Mindy said.

"Okay, then it seems we will have to carry you out to the car," Charlotte said, winking to me.

I nodded to her and we moved to the couch and lifted Mindy up. I grabbed her from under her shoulders and Charlotte grabbed her legs, since she had more strength to control Mindy's legs flailing all over.

"Let me go! I don't wanna! It's cold out there," Mindy whined as we carried her towards the front door.

"You three be safe out there," my mom said from the kitchen.

"You aren't gonna help me get them off me?" Mindy cried out to her.

"Nope," my mom said with a wink to her.

"Dammit, Everett!" Mindy shouted as Charlotte opened the door.

"Bye, Miss Everett," Charlotte said with a small smile.

"Bye, Mom," I said, carrying Mindy out the door.

"Seriously, you guys can let me down now. I'm already outside," Mindy said.

"You want down?" Charlotte asked her.

Mindy nodded.

I caught on to what Charlotte wanted to do and nodded to her and we swung her towards a small snowbank. Mindy landed on her back with a soft thud and a groan.

"You guys are assholes," Mindy groaned. She stood up and dusted the snow off her back, legs, and butt.

"Yep, you bet your bottom dollar," Charlotte said. "Now get in the damn car."

"Yeah. Or we'll *throw* you in the back seat too," I threatened.

"And yet you call me impatient," Mindy groaned as she started off for the car.

"Well, I'm the one driving us to a mall. On Christmas Eve. And with a crazy-ass blizzard about to cover us in several feet of snow," Charlotte noted, digging in her pocket for keys.

"Listen, it won't be that bad. When is the weather channel ever right?"

"Well, with this storm, they have been tracking it for quite a few days now," Charlotte replied to her.

"Yeah, but I doubt it'll be that bad," Mindy said with a scoff.

"Did you not see the pictures of New York? The whole city was grinded to a halt because of how much snow they got. And we're gonna get just as much. We might even get more than that because *Canada*," Charlotte stated.

"Yeah, so get the hell in the car and shut up," I butted in.

"Jeez, okay," Mindy said, defeated.

We got to the little four-door sedan that Charlotte drove us around in. Wasn't much, but it got the job done for us. It used to be all black, but the paint started chipping away over the years that the previous owner had it sitting in his garage, so we had to mix up paint for it, now it looks more like *Fifty Shades of Grey* splattered all over it. Get it? All well, the car will be stark white by the time we're done at the mall.

{Chapter: **Two**}

The roads were pretty bad getting to the mall, but we actually managed to get here alive and well. Charlotte's a pretty good driver, especially for someone who isn't used to driving around on snow, ice, and nasty slush-covered parking lots. Scared to see them now after a few hours of shopping though.

"How much snow do you think is outside now?" Mindy asked as we all looked up at the big clock in the centre of the mall.

"Probably a lot," I said.

Mindy sighed. "I gotta get going soon, guys."

"I'll get you out of here soon, don't worry. It's only 5:30, you got lots of time," Charlotte said.

"When does the mall close?" I asked.

"I think it closes at either six or seven today," Charlotte replied. "Why?"

"I wanted to go buy some clothes for me."

"Want me to take all your stuff home for you when I take Mindy?"

"That would be very nice of you," I said.

"'Tis the season," she said with a shrug, and then she reached for the bags in my hands and took them from me. "I'll make sure that nobody sees what you got for them."

"Good girl. Don't ruin the Christmas surprise for everyone."

"I'm hungry," Mindy whined.

"Shut up, Mindy," Charlotte barked.

"You're mean."

"Charlotte is always mean. It's her shtick," I said.

"Shtick or not, she shouldn't be so mean to her best friends," Mindy argued, which was a fair argument, I guess.

"Take her for food when you leave too. I doubt you wanna listen to her whine all the way home," I said to Charlotte.

Charlotte nodded. "Probably should."

"I want burgers," Mindy growled loudly.

"Calm down there, Rambo," Charlotte said teasingly.

"Look," I said, pointing up towards the large dome-shaped glass roof above us.

We all looked up to see snow starting to fall on the glass. It was slowly blanketing the dome in the familiar cold white of winter. And beyond that, a dark sky of clouds, with heavy winds, heavy snow, heavy thunder, and even a flash of lightning that lit up that dark sky.

"Looking spooky," Mindy said as we stared in awe.

"We should probably get finished here then," Charlotte said.

I let out a loud yawn. "Yeah. I'm feeling extra tired today too. I wanna go home and take a nap before I pass out in the middle of the mall."

"Mindy has places to be, and you want to go home and sleep. Let's go grab something for dinner real quick and then be on our way out of here," Charlotte said, turning to look at me and not the *spooky* sky.

"Sleep sounds so good right now," I whined as the three of us turned and started to walk towards the food court of the mall.

"Are we gonna go to Baker's Tacos?" Mindy asked.

"I thought you wanted burgers?" Charlotte asked.

"Well, I want tacos now. Deal with it."

"Why don't we get both?"

"Tacos and burgers, what a good combo," I butted in.

"Don't be sarcastic, okay?" Mindy barked at me. "Sometimes it's good to expand your definition of a proper meal."

"But burgers and tacos? That's way too much greasy ground beef at one sitting, isn't it?" I questioned.

"Yeah, but ground beef is delicious, so what are you complainin' for?" she asked.

I shrugged. I guess burgers and tacos would be okay for now, I could always go home and make some salad or something. I hated eating just meat for dinner, I need to have vegetables to balance it out.

"Hard or soft tacos?" Charlotte asked.

"What, are you paying then?" Mindy asked.

"Yeah. Goodbye gift for you and a Christmas gift for Spencer. Duh."

"Then both," Mindy said, answering the initial question.

"And for Dill Pickle?" Charlotte asked, stopping and turning to me as we got to the food court.

"One, don't call me that," I demanded. I hated that stupid nick-name. They call me that because I once ate a whole jar of dill pickles to myself, and I even drank the pickle juice after. It's not even that embarrassing, but I think that's why I hate the nickname. It's just dumb. "And two, I will also have both."

"What's wrong with calling you Dill Pickle?" Charlotte teased, pulling her wallet out of her purse.

"It's a stupid, childish name. It makes me feel seven," I told her.

"Well—"

"Don't say it," I snapped.

"What?" Charlotte asked, trying to sound innocent.

"You know what."

"She was just gonna say that you look like you're seven," Mindy chimed in.

"I'm gonna punch both of you so hard *in the face*," I growled.

"I didn't say shit," Charlotte said with a devious smile. "Now, you two go find a table and wait for me. I'll go get us some tacos and burgers."

"We do look like fifth graders," Mindy said.

"We do not," I argued, turning and walking over to a table.

"We're short, and stupid—"

I faked a cough to interrupt her.

"Okay, I'm stupid. But we're both short and cute and we act immature sometimes. The only reason people can tell that we're not, like, thirteen is that we got these," she said, proceeding to grab her boobs.

"Why do I even talk to you?" I asked jokingly.

"Because you love me," Mindy said.

I shrugged. "Yeah. I guess I do. Only a little."

"Are you gonna miss me when I go to Toronto?"

"Yeah. Obviously. You've been my friend for ages. If I didn't miss you, then I'd be a horrible friend."

"I'm nervous though," Mindy said.

"But why?"

"It's been a while since I've seen her and kissed her, right. *And* I have to meet her friends and family. I am nervous as hell," Mindy explained.

"Relax, dude, it'll be fine," I told her.

"Well, I can handle Emily, she's my friend and the reason why I met Haley in the first place," Mindy whined.

"Just relax," I told her sternly.

"Is Mindy being whiny again?" Charlotte asked, sitting down.

I didn't know how the hell Charlotte got our food and then got over here so quickly, but alright. She's a wizard. Or Mindy and I spent more time talking about being immature than I thought.

"I'm not whining," Mindy barked, turning to me. "Tell her, Spencer."

"She was whining," I stated.

"Wha—"

"You said I was seven," I reminded her.

"Stop bickering. Eat up," Charlotte said, dumping a plethora of tacos and burgers onto the table in front of us.

"Hells yeah!" Mindy shouted, grabbing a burger and two tacos, unwrapping and stuffing her face with one of the soft tacos.

"You love food way too much," Charlotte said, grabbing a taco.

"You still wanna go and get clothes?" Mindy asked with a mouthful of taco and burger.

"Oh, yeah," I said, unwrapping a burger.

"Well, hurry up and eat," Mindy said.

I glared and her and took a bite. "I'm trying," I said, my mouth now full of food. Obnoxiously chewing to try and piss her off a little bit.

"You two are such pigs," Charlotte said, referencing our poor table manners.

"Sorry, not sorry," Mindy said, barely able to speak from a mouthful of food.

"Seriously," Charlotte groaned, noticing the little bit of food Mindy had spat up when she spoke.

"Sorry, for real that time," Mindy said, wiping her lips with a napkin.

"Yeah," I said, swallowing a mouthful of burger. "Me too."

So we ate as much as we could as quickly as we could, but time wasn't really on our side. It was already almost six, and that's when the mall closes. Or maybe a half hour later than that. But regardless, it's closing soon.

"Alright, I'm just gonna take this last taco to go," I said, standing up from the table.

"Good idea," Charlotte said, unwrapping the last taco and standing up.

Mindy belched loudly and stretched as she stood up. "Mm, that was some damn good eats."

"You're a pig," I joked, unwrapping my taco.

Mindy scoffed and stuck her tongue out at Charlotte and I. And she called me seven?

"C'mon, let's just go see if we can get your clothes shopping over with," Charlotte said, shoving Mindy so she would start walking.

"Okay," I said, yawning after.

"Where did you wanna go?"

"I dunno. Over that way," I said, pointing towards a faraway store all the way down the mall.

"Let's go," Mindy groaned, turning and walking towards where I had pointed.

"I'm so friggin' tired," I said, yawning again.

"What's got you so tired?" Charlotte asked.

"I stayed up all night marathoning *How I Met Your Mother* on Netflix," I told her.

She scoffed and shook her head. "Typical Spencer."

"Yeah, and now I'm paying for it," I said.

"Let's go, you slowpokes," Mindy whined from a few feet in front of us.

"Dill Pickle is too tired to walk any faster than this," Charlotte stated.

"Dill Pickle gonna beat yo ass," I muttered to her.

"Dill Pickle is *not* that scary," Mindy chimed in.

"Just walk," I growled.

I just wanted to get shopping over with. I could really use a nap before Taylor comes over later. I missed my sister, and I don't think she'd like it if I went to sleep early and didn't see her tonight. So nap, just a quick little two-hour nap, and then I should be good. She'll be there at seven, I think. So if I nap until nine, we still get some night to spend together.

"This taco is my limit. I'm so full," I groaned, trying to chew the halfway bite of the taco.

"Hey, watch out!" Charlotte shouted.

I turned to see why she shouted that, and then I found out. Some guy accidentally tackled me as he ran past us. Him bumping into me that fast and hard caused me to lose balance and fall onto the ground, which caused my half-eaten taco to go flying out of my hand too, not that I really cared. Stupid kid, with his stupid beanie and plaid shirt. Why was he running so goddamn fast in a mall?

"Dammit," I groaned from the cold tile floor.

"Hey, watch where you're going!" Mindy shouted after the guy, even though he was already long gone by now.

"C'mon," Charlotte said, reaching a hand down to me. "Let's get off the floor now."

"Yeah," I groaned, grabbing her hand.

Mindy came over and helped to pick me up from the ground. "That guy's a douche," she said as I stood up straight.

"You don't say," Charlotte sassed her.

"My ass hurts," I groaned, rubbing the sore part of my butt.

"You're okay."

"But lemme at that douchebag. He won't be okay after I'm done with him. Run into my friend like that and think you get away with it, not up in here," Mindy shouted in the direction where he had ran.

"Mindy. *No one* is scared of you. You're about as threatening as a wet cat without claws or teeth, okay?" I said to her.

"But… Fine, whatever. You suck," she said with a pout.

"Sorry 'bout the loss of your taco though," Charlotte said jokingly.

"Yeah. That was a total loss, eh?" I said, turning and looking at the taco on the ground a few feet away from where the three of us stood.

"Rest in peace, beautiful little Mexican snack food," Mindy said, resting a hand on her heart and feigning sadness.

"You're getting increasingly weird as you get older, you know that?" I said to Mindy.

She shrugged. "Yeah. I do know. And I don't mind it. I like being weird, it gives me a certain *je ne sais quoi.*"

"Stop speaking French," Charlotte butted in. "Okay, so… the store. Wanna get going now? You might be able to make the ride. I'm leaving in ten minutes with Mindy."

"I will try to be quick," I told her.

"Good, let's go, then," Mindy said, walking in front of Charlotte and I again.

"Chipper little thing, that one," Charlotte joked.

We started following Mindy towards the store I had pointed to. My ass still hurt from that stupid kid tackling me though. Not fun. Anyway, when we got to the store, Mindy started trying to get me to buy this one hideous dress that she saw as soon as we walked in.

"C'mon. It really isn't that bad," Mindy whined. She was really pushing this dress on me.

"Mindy. It's the middle of winter. Why would I even need a dress?" I asked.

"For my wedding, duh," she replied, giving me a weird look.

"You aren't getting married anytime soon," Charlotte butted in, walking over with a pair of jeans for me. Friends are great when they're actually helpful.

"Frick you," Mindy mumbled.

"These better fit you," Charlotte said, handing me the pair of jeans. It's weird how they're called pairs of jeans when it's really only one piece of clothing.

"I'll try them on," I said.

"Do we really have time for that?" Mindy whined.

"You can go now if you want."

"You sure? I don't mind waiting a little longer," Mindy said.

"No, no. I don't want you to end up any later than you already will be with the roads being all bad," I said.

"Want me to come back for you or something?" Charlotte asked.

"Nope. I'll call Tim and he can come get me. You guys just relax. Take the night off, sheesh. It's Christmas, you don't have to babysit me. I'm gonna go and try these on, and then I'll call Tim. You two get out of here and I will call y'all tomorrow," I told the two of them.

"You're 100 percent sure?" Charlotte asked.

"Yes. I'm completely sure. You two get out of here," I said.

"I'm gonna miss you," Mindy said, grabbing my arm and turning me and then wrapping me up in a 'tight' hug.

"I'm gonna miss you too," I said, hugging her as tightly as I could. "You're gonna do so great in Toronto."

"I'm gonna call you lots, okay?" Mindy said with a few tears welling in her eyes.

"Why are you crying?"

"I'm so bad at goodbyes," she whispered with a small smile.

"You're gonna be okay," I whispered back.

"C'mon, you overemotional loser," Charlotte teased Mindy.

"But, I don't wanna leave my Dill Pickle," Mindy said as she let go of me.

"I'm gonna miss you so much," I said.

"I'll call you the morning after I get there."

"Why not the night you get there?"

She winked playfully. "Do you really think my mouth is gonna be available for talking?"

"Ohh, okay, got it," I said.

"Okay, but we have to get going," Charlotte said, grabbing and pushing Mindy towards the exit.

"Be gentle with her," I joked.

"Will do," Charlotte said, turning and walking away with Mindy. She turned back just before leaving the store. "And you better remember to call me tomorrow, you little shit."

"I will," I shouted back at her. I turned and walked over to the lonesome saleswoman that was still working. I think she was the last one working here. She looked pretty tired herself. I know I was. Stupid marathons of TV shows.

"Hi, um, could I just go and try these on real quick?" I asked her.

"Mm-hmm. The doors are all open, just go in and pick a room," the woman said to me.

Not the best service in the world. "Thanks," I said to her, and then I turned and walked towards the small changing rooms. I picked one of the changing rooms at the far end, number 41. The numbering of their rooms started at 40, which was weird.

I stepped in and locked the door behind me. I sat down on the bench and peeled my boots off my feet and then my jeans off my legs. Then, somewhere between getting up and putting on the new jeans I wanted to buy and sitting back down, I fell asleep on the little wooden bench in this quaint little changing room in this big mall in the middle of a freak blizzard.

{Chapter: **Three**}

I woke up in a really uncomfortable position. I was halfway on and halfway off of the little wood bench in the changing room, with my jeans halfway down my legs. I rubbed my eyes and looked around. Doesn't feel like a lot of time passed. Maybe I just slipped under for a couple minutes. I was so, so tired.

"Ugh, my back is sore as hell," I groaned, standing up from the bench. I looked at the bench and wondered how I even managed to sleep on that thing at all. The size was way too small, even for me.

I grabbed the waist of the jeans I was trying on and pulled them up. I'm half asleep, so there isn't any way I'm changing the jeans I'm currently wearing back to my older ones. I fixed my shirt and wiped up the little bit of drool that had found a home on my cheek.

I opened the door to the changing room and walked outside. It seemed pretty empty in the store, and by that, I mean that the saleswoman had left.

The lights were still on in the mall, probably on a timer to shut off at a certain time though. It's still pretty creepy if you ask me.

I walked out into the store and dropped my clothes onto the sales counter as I noticed a large metal gate over the front of the store. The saleswoman had left me locked in the store. She left me to sleep in the changing room. Forgotten.

"Well, this is just great," I grumbled, walking over to the metal gate. I bent down and tried to pull it up, but it was locked, but I figured that she'd have locked up the store before jetting off. "Dammit," I muttered. How am I gonna get out of here?

I stood back up and walked to the sales counter and started searching for keys or at least something to pry the gate open.

I rummaged through the desk and, to be honest, I made quite a mess of things. I gave up on searching the sales counter for the key to the gate. I guess I have to suck up the fact that I might be stuck in here for a while.

I walked back into the changing rooms and got my phone to find that, with my luck, it was dead. I should have charged it when I had the chance. Dammit. I was stuck in a mall with no phone to call for help, and since cell phones are a thing, all the payphones that used to be in this mall were removed because they were costlier to keep than to get rid of.

I put my useless phone back into my pocket and then I walked out of the changing room and noticed a door in the back that was slightly open. Maybe the keys would be in there.

I walked in and flicked the light on. Hmm, *seems* like the place someone would store keys and various other items for upkeep and whatnot.

I rummaged through a few desks until I found a small cabinet, I pulled the little door open and inside I found a few different keys. I grabbed them all and looked at them closely. Any one of them could be the key to the gate, so I decided to just bring them all back with me.

I walked back to the gate and started trying each one of the keys. Key after key, and I was having no luck. And then, the third last key in my hands finally slid into the keyhole and unlocked the gate. I quickly pulled it up and tossed the keys back into the store. I'm sure someone else will clean up my little mess.

"Okay, now where is the exit," I asked myself, looking around. I started walking towards the main clock in the centre of the mall so I could check the time. I got there after a minute or so and looked up to see that the time was 7:32 PM. I had taken an almost-two-hour nap in a changing room, goddammit.

I turned and started walking at a faster pace. I might be able to walk home if the blizzard hasn't gotten too bad outside. But judging from the glass dome above, there was a lot of snow, and it looked windy and just horrible out there. I kept walking towards where the back emergency exits were located. I knew the main entrances would all be locked up, and I don't feel like looking for keys for those or breaking out.

I walked past all the empty and closed stores, only about half of them had the metal gates closed, I bet even less had them locked. It was like a ghost town, like it had been deserted really quickly. Which was weird, because even on slow days, the mall was so busy and full of noise, and now it's so empty and echoing with silence and my footsteps.

I continued along on my walk, taking in all the eeriness of the silent mall. I passed the food court, which was dark and desolate now. I passed by the movie theatre, which was also dark and desolate. The whole mall was shut down, except for the lights and heating. I mutter to myself, "I really hope I can get out of here. Being stuck in a mall would suck."

After a few minutes of walking and enjoying the views of a deserted mall, I found the back hallways. These halls would surely have an exit door that doesn't have an outside handle, meaning that I could easily get out that way. I continued my trek down through the back halls.

And then I heard a banging.

It was a loud banging coming from somewhere down the hallway. It was followed by a cry for help. It sounded like a guy. Maybe he had gotten stuck somewhere too, or maybe he was hurt or something. I picked up my pace as I jogged towards where the banging sounds were coming from.

"Is anyone out there? Hello?!" the voice shouted out from behind some door down one of the new hallways approaching me. What were the odds someone else was in here?

I made the quick turn right and down to where the shouting had come from. I slowed down and listened to the thudding of someone's fist on the door and I used that to hone in on exactly what door was being banged on.

I finally reached the door and looked up to the sign. It was the boiler room. Some poor idiot got locked in the boiler room.

"Hello?" I said loudly to the door.

"Oh, finally. Hey, so I'm kinda locked in here. Can you help me get the hell out of here?" the man's voice replied.

"Um, I don't know how. I'm not a worker here," I stated. Man, it's so weird talking to a stranger through a metal door like this.

"Well, then, what help are you gonna be?" he sassed.

"None if you get saucy with me," I barked.

"I'm sorry. Just go find they keys or something. I don't know why they lock it from the outside, but this is bullshit."

"Where would they have the keys?"

"Probably in the security office. They'd at least have copies of all the keys in there," the guy told me.

"That's all the way back across the mall though," I said.

"Well, I'm not going anywhere."

"Alright. I'll go find the keys to the boiler room, and then you owe me one."

"We can talk about that later. Just help me get the hell out of here, please."

"I'll be back," I said to him, turning and walking away.

"Hurry," he shouted as I walked away from the door.

I jogged back out into the mall and looked around. I settled on the way I had come from and I ran all the way back to the store I had broken out of. I continued from there toward the elevators, they would be able to take me up a floor to the security office. I ran over and clicked the call button and waited impatiently for the slow-ass elevator to come down.

The doors slid open and I stepped in, hitting the button for the second floor. It took way longer than it should have to get up that one floor. Seriously, these elevators are way too slow. A snail could climb up the walls to the second floor faster than this. But, I digress.

I walked out and started running, any direction, really. I didn't care where I went, as long as I ended up at the security office. I think looking at a map would have helped, but I didn't care. I just ran until I found the security office. Which I did, but it was after a ten-minute zig-zagging jog. I guess partaking in the cross-country club in high school paid off after all. Score one for Spencer's foresight.

I searched through the desks of the security office and then the cabinets. I didn't see any keys or anything that looked like it might store keys inside of it.

"I'm about to lose it," I groaned, opening another desk drawer. I rifled through four more drawers nearby and then slumped to the ground. I give up. There isn't any way I'm gonna find keys. That poor dude is gonna stay stuck in the boiler room for the time being.

I sighed and looked around the room from my seat on the tiled ground. Stupid security office, stupid keys for everything. I feel bad now that I can't help that guy get out though.

After a few moments of sitting and chewing off some dead skin from my lip, I got up and took one last glance around the room, hoping that a big corkboard full of keys had magically appeared somewhere in the room, but there was nothing. It was just messier than when I had come in. I should probably stop making messes everywhere now that I think of it.

I turned and went to walk, but I was stopped short of a full stride. I looked down and saw a little wooden cabinet that I had missed while I was tearing through the desks in the office. I leaned down and opened the door. Inside the cabinet lie several keys. "Just my luck," I mumbled, realizing I would have to try an assortment of keys on the lock until one of them unlocked the door and let that dude out of the boiler room.

I grabbed the plastic bag from the small garbage can next to me, and thank God it was an empty bag. I didn't wanna have to make another mess. I quickly scooped all the keys into the bag and then slipped the handles around my wrist so I wouldn't drop it. I ran back to the elevator and went back downstairs. I jogged my way back to the hallways and then to the boiler room door.

I knocked loudly on the door. "Hey. Still in there?" I teased.

"Did you find the key?" the guy asked.

"I don't even get a hello?"

"Sorry," he said. "Hello. Did you find the key?"

"I found about thirty *the keys*," I stated.

"Well, start sticking them in the lock and seeing if any of them work," he said rather demandingly.

"Not until you learn some damn manners," I barked.

"Can you please start sticking some keys into the lock and seeing if any of the will get me the hell out of this boiler room?"

"That's better," I told him, reaching into the plastic bag for the first of many keys. I grabbed the first key and shoved it towards the lock, and it didn't go in. Figures. This pattern continued for a good thirteen more keys. And then, by some miracle, I found the key that unlocked the door. The sound of the tumblers turning and clicking and unlocking was music to both of our ears.

"Open it," he whined.

I pulled the key out of the door handle and I pulled the door open the way you fall asleep. Slowly at first, and then all at once. "I never thought I was gonna get out," the guy said, stepping out of the room.

I got a good look at him now. He was wearing a red and black plaid shirt, jeans, and a deep grey beanie that ended just where the front of his hair puffed upward. He had a nice face and a slight beard. And his eyes weren't too bad either, a nice and calming pale blue colour. I was actually taken aback by how attractive I found this guy. Maybe he's close to my age too. Well, hopefully he is. I wouldn't wanna be stuck in a mall with some middle-aged dude.

"Um, you wanna tell me how you got locked in there?"

"No. Not really," he said firmly. "But, uh, thanks for, y'know, getting me out of there."

"Ah. Don't mention it."

"Yeah, I probably won't."

"You're really not gonna tell me why you were in there?" I pried.

"Nope."

"Why?"

"You don't need to know," he grumbled, fixing his beanie.

"I think I do need to know. I just saved your ass," I reminded him.

"You don't need to know. So just drop it. I don't even know you, and you don't know me," he stated.

I also liked this boy's voice. It was soothing and calming and I wanted to listen to it for hours. It was one of those kinds of voices. Soothing, welcoming, and warming.

"Is the whole mall empty?" he asked, turning to me and snapping me from my thoughts.

"Yeah. It's just the two of us from what I can tell," I told him. "Or maybe there are other people stuck somewhere too. I don't know."

"Well, uh, do you know what time is it? My phone's dead."

"Uh, well, when I checked last, it was almost eight."

"Almost eight?" he asked, surprised. "I've been in there for at least two hours if it's eight right now."

"Well, since I rescued you, can you come and help me clean up the security office?" I asked.

"Why? What did you do, rip it apart?" he asked.

I stayed quiet and nodded slightly.

"You idiot," he groaned. He glared at me slightly. "Okay, fine. Lead the way then." He nodded down the hallway.

I started walking down the hall and I heard his footsteps following close behind mine. At least he isn't just gonna ditch me here. That would suck. I didn't wanna clean the security office by myself. And he should help since it's his fault I made the mess. "You still have to tell me why you were in there," I tell him as we reach the elevator.

"I'm not telling you, so you might as well let it go."

"You're gonna tell me what you were doing."

"Why's that?" he asked as we stepped into the elevator.

I reached over and pressed the elevator button for the second floor as he took a spot in the corner of the elevator, tightly grasping the railing on the side. "Because you owe me that for rescuing you."

"I thought I was helping you clean the security office because you rescued me?"

"No. You're helping me clean because it's your fault that I had to search for that key to recue you," I stated.

"Stop saying rescue. I wasn't dying or anything. Just stuck in boiler room," he said as the elevator doors slid open.

"And you're gonna tell me why you were stuck in the boiler room. You're not leaving this mall until you tell me."

{Chapter: **Four**}

The boiler room guy and I reached the security office, and after a few minutes of me pestering him to tell me why he was in the boiler room, he seemed more annoyed at me than anything else.. I'm just shocked that he didn't wanna just fess up about it. I'm gonna find out one way or another anyway. I swear I will.

"This one," I said, sliding the small wooden cabinet that had held the keys in it before I took them all. "Put the keys in here." I dumped the baggy of keys onto the floor and they poured out like a little silver and bronze waterfall, clattering all over the floor with a bunch of metallic clangs.

"And then I can go?" the guy whined at me.

"Not until the *whole* office is cleaned up," I told him.

"Oh, come on," he groaned. "That's not fair."

"It is."

"I was stuck in a boiler room. I shouldn't have to pay for you being a good person and getting me out."

"I'm not a good person," I lied. I mean, I was a pretty good person in comparison to a lot of other people out there, but that's beside the point right now.

"That's bullshit. If you weren't a good person, why did you actually come all the way to the security office, and tear it apart, looking for a key to save a stranger?"

"Um. I thought I would maybe get a reward. Or maybe a news story," I said, blatantly lying, and I'm pretty sure he could tell that I was.

"See. You're a good person. But, I'm also in your debt, so I guess I'll help," he said, sitting down in front of the heap of keys I had left on the floor for him.

"That's frickin' right you'll help," I said with a smirk.

He shook his head and grabbed the pile of keys with his hands, pulling them in towards his crossed legs on the ground so he could reach them easier.

"Are you gonna reorder them or something?" I teased.

"Yeah. I might as well see if I can put them where they're supposed to go. They look labelled to me. Which begs the question, why did you bring them all and not just look for the key under the boiler room label?" he asked, looking up at me.

"They were all messy when I got here," I said.

"Okay, but the boiler room is key 41, and you could have checked the numbers by the labels and found out that the key for the boiler room was 41. It would have saved you, like, twenty failed attempts at unlocking the door."

"Okay. So I had a momentary lapse of thought. I was trying to get some idiot out of a boiler room. Gimme a break."

"I'm not some idiot," he argued.

"Only idiots get themselves locked inside a boiler room."

"Yeah, you said that already."

"Paraphrasing it over and over again helps people retain the information," I stated.

"What, are you some kind of teacher or something?" he asked with a slight and subtle scoff.

"No. I'm only a freshman," I replied, joining him on the floor. I grabbed half the pile of keys from in front of him and started to look at them. I noticed the different numbers on each of the keys. I guess, in my rush, I forgot to even check if they were labelled. Stupid me.

"Are you sure?" he asked with a wry laugh.

"I'm sure. I'd never want to be a teacher anyways. Kids suck and teenagers are too rowdy for my liking," I stated.

"Well, Miss, do you at least have a first name?"

"I do, indeed, have a first name."

"So…?"

"So… what?" I asked, pretending to be clueless so I wouldn't have to give up my name first. I was a little self-conscious about being the first to introduce themself.

"Do you wanna tell me your name?"

I gave him a half-assed excuse for a shaking of my head.

"Okay. Well, my name is Evan. Evan. Me, Evan."

"Hi, Evan."

"And you are?" he asked.

"Spencer," I begrudgingly told him.

"Isn't that a nerdy dude name?"

"Screw you and your sexism."

"Don't be mean. I'm just playing around. I actually like it. I think it suits you pretty well."

"How so?" I asked him, curious as to how my name could suit me at all. It was just a name after all.

"Spencer. It just sounds like some smarty-pants name. And I guess it's also kind of cute, which fits you," Evan stated, finally starting to reorganize all the keys.

"It means guardian."

"Hmm?"

"The name Spencer. It means guardian. Or at least something like that," I told him.

"See, how weird is it that you were my guardian angel tonight and saved me then?"

"Not at all. You're just looking for reasons for it to be weird and coincidental."

"Stop being smart," he said with a soft pout of his lower lip.

"I can't help it. I like reading and writing and math and science and history and photography and medicine and just… learning. It's all I'm good at."

"So you're a freshman? College, right?"

"Yeah. You?" I asked.

"Same. Freshman because I'm so fresh, man."

I furrowed my eyebrows at him and sighed.

"Let's pretend I never said that," he mumbled. "That was a really bad joke."

"Right, well, anyway, what are you taking?"

"Business," he replied softly, almost as if hat embarrassed him or something.

"Why'd you say it like that?" I asked.

"Like what?"

"Like you were embarrassed."

"Oh. I don't know. I just thought I woulda been doing something cooler than lame old business stuff," he explained.

"Oh. Okay. Yeah. I guess I feel you on that."

"What did you take?" Evan asked me.

"You mean, what am I taking?"

"Don't be a smartass," he snapped.

"I'm taking a foundations in art and design course. It's a one-year program, but it's only meant to help me get into another program next year," I told him.

"I gotta be honest, that's pretty cool."

"Oh, you really think so, eh?" I asked. I didn't think it was cool. I just figured that an arts and design course would be best for me, because if I wanna get into all the CGI artsy stuff, I need to take this foundations course. I mean, I'd still have ridiculous amounts of schooling left after this year, but it still helps me along on my way.

"Yeah. It's probably a lot better than a business class," he said with a soft chuckle.

"You go to the—"

"Local college? Yeah," he said, answering me prematurely.

"Don't interrupt me," I said. "Here, finish putting these keys away." I slid the pile of keys I had back to him. It was more calming to watch him sort them and put them back into the little cabinet on the floor than it was for me to actually put them in myself.

"So much for you helping me," he muttered.

"Well, sorry. I'm bad at sorting things."

"You're all smart until something has to be sorted?"

"Yeah, basically," I said.

"Tidy up all the papers all over the floor so we can leave," he told me, nodding towards the mess of paperwork strewn about.

"Fine," I groaned, crawling over to the mess of paper in front of one of the desks.

"So, um, why were you still in here after hours?" Evan asked.

I turned and shrugged. "I'm a thug," I joked. I didn't want to tell him that I fell asleep in a changing room. I felt like it's just maybe kind of embarrassing.

"A thug? You're a mouse if anything," he joked.

"Is that a shot at my height?"

"More than a shot," he teased, winking at me.

I started piling papers into a stack so they would be neat. "Well, I'm a junior thug, okay? I'm in training."

"For real, why are you in here?" he asked. "Tell me. Please?"

"Why don't you tell me why you were in the boiler room first?"

"Ladies first."

"I'm not about that whole *ladies first* thing," I stated.

"Fine. Do you really have to know?" he groaned, dropped the last key into the cabinet.

"Um, yes. Why the hell would I ask you so many times if I didn't even want to know? So, go on, fess up, let me hear the story."

"Okay, but after you tell me yours," he stated.

"Why?"

"I told you my name first," he said, shrugging with one shoulder.

I groaned and rolled my eyes. "Okay, fine."

He smirked at me, like he had just got me to confess to a murder or something.

"I fell asleep in the changing room at some store," I mumbled, trying to keep my voice low enough that he either couldn't hear or couldn't understand.

"I didn't catch any of that. Stop mumbling."

"You sound like my mom when you say that," I stated.

"That's cool and all, we can talk about why I don't sound like your mom later on, like, after you tell me why you're in this mall right now," Evan stated firmly.

"I said, I fell asleep in a changing room," I mumbled just as low as before. I didn't *want* him to hear me.

"Seriously. What is so embarrassing that you have to speak like you have a mouth full of peanut butter?"

"I fell asleep in a frickin' changing room, okay?" I finally spat it out.

"You wha—" Evan began, cutting himself off with his own burst of laughter.

"It's not funny," I snapped.

He kept laughing his ass off. Completely cut off from reality, just laughing.

"Stop," I said, kicking his shoe.

"Sorry," he said, his laughter dying out. "That's just horribly funny to me. And a little sad when I think about it."

"Shut up," I grumbled.

"So, how did you manage to fall asleep in the changing room?"

"I don't know. I was trying to get jeans on and I fell asleep."

"I still can't believe that. That's gotta be a first," he said, still chuckling softly to himself.

"Shut up," I barked. "Okay. So you owe me your story now. Why were you locked in the boiler room?"

"I was running from these dudes who wanted to kick my ass and steal my shit. No biggie," he told me.

"No biggie? Dude, getting your ass kicked and having your shit stolen is a biggie."

"Nah. I'm pretty good at running, so it's never a biggie. I took track in high school. Even got some first places in the regionals," Evan stated.

"Wait. Wait a minute. Hold up."

"Yeah?" he asked, cocking his head as he looked over to me.

"You ran into me earlier," I said.

"Huh?"

"Yeah," I said, remembering the kid who had knocked me over and ruined my last taco. "You ran into me earlier and it made me fall over, you jerk."

"I'm so sorry. Oh, my God. I didn't mean to, obviously."

"You owe me a taco now," I said with a stern look.

"You were okay, right? I really feel like an ass now. I'm sorry," he rambled out.

"I'm fine. My butt got hurt a little. It's still a little sore, actually. Might be a bruise," I told him. "But other than that, I'm fine."

"Want me to, uh, massage it better?" he asked with his empathetic smile turning into a flirty smirk.

"No. You touch my ass, and I will throw you off the roof. Don't you even tempt me."

"I just feel bad about it. I didn't mean to run into you. I was just sorta in 'save my own ass' mode."

"You owe me."

"What do I owe you now? Isn't cleaning up all of *your* messes enough?" Evan groaned.

I shook my head and smirked.

"I don't like the look you're giving me right now," he stated.

"You owe me."

"What do I owe you though?" he asked.

"I don't know. I haven't thought about that. I'm sure I'll figure out something though."

"Okay, well, whatever. So, you stacked all the papers, and I made sure the keys are all put away. So now can we get the hell out of here, right?" Evan asked, standing up and stretching out his legs and back.

"Yeah. I wanna get home," I said, standing up. I let out a yawn and stretched my arms out wide. "I'm still tired. That nap didn't even help."

"Okay, come on," Evan said, walking out of the security office.

"I'ma coming," I said, following him out. I closed the door behind us, not like it would really make any difference.

"So, where the hell is our exit?" he asked as we reached the elevator. He clicked the call button so the doors would open.

"We're gonna go out the back way, down by the boiler room."

"Why's that?" he asked as the elevators doors opened and we stepped inside.

"Well," I said, pressing the button for the main floor. "The main entrances are all locked up with chains and padlocks and whatnot because the mall is on lockdown, I guess. We wouldn't be able to get out those ways, and I'm not even gonna try to smash the glass, it's too thick and strong. So we have to go out the back way. The service doors don't have handles on the outside, so we could just push the big handle on the inside side of the door and then we're free," I explained to him.

"Oh. Okay. I gotcha now," he said as the elevator lurched to a stop and the doors slid open again.

"Yeah. And then we get to walk through the blizzard, unless you have a car, maybe?" I said, following him out of the elevator.

"I do not have a car here," Evan stated.

"Well, shit. We're gonna be stuck walking home."

"How far do you live?" he asked as we walked past all the empty and deserted stores.

"Pretty far. On a good day it would take forty minutes to walk home from here. So with all the snow and ice it might end up taking an hour and a half… or more. And then there's the frostbite. That's always fun," I whined. And whine with a good reason, I did.

"Damn. I live just as far though," Evan said. "So I can't invite you to crash at my place or anything then."

"Why would you let me stay at your house?" I asked.

"Well. If I lived, say, ten minutes away, I would let you stay with me until the storm was over. I wouldn't want you to walk all the way home in this shit."

"Aw, see. You're a good person too. Now tell me you do live ten minutes away so we don't have to die on our walks home."

He shot me an apologetic look. "Sorry, dude."

"It's fine. I guess the cold isn't that bad," I said, slightly lying as I pushed open the door to the back halls of the mall.

"Yeah, negative thirty degrees with the wind chill is nice and frickin' cozy," Evan joked as we started off down the hall.

"I think that's the door up there," I told him, noticing two metal doors directly down the hall from us.

"I don't even have my coat," Evan said, looking down and noticing his lack of winter attire.

"Yeah, neither do I," I said, looking down at my lack of winter attire.

"Okay, we'll make sure we can get out this way, and then we can go back and grab our coats," Evan stated. "Good plan?"

"Okay. Good plan," I said, stopping in front of the door. I started pushing the metal push panel to open the door, but the door wasn't budging. It must be frozen shut or something.

"Move," Evan said, pushing me lightly out of the way.

"What are you gonna do?" I asked, turning to see him backing away from the door.

"Gonna bust it open, duh," he said. He narrowed his eyes and started running for the door. He tackled the door and it snapped open a little bit, causing Evan to fall down in front of it. A cascade of snow plummeted down on top of him as he plopped onto the ground. "That is *so* goddamn cold. Holy crap."

I started to laugh as he got the snow off of himself.

"It's cold!" he yelped. "It's going down my shirt." He stood up and started trying to get the snow out from the inside of his plaid shirt. "It's not funny." He gave me an angry glare as he noticed me laughing.

"That's a lot of snow," I said, looking at the door he had budged open. There was a pretty huge pile of snow right outside the door. This blizzard really wasn't messing around with us.

"I think the winds piled it all up onto the doors," he said as he stopped freaking out about the snow in his shirt.

"Can we just dig ourselves out?" I asked.

"No. That's all ice and snow. It's deep and it would take way too long to dig ourselves out if we did it safely. And if we didn't do it safely, we could end up stuck in the snow and then dead from suffocation or hypothermia, whichever would come first," Evan explained.

"So… does this mean—"

"That we're stuck in here? Yeah. I'd make the smart bet of saying that we are."

"Shit," I muttered, walking over and pulling the door closed to keep the cold air and snow out of the mall. "Now what?"

{Chapter: **Five**}

"So, since we're stuck we can go and eat food from the stores, right? Like, we could die if we don't eat or drink," I said, pushing open the door that leads back to the main part of the mall.

"Usually the law will overlook that, so yeah," Evan said, taking his beanie off and ruffling his hair as we walked out of the back hall-way.

"Well, let's go get food. I'm hungry," I stated.

Evan chuckled as we walked in the direction of the food court. He put the beanie back on and followed close behind me as I started to lead us through the mall.

"They probably have food already made and in the heating trays. I mean, the mall did close rather quickly today," I said.

"Yeah. Saves us from cooking our own food," Evan said.

"Come on, keep up."

"Sorry," he said. "Just admiring all the empty stores. I'm so used to this place being full of people and being so loud and brightly lit. Now all the stores are dark and the only sound is our footsteps. It's just weird."

"I know. It's pretty cool though. We have the mall to ourselves all night," I said.

"Or for the next few days."

"Wait, why?"

"The storm. It's supposed to last for a pretty long time," Evan told me.

"Oh, crap. I forgot. I hope we aren't stuck in here for that long, man. I got things to be doing," I said.

"I'm sure it'll let up by tomorrow. Just stop worrying for now."

"Oh, no. No reason to worry that I'm stuck in a mall for the night with some guy I barely know, some *stranger*."

"I'm not a stranger," he said.

"Yeah, you are."

"Nope. Strangers are people you don't know at all. You know where I go to school, what I'm going to school for, that I took track in high school, and my name. That makes us acquaintances at the very minimum," Evan explained.

"Just shut up," I snapped.

"Rude."

I sighed softly and continued leading us towards the food court. I liked the food court. It was big and open and it led up to the second floor via a staircase. The second floor overlooked the food court. It had even more food stores, mostly snacks and sweets, which circled the dining area below.

"Voila," I said, stopping at the start of the different coloured tiles of the food court.

"I've been to the food court before," he said, nudging my shoulder with his arm as he walked by. God, I hate being so short.

"Well, let me pretend to be a tour guide, dammit."

"Nope," he said as I started to walk after him.

"You're so mean." I jogged my way back up to him as he stopped in front of a Thai food place.

"This'll be good, right?" he asked, glancing down and over to me.

"Thai food?" I asked.

"Yeah, I feel like having some stir-fry. You like stir-fry, right? Or are you one of those weird people that don't?"

"I like stir-fry," I told him.

"Okay, good." He hopped over the service counter and went into the back of the store.

I watched as he walked around the kitchen and picked up stuff and did some things and stuff. I couldn't really see back there, and I'm lazy, so I am not hopping over the counter just to get a peak at what he's up to.

"Want a *little* bit of chicken or a lot?" he asked, popping his head out from behind one of the ovens or something in the back.

"Um, lots of chicken," I told him.

"Okay. I'm just whipping somethin' up for us," he stated, and then he disappeared behind the oven, or dishwasher, or fridge, again.

"Okay. Well, don't hurry or anything," I said sarcastically.

"Don't get sassy with me. I'll spit in your food," he threatened.

"You better not!" I shouted at him.

"I won't," he said, walking back over to me with two Styrofoam containers of food.

"Those smell good," I told him as he placed the containers on the counter.

"That'll be thirteen dollars, ma'am," Evan said, as he walked back over to the front counter.

"Just shut up and give me my food," I barked. "I can't believe I'm stuck with your dumb ass all night. You can sleep on the roof or something."

"Oh, screw you. I'm not sleeping on the roof in a blizzard."

I grabbed the two containers of food from the counter. The food smelt so good and the containers were nice and hot in my hands.

I turned around and nodded for him to follow after me. "Come on. Let's go and eat."

Evan hopped over the countertop with a slight grunt. "Lead the way," he said, nodding towards the sea of empty food court tables.

"Okay."

I led us through the rows and rows of tables until I reached a booth. I slid in on one side and Evan slid in on the other side. I slid his container, which had his name on it, over to him.

"Good seat."

"It's okay, I guess."

"I never get the booth seat here. Always some group of whiny cheerleaders or something in them," Evan stated, opening up his container of food.

"Me and my friends are not whiny cheerleaders," I snapped.

"Well, either way, I didn't know you till an hour ago."

"We weren't cute enough for you to approach before?" I teased him, opening up my own container of food. Hmm, he's a decent preparer of food. This food did look pretty good.

"I didn't even say it was you that I was talking about."

"Well, why didn't you ever just go up and talk to them? Girls aren't that scary."

"They are. They're always in groups and it's awkward when you try and hit on one of them when they've got two to five of their closest friends watching and listening, waiting for you to leave so they can crack jokes about you," Evan stated.

"Y'know, I'm not even that hungry," I grumbled.

"I thought you were."

"Well, I did eat a really big dinner of tacos and burgers. My stomach still aches from that. I just liked the idea of eating more food," I said. "Whatever though. I can just save it for later."

"Yeah. I don't think I want this food anymore either," Evan said, closing his container.

"Well, it would have gone bad anyway, so don't feel too bad about wasting food."

"Oh, I never do. Ignorance is bliss."

I gave him a sort of vacant death stare.

"I'm kidding," he said with a chuckle.

"Just save the food for later. A midnight snack," I told him, closing and sliding my container towards him.

"Good friggin' idea." He put my container of food on top of his and then leaned back, trying to get comfy against the booth seat.

"So, um… what do you wanna do for the rest of the night?" I asked.

Evan glanced at me and shrugged. "We have the entire mall to explore. I'm sure we'll find something."

"There's games and stuff."

"Like, board games? Video games? Card games? Hunger games?"

"Video games, maybe board games, probably not card games, and trust me on this one, but I would kill you in the initial bloodbath," I stated.

"Bitch, please."

"Do you really think you could get the drop on me, buddy?" I asked tauntingly.

"I'm bigger than you."

"I took kickboxing classes," I told him, smiling like a show-off.

"I'm still bigger than you," Evan stated.

I scoffed. "That doesn't mean anything. Just 'cause you're bigger, doesn't mean you're stronger or tougher."

"I'm tougher," he said with a cocky smirk.

"Shush." I slid out of the booth seat. "Come on. Let's go find something fun to do."

"What did you have in mind?" he asked, sliding out and picking up the containers from the table.

"Games."

"That involves breaking into a store. I'm pretty sure *that* is illegal as hell," Evan stated as I turned and started off towards a gaming store.

"Just come," I told him, leading the way towards the store. I reached the metal gate that covered the front of the store. I bent down and pulled on the handle. I tried with all my strength to lift it, but it was locked shut to the floor. Dammit.

Evan started chuckling to himself as he watched me try to get the gate open.

"What's so goddamn funny?" I yelled, standing and turning towards him.

"You."

"What the hell about me is funny?" I asked, annoyed.

He smirked and nodded his head towards the gate, just past where I was.

I turned and looked at what he was nodding towards and then I realized why he was laughing at me. There was a little doorway in the gate that was wide open. So I was trying to open up the gate for no reason at all. "Oh."

"You don't even check things, do you?" Evan taunted, walking over to the door. "I mean, like, come on. This thing is wide open."

"Shut up, okay? I didn't think these things even had doors," I stated, following Evan into the game store.

"Well, now you know that they do."

"Why'd you let me struggle trying to open a locked gate then?"

"It was kinda cute, kinda funny," Evan said, shrugging slightly.

"Where's the light switch?" I groaned, ignoring Evan.

"Here," he said from somewhere behind me.

The overhead lights then illuminated the store. Rows upon rows of shelves of games and consoles, and even TVs, all just appeared from the darkness. And, thankfully, there was already a gaming area set up in the corner of the store. That saves us the time and hassle of trying to set up a TV and console.

"Call of Duty?" Evan asked, walking over to the couch and gaming setup.

"No. Let's play a racing game. Or something co-op," I told him, following him over to the couch. I took a seat while he went over to the console and TV.

"Wanna play Mario Kart?"

"Um. Yeah, sure," I replied.

"Just a warning, I'm pretty awesome at Mario Kart. I'm probably gonna whoop your ass."

"Bitch, please. You wish you were as good as me."

"So let's settle this. First to three wins is the better racer."

"You're on," I said.

"Care to make a wager?" Evan asked, turning the TV on.

"Like what?"

"A wager. Just a few bucks or something."

"Okay. Let's make a bet of, oh, I don't know, fifty bucks?" I suggested.

"Whoa, whoa, whoa. Where the hell am I pulling an extra fifty bucks from, my ass?" Evan bemoaned.

"I'm just messing with you. Loser has to make the winner a coffee at the Starbucks on the second floor," I told him.

He smirked and outstretched his hand to me. "You're on."

I took his hand in mine and shook it. "You're gonna lose, you know that, right?"

"Don't be so sure," he said, handing me a Wii controller.

I took the Wii controller from him and we took our seats on the couch. It was pretty comfy for a public-used couch that was probably crawling with lice or something.

39

"You should be Bowser," Evan said.

"What the hell? No. I'm gonna be Mario, you be Bowser."

"I don't wanna be a boring main character," Evan groaned.

"But… Mario versus Bowser," I said whiningly.

"Okay, fine. I'm still gonna win," he said as he began to set up a race for us.

"Wait. I gotta go pee first," I told him.

"Yeah. I'll come with so I don't have to go in the middle of me kicking your ass," Evan said, setting his controller down on the couch.

I tossed mine onto the couch and stood up. I walked out of the store and heard Evan walking behind me. Good thing he can at least keep up in real life, 'cause he's gonna be chasing my muffler smoke in Mario Kart.

"Are you gonna be okay without a group of girls escorting you to the washroom, or should I go get some female mannequins or something? Because I will if you want me to," Evan joked as we walked back to the food court.

"Shut up. I don't even go to the bathroom with other girls. Not all girls do that shit, y'know."

"Just asking."

"And I think a mannequin watching me piss would just be really creepy and disturbing, so…"

"You've made your point," he said as we reached the bathrooms.

I went through the bathroom door and quickly ran over to the stall. I swear I was about to burst like a broken fire hydrant. After a relieving bathroom trip, I walked outside to find Evan standing on top of the table looking up at the second floor.

"What are you looking at?" I asked.

He turned to me and shrugged. "I thought I saw something up there."

"Like what?" I asked, walking over to him. I noticed how my voice carried so well in the empty mall, usually I'd have to yell for someone to hear me at this distance.

"Like a person or something, I don't know." He hopped down from the table and started walking beside me.

"Well, let's just go back so I can whoop your ass in Mario Kart," I

40

told him, glancing up at the second floor. It looked creepy because it was mostly dark now, but there definitely wasn't anyone else in here with us. We'd have known by this point.

"You mean so I can kick your ass?"

"Listen, Evan, I know you've got all this pride in your talents as a racer, but I'm here to prove you that you suck."

"If this were real life, you wouldn't even be able to see over the steering wheel," he teased.

"That's a low blow, man."

"I have to hit you low. All of you is low."

"Okay. I'm gonna *wreck* you," I said, determined as hell to beat him. I took my seat on the couch and Evan plopped beside me.

"I'm glad I'm not a nice guy," Evan said, starting up a race.

"Why's that?" I asked.

He turned and smirked. "Nice guys always finish last."

"Well then, you're the nicest guy I know," I taunted him.

We did this for four races. We just sat and played and kept taunting each other and making jokes at each other's expense. I know he's a stranger, but it all felt so natural with Evan. Neither of us had to try. We just let go for a bit and had fun trying to beat one another in a game.

"Only one more lap," I said, taunting Evan because I was leading the race.

"I refuse to lose to you for a third time, dammit," Evan groaned.

"I'm gonna win! You suck so bad!" I shouted.

"Nope, shut up. I'm coming up," he said, somehow managing to catch up to me.

As we were coming down toward the finish line, we were neck and neck with each other. It was anyone's win now.

And then, a loud and quick whirring sound overcame the mall, and then darkness settled itself all around us. The power had just shut off, or been cut off from the blizzard, and now Evan and I sat on a couch in the dark with useless controllers in hand.

"*I was winning,*" we said at the same time.

{Chapter: **Six**}

"I'm just going to go ahead and assume that neither of us has a flashlight," Evan said, his voice pitch perfect in the darkness.

"You'd be assuming correctly, good sir," I said back to him.

"Damn. Well, okay. We should probably go and find some flashlights, then," he stated, getting up from the couch. Well, it felt like he got up from the couch anyway.

"You gonna go by yourself, that's so nice of you," I said, slightly joking as I stood up.

"You're coming with me, Spencer," he commanded, grabbing my arm and pulling me towards off of the couch and toward the slightly brighter exit of the game store.

"But I don't wanna." I dragged my feet as I followed him into the very dimly lit mall. The only light seeping down form the glass domes in the roof of the mall. At this point in the day, the sky was basically all dark anyway though.

"Okay. Where would they keep flashlights?" he muttered.

"Hmm. Security office would have some," I suggested.

"I'm not going all the way across a pitch-black mall to find the stairs up to the second floor. We'll just have to find flashlights down here. It'll be easier."

"You're no fun," I groaned. "Let's go upstairs."

"If we can't find anything down here, then we'll go upstairs," Evan said, defeated.

"Okay. So now where are we headed? I don't wanna just stand around in the dark," I said, waiting for Evan to start walking somewhere. Thankfully, my eyes had adjusted to the insane darkness of the mall. I could *just* make out the figure of Evan in the darkness at least, but it was too difficult to see more than ten feet in front of me. I could barely manage to see the difference in the white and dark brown tiles on the floor of the mall.

"Um, I think the hardware store is off this direction," Evan stated, walking to the left of the game store.

I turned and followed him, making sure to keep close to him so I didn't lose track of him. "Do they have flashlights there though?"

"Well, they should. It's a hardware store."

"What if there's a gate over the entrance though?" I asked, noticing the slight shimmer of the metal gate in the slight moonlight that filtered in from the overhead skylights.

"Then we improvise," he said.

"Nothing illegal," I said.

"Pfft, I wouldn't dream of it," he said, obviously lying, but whatever. I wasn't about to argue that.

"Just don't do something *too* illegal, okay?"

"I can't make any promises," he said, walking farther out in front of me. Frick, it was hard for me to keep up with him. He should know that I have short legs. It's harder for me to walk fast.

"It's bad enough that we got stuck in here. I don't wanna be breaking all kinds of laws and shit," I told him.

"You won't be breaking any laws. We'll just say it was like this when we found it."

"And how would we get away with that?"

"In the store owner's rush to get out at closing time to beat the storm and traffic, he broke the lock," Evan stated.

"Oh, so to get a flashlight from the hardware store, we need bolt cutters?" I asked. "Which we would find in the hardware store."

"Yeah. I didn't think that through," Evan said, sounding slightly embarrassed.

"You idiot."

"Shut up. We'll figure something out."

God, I hope so. I don't wanna spend all night walking around the dark mall with this total not-so-strange-anymore stranger.

"*You'll* figure something out," I corrected him.

"Shut up. You have to help too," he said.

"I got you out of a boiler room and you knocked me over earlier. You still owe me."

He scoffed. "You're never gonna let the boiler room thing go, are you?"

"Probably not, no," I told him.

"Well, at least I didn't pass out while trying on pants," he teased.

"Shut the hell up," I snapped at him. "You're the one who's getting us lost in the mall."

"It's completely dark in here. Of course we're getting lost," he argued. "It's all disorienting and shit."

"Yeah, keep making up excuses," I teased him.

"I will smack you," Evan threatened.

"Bring it on," I bellowed, shoving him from behind.

"You don't get a massage now," he said, regaining his balance.

"Maybe I don't want any of your damn massages, you little shit potato," I growled.

"You seriously just called me a shit potato?"

"And a little one at that," I stated.

"Follow me to the stairs so I can promptly throw you down them."

I laughed. "I may be small, but my might knows no bounds," I shouted out into the empty black abyss.

"Calm down, Braveheart."

"But when else will we get the chance to be all loud and shit in the mall?" I asked. "We can be as loud as we want," I howled out.

"You better shut up, Spencer. You're gonna wake up all the demon cannibals that sleep in the mall," Evan said.

"We're all alone. Nobody else is here. Stop trying to scare me," I said.

I followed his shadowy figure around a corner. There was a store on the corner that didn't have any metal gate. It was kind of creepy looking though, to be honest.

And then, something from in the store fell or something, followed by Evan screaming a little. "Evan?" I asked, peering into the dark store. "Not funny. I'm leaving you in there to get eaten by the homeless people. Bye."

I turned and started walking off towards the hardware store. If he wants to pretend to be dead in a makeup store, then so be it, but I'm not standing around waiting for him to pop up and grab me from behind or something.

I continued along on my walk away from the store. I enjoyed the darkness of the mall, actually. It, much like the emptiness, was rather calming to me. I heard some footsteps running up behind me, which meant it was perfect time to do to Evan what Evan wanted to do to me.

I turned sharply to the left and into a store that sold stuffed animals. I could see all the insanely creepy and dim lit stuffed teddy bears at the front of the store. I always hated teddy bears.

Anyway, I crouched down behind one of the shelves at the front of the store and waited for Evan to stop in front of the store, which he did, because he's stupid.

"Spencer?" he called out.

I held back my laughter as I thought about all the ways to screw with his mind a little. Perhaps a jump scare? Maybe I throw some teddy bears at him? Hmm, maybe I beat him to the hardware store and chase him down with a chainsaw? Yes. The last one, I like the last one the best.

I smirked to myself as I slinked out of the store and around where Evan was. Boy was so oblivious to the fact that I was barely fifteen feet behind him right now. I snuck around him as he walked into the stuffed animal store. I bet he likes brightly coloured plush toys anyway.

I continued my slow crawl until I got far enough away that he wouldn't hear my footsteps. I lifted myself off the ground and back upright to continue walking towards the hardware store. "I really hope that hardware store is open," I muttered to myself as I walked along.

I finally reached the hardware store, and guess what? It was wide open for me to go on in. Thank God too, if it had been locked, well, my plan of scaring Evan would have gone straight out the metaphorical window.

I walked in and felt around until I found the bin that usually held the flashlights. I pulled one out and ripped open the packaging, quietly of course. I fiddled with it until it turned on and a beam of steady light shot across the store where I aimed the light. I better be quick, or else Evan's gonna see the light from the flashlight, and then it would be plan-out-the-window time for me again.

"Okay. Gardening tools, gardening tools. Where art thou, gardening tools?" I mumbled to myself, turning and walking towards the gardening section of the store.

It wasn't very hard to find the gardening sections, it was surrounded by bags of fertilizer and topsoil and the like. I walked up and down the aisles with the flashlight on the dim light setting. I hoped that the dimmer light wouldn't draw Evan in here yet.

I waddled around in the dim light until I stumbled upon what I was looking for. Chain-freaking-saws. No, they were just regular chainsaws, but I was very happy about seeing them. I grabbed one from the wall and went over to the little pre-filled jerry cans and filled the fuel tank of the chainsaw.

Don't you just love the smell of gasoline, by the way?

After filling the chainsaw, I walked back to the store entrance and set the flashlight down on the ground so it would illuminate the entire entrance to the store. Oh, Evan, you're in for it now.

From the darkness, I saw Evan's figure approaching. And as he walked closer towards me, he became more and more defined. I could see the colour of his eyes shine when he picked up the flashlight from the ground.

"Spencer?" he called out into the dark, aiming the flashlight around in the dark, which caused me to duck behind the shelving so he wouldn't be able to see me.

"Idiot," I whispered to myself, laughing in my mind.

"Spencer, come on. I know you're in here," Evan said as he started walking down one of the first aisles. Thank God he didn't walk towards my aisle though. There wasn't anywhere for me to hide with this chainsaw.

I snuck my way over to the welding section of the store and

grabbed myself one of those scary-looking welding masks. I slid it onto my head and started to walk back to where the beam of light was coming from. It was kinda funny watching Evan walk around looking for me.

"Evan!" I screamed as loud as I possible could. I made sure that it wasn't any regular scream, no, I made sure it was a bloodcurdlingly loud and high-pitched screaming.

"Spencer?!" he shouted back, the beam of light swinging around and heading my way.

I walked down one of the aisles and waited for him to pass by me. I walked out behind him and pulled the cord of the chainsaw and it roared to life. And I do mean roar. The emptiness of the store really helped echo the sounds of the chainsaw. "You're next!" I hissed at him.

He swung around and let out a yelp. The sound he made was barely even human, if human at all. It sounded like a baby poodle or something equally as unmanly.

He ran as I started chasing him with the chainsaw, but I gave up after ten seconds from laughing too hard. Plus, he tripped and fell anyways, dropping the flashlight on the ground as he did.

I killed the engine and dropped the chainsaw to the side. I fell to the ground and took off the welding mask, still laughing harder than I have in recent memory. "You should have seen your face," I said through my cackling.

"You piece of shit!" he howled, rolling over and aiming the light towards me. "I almost had a heart attack," Evan said, trying to catch his breath.

"Your face was all—" I said, making an overly exaggerated scared face at his expense.

"Screw you," Evan muttered, getting up from the ground.

"Come on. It was funny," I said, trying to withhold any more of my laughter.

"It was not funny. It was cruel. Who the hell chases someone through the dark with a chainsaw?" he shouted.

"Someone who wanted to scare the shit out of someone else, obviously," I replied flatly.

"Well, it worked. Jesus. I swear my heart's beating so fast that it's gonna break my ribcage because of you," Evan stated.

I turned and started walking down one of the aisles. "Whatever. I had my fun. Let's go get more flashlights and get on with our night."

"You better sleep with one eye open tonight," Evan said, following behind me, shining the light in front of the both of us.

"Yeah, yeah."

"Seriously, that was so not cool of you. You took a simple prank scare to a whole new damn level."

"That was the point. See, now you'll always remember this night. The night that I, Spencer, scared the bejesus out of you," I explained.

"And you'll always remember this as the night that I, Evan, tied you to an air conditioning unit on the roof."

"We should totally go on the roof tomorrow morning," I said.

"Nope," Evan stated. "We're gonna get the hell out of here tomorrow morning. I don't wanna spend any more time at the mall than I need to."

"But, we have the entire mall all to ourselves."

He sighed. "Okay, but some people actually have lives to go back to. And it's also Christmas time. I'd like to go and see my family and friends."

"Lame, but you make a good point," I said, stopping in front of the flashlight bin. "How many should we take?"

"Like, four or five."

I grabbed a handful of flashlights and handed them to Evan, exchanging them for the already working flashlight.

"Yeah, no, just take the good flashlight," Evan muttered.

I stuck my tongue out at him and blew raspberries at him. "You can shut up."

"You're so dumb. Just lead the way back to wherever it is we're gonna make ourselves a home for the night," Evan said.

I turned and headed back towards the main part of the mall. Time to search for a nice little cozy store to sleep in. "Wanna just leave these flashlights by the game store and then go to the roof right now?" I asked.

"Why?"

"Well, I wanna go up to the roof, if we can even get onto it, and since you don't wanna go tomorrow morning, we should go right now," I told him, trying to sell my case.

"Will it make you shut up about it?" he asked, sounding very, very annoyed with me already. Maybe he was getting tired already and, therefore, cranky.

"It would not make me shut up, but… it might make me a whole lot less whiny with you about it."

"Fine. We can go to the damn roof," Evan said with a groan.

"Hell yeah."

"We'll need to grab coats first," he added.

"Right," I said, making a sharp left and walking into a store. "You're a large, right?" I asked, tossing to him the very first coat I saw.

"Yeah. Thanks, homie," he said, somehow managing to catch the coat and not drop a single flashlight out of the five flashlights he was holding in his arms. "New coats are better than our old coats."

"You are so very welcome," I said, grabbing myself a coat from one of the racks at the front of the store. Thank God for mall stores that specialized in winter coats and suits. The suits part isn't important. I just don't wanna discredit what the store does.

"Okay. So how does one get to the roof?" Evan asked, ripping the flashlights open.

"Well," I said, pausing to think. "I don't actually know."

"Figure it out," he said. He placed the flashlights into his coat pockets for safe keeping.

"You figure it out," I snapped.

"Follow me," he barked, grabbing the flashlight from my hand and walking off.

"Pfft. Rude."

"I'm for sure not rude."

I rolled my eyes and sighed a little. "Whatever you say, buddy. Lead the way."

{Chapter: **Seven**}

Watching Evan saunter through the darkness in a coat that had pockets filled with flashlights was pretty funny. He dropped all but two flashlights onto the couch when we got to the game store. He tossed me one so we would both be able to see where we were going.

"Roof," I groaned as we walked out of the store.

"What is your infatuation with roofs?" he asked.

"You can see the sky and nothing but," I replied.

"Turn your light on."

I looked down at the flashlight in my hands and fiddled with the knobs and buttons. Why was this one so complicated? It's a flashlight, goddammit. Finally, I got the stupid thing to turn on. "There we go." I aimed the light at Evan's face and giggled.

"Stop that," he whined, shielding his eyes from the bright light.

I pushed Evan towards the general direction of the staircases that would take us up to the third floor, though I'm not too sure where to go from there to get to the roof.

"Um, hmm. The mall seems cooler when it's this dark inside," Evan noted as we walked along the row of stores.

"Yeah, kinda like a crazed chainsaw murderer is about to chase you through a hardware store, huh?" I teased.

"I was serious. You better sleep with one eye open tonight. I want me some kind of payback for that stunt."

"But if you get payback, I'll need payback for your payback, and then, boom, endless cycle."

Evan sighed. "Okay, no. If I get payback, that's it. You pranked and scared me half to death, so I get one payback prank."

"Right. But if you get payback, I need to get payback because you would have pranked me, and I have to have the last laugh."

"I'll just be the bigger man here and not prank you at all then," Evan grumbled as he led me towards the big main staircase of the mall.

"That's right, *France*, surrender," I taunted. I guess aggravating him would only make him want to get me back more and more, but dammit, it was just so fun.

"I'll push you down the stairs," Evan threatened as he started up the second set of stairs, the ones to the third floor.

"If you did, I'd take you right down with me."

"Okay, then. I'd like to see you try."

"Just keep walking, you sack of crap," I whined, pushing him on his back to try and get him up the stairs, granted there were a fair bit of stairs.

It was so weird that we just met a few hours ago, but we're already this verbally abusive to each other. It's like we're long lost friends or something. Maybe we were friends in a former life. Or maybe we were enemies. Probably the latter.

Evan stopped after we got to the top of the stairs and turned to me. "Are you tired?" Evan asked.

"Kinda. Why?"

"'Cause you're getting kinda cranky," he stated.

"Ha. Oops," I said. I turned him around and pushed him again. "Let's go to the roof. I just need fresh air. I'm getting mall fever."

"If it'll make you stop pushing me every three seconds," he whined as he headed off down the hall.

Hmm. I've never been to the third floor of the mall. It felt more like a dental office, which made sense. The third floor did house a dental office. It also housed the abortion/sex clinic, a plastic surgeon's office, some other offices and crap, and a small coffee shop. I guess people up here still needed their coffee.

"How do we get to the roof?" Evan asked after we reached the end of the hallway he had chosen for us to walk down.

"I don't know. I was following you," I told him.

"You shouldn't follow idiots."

"You shouldn't be an idiot."

"Touché," he said, turning around to face me.

"Do you see any fire escape signs?"

"Okay. Think this through. Why the hell would there be fire escape signs that lead us to the roof?"

"*Right.*"

"How did you make it this far in life, you silly little nincompoop?" Evan asked jokingly.

"I don't know. I'm just tired, okay?"

"I'll make you some coffee. The coffee shop is on the way back anyway," Evan stated, walking past me and back toward the main area of the third floor.

"You'll make me a coffee?" I asked.

"Are you deaf? I just said I'd make you some coffee."

"Sorry. Like I said, tired."

Evan chuckled as he stopped in front of the little coffee kiosk. "You want a tea, hot chocolate, or just coffee?"

"Gimme a coffee. Double-double," I said.

"Coming right up," he said.

Evan put the flashlight in his mouth and hopped over the counter to get behind it. He started fiddling with some coffee machines, even though the power was out, so I hope he has a better plan than hoping electricity works magically for coffee shops.

"How are you gonna warm up the coffee there, bud?" I asked teasingly.

"They have a gas-powered grill in the back. I was gonna boil the water and make it the old fashioned way," he said, grabbing cups and coffee and filters for the coffee. He walked into the back, and I could only see the occasional flash of light from him moving the flashlight around.

"Hurry. It's frickin' creepy out here," I said, looking back and forth down the long and empty hallway.

"Oh, shut up," Evan sassed back from somewhere in the dark.

"Not gonna happen," I said.

"I'll pee in your coffee."

"No, you won't."

"Well, who's gonna stop me?" he asked.

"I will," I shouted, climbing onto the counter and then sliding and falling off on the other side of it. I heard Evan start laughing his ass off at me. Jerk.

"You're not too bright," he said, walking over and offering me his hand to help me get back on my feet.

I reached for his hand and he helped me back to my feet. "Thanks, but I coulda handled standing up by myself."

"Shut up," Evan said. He picked up my flashlight and handed it back to me. "Are you okay? Nothing's broken, is it?"

"No. I'm fine. Thanks," I said begrudgingly, fixing my pant legs and shirt.

"Well, coffee's almost ready. Wanna just hop back over?" he suggested.

I shook my head.

He sighed. "Okay, you come hold the light for me."

"Okay. I can handle that," I said, following him into the back of the coffee shop. The kitchen was so creepy in the dark, but then again, everything in the mall was creepy in the dark, but then again everything was creepy in the dark.

"Shine the flashlight over here, please."

I did as he commanded and shined the light towards the countertop where he was fiddling with something. I wasn't really paying attention to him. I was using my other flashlight to look around the kitchen instead.

"You're drifting," he said.

I turned and fixed the lazily drifting beam of light. I couldn't help that my arm didn't wanna hold it where he wanted it when I wasn't paying attention.

"Hurry up," I whined.

He scoffed and poured some coffee into the cups he had gotten from the front counter. "Done," he said.

"'Bout freaking time," I grumbled, taking a cup of coffee from him.

"Here," he said, sliding a little black lid across the counter.

I set one of the flashlights down on the counter. "Thanks," I said, picking up the lid and putting it on the top of the cup.

Evan walked over to me and grabbed my coffee from my hand. "Climb back over the counter carefully and you can have your coffee back."

"You're a jerk," I groaned as I walked back to the counter.

"Just looking out for you. Sorry."

"Yeah, yeah," I groaned, climbing onto the counter and then hopping down on the other side.

"See," he said, placing my coffee on the counter. "You did it. And also, that'll be four bucks."

"Four bucks for one coffee?" I asked, taking the coffee from the counter.

"Well, no. You're paying for mine too," he stated.

"Oh. Well, sucks for you, I'm broke."

He climbed over the counter, somehow, with his coffee in one hand and the flashlight in the other. How the hell does he do that? "Then we better run. I don't have any money either."

"You're so strange sometimes," I said, walking back to the area where the stairs are.

"Agreed," he said, following behind me. "Look."

I turned to see him pointing his light towards a sign on the wall that had a directional arrow and a symbol for the roof. At least, I think that's what the symbol was.

"I found it," he said. "Let's get to da roof."

"I'm very excited right now."

"You don't seem it."

"The key to being excited is to not show excitement."

"What kind of drugs is this girl on?" Evan mumbled, shaking his head as he walked down the hallway that the arrow pointed to.

"I don't know, to be honest."

"Have you ever even done drugs?" he asked.

"Um. Yes. I have. One of my close friends is a pothead," I told him, obviously referencing Mindy, but he didn't know that, but now *you* do.

"Do you have any with you?"

"I said I've done drugs, not that I'm addicted to them."

He glanced back at me and smirked a little. "Relax. I wasn't serious anyway. I don't like pot all that much. I'm more of a crack cocaine kind of guy."

"I don't doubt it. Only crackheads get locked inside of boiler rooms."

"Well, only potheads fall asleep in changing rooms," Evan rebutted.

I pushed him against the wall. "Shut up."

"I don't wanna shut up though," he said.

"Well, can you please?"

"Oh, look. I found the stairs to the roof," Evan said, turning to a door with a sign that had the same roof symbol on it. Why not just write roof on a sign? What the heck is the symbol actually needed for?

"Let's go up it then," I said, opening the door. I looked in and saw a pretty small stairwell, which made sense. Why would you need a super long staircase for a roof that's only one floor up?

Evan pushed past me and walked up the stairs. "Grab a chair or something to keep the door from closing over."

"What door?" I asked, walking over and shining the light to the top of the stairs where he was standing.

"This one," he said, kicking the metal door in front of him.

"Give me a sec," I groaned, laying down my cup of coffee on the stairs.

"Hurry up," he whined.

I sighed and walked back to the hallway. I flashed the light around the hallway, searching the darkness for a chair or something. Unfortunately, there were no chairs in the hallway, just one of those water dispenser things. I walked over and ripped the big-ass water bottle out of the machine.

This'll have to work.

I walked back with the bottle of water, barely able to carry it because of the weight of the water inside. Water is so heavy.

I walked over to the stairs and dropped it down. "Will this work?"

Evan came down and picked up the jug of water. "Yeah. It just has to stop the door from closing on us." He took it and walked back up to the door.

I picked up my coffee and walked up after him. My shoes were causing a little echoing because of the metal stairs and concrete walls. Kinda spooky.

"Open the door, nerd," I said to Evan.

Evan scoffed at me, and then scoffed again. "Here goes nothing," he said, pushing the door open.

A gust of cold air swept over us, thank God we had put on coats. Evan put the water bottle down and tested it to make sure it would hold the door open. It did.

We walked out onto the roof with our coffees in hand. We switched our flashlights off and put them in our pockets. It was kind of pointless to have flashlights on when you're outside. Besides, the light from the sky was still plenty bright enough out on the roof for us to be able to see pretty well. Well, not really, but we still didn't need flashlights.

"The sky looks so pretty," Evan joked. The sky was a deep and dark grey colour. You know, because of the storm-of-the-century blizzard currently raging all around us. There was a lot of snowflakes falling all around us too.

"All this snow falling does look pretty though," I said, walking with Evan towards the edge of the roof. There was a half wall instead of a railing as the guard. Evan leaned over with his elbows on the concrete wall, so I decided to do the same.

"I think the snow would look cooler if the sky was a deep purple-pink colour," Evan stated.

"Yeah, but blizzards kinda make seeing the sky a bit impossible."

"It's still nice out," Evan said, fixing his beanie. The wind was probably gonna blow it right off his head, which would honestly be pretty hilarious.

"I guess."

"You don't seem to excited to be up here."

"I had hoped the storm woulda let up a little by now. I thought the sky would look all pretty because of the power outages, but apparently not yet," I replied.

"Maybe tomorrow night," Evan suggested.

"Tomorrow night?"

"Well, look at all this snow and ice. I don't think we'll be getting out tomorrow." His face almost looked defeated when he spoke.

I looked out at the endless blanket of snow and ice that had coated the entire town with its shimmering sheen. Was that poetic enough?

"I wish we had syrup for snow cones," Evan said with a sigh.

"Just eat the yellow snow," I told him.

"There isn't any yellow snow up here."

"Right. Look the other way and I can change that for you."

"You're gross. I'm not eating your nasty pee snow," he stated.

"Looks like it's just more for me," I joked.

"You're gross."

"Mm. My dad tells me that a lot," I said.

"What for?"

"He's my dad?" I said, raising an eyebrow at him, not even sure if Evan could see it or not.

"You have a good relationship with your dad?"

"The best. Well, kind of," I said.

"Mm? Go on."

"Well, he just doesn't seem to have time for the family anymore. Maybe it's just because we're just getting older. I don't know though. I hate how different things are with him now. Like, we used to do everything together. I was such a daddy's girl growing up, so it sucks that he isn't around as much now," I explained. "Sorry for the whining."

"No, no. Don't be sorry. Sometimes, it's nice to just vent and get out all those emotions and whatnot," Evan said.

"What about you? What's your dad like?" I asked.

"Wouldn't really know."

"Why's that?" I pried.

"He left us when I was seven," Evan replied. "It's hard to remember someone who left over a decade ago. His face and voice are just, y'know, distant memories now."

"Oh. I'm sorry to hear that," I said, resting my hand on Evan's. Lucky thing that his coffee was in his other hand.

"Don't be. I was young. I don't think it affected me anywhere near as much as it tore apart my mom," Evan stated. "She cried for weeks. She was angry, hurt, upset, pissed off, jealous, envious, and regretful. I mean, like, she told me at least once a week that she was so sorry for him leaving and she made sure that I knew it wasn't my fault that he left."

"Do you ever feel like it is?"

"No. It was his fault he left. He wanted a life of cheap skanks and drugs. He wanted a life that a wife and son couldn't give him."

I squeezed his hand in mine and he flashed me a small smile. "Your mom sounds strong."

"She's been sober for two years now, actually," Evan said.

"See."

"I've never seen anyone's hands shake as much as hers did the night he left. She could barely open the bottle of whisky that she jid under her bed," Evan said, chuckling softly.

"What's funny about that?"

"Life. Life is funny. I mean, it was so long ago. My mom even laughs about it now." Evan took a sip from his coffee. "Funny how when you're broken, you never think you'll be fixed. And then, when you're fixed, you never remember *why* you were broken."

{Chapter: **Eight**}

After an hour and a half on the roof, I started to get way too cold to want to stay up there for much longer. I just didn't wanna be *that* guy or, in this case, girl. I figured Evan liked it out here. He was pretty talkative, though we avoided anything too deep after he had told me about his dad leaving him when he was younger. We talked about school and work, mostly.

"Evan," I said, cutting off one of his sentences in some story he was telling me about his old school.

"Yeah?"

"I'm freezing," I said, which also probably audibly noticeable because of my slightly chattering teeth. It was that cold, yes.

"Wanna go back in?" he asked.

I nodded.

"Okay, come on," he said, letting go of my hand and walking back towards the door. He didn't stop holding my hand from after I had held his. It was actually kind of nice that he didn't stop till just now. Made me almost forget about how cold it got.

"You can't just leave your empty cup up here," I scolded him as I grabbed his cup from the concrete ledge he had left it on.

"Sorry, tree hugger," he joked, opening the door for me as I walked over.

I sighed as I walked past him. "You're an idiot."

"I know," he said with a grunt as he lifted the water bottle and brought it just inside the door, laying it down next to the door for future use.

"We should make more coffee," I said.

"Can we go and make it in the food court?"

"Why?"

"Because I don't wanna hop the counter or go all the way around to the employee entrance, okay? The coffee shop at the food court has an entrance right in the front, dang," Evan said in a whiny tone.

"Whatever. Let's just go," I said, starting to walk down the stairs. "My bones are freezing."

"I can only go as fast as you're going," Evan said.

"Shut up," I snapped, pulling my flashlight out of my coat pocket. I turned it on and it helped tremendously with seeing in the dark.

"We're gonna need to make beds somewhere," Evan said as we walked back into the hallway.

"Really? Wow. I sure didn't think of that at all," I said sarcastically.

"You can make your own coffee now," Evan muttered as he walked past me with his flashlight aimed toward the staircase leading back to the main parts of the mall.

"Wait. I'm sorry. Please make me coffee," I said, walking after him.

"What do I get out of it?"

"I promise to make you a super awesome breakfast."

"Nah. You can't even make coffee. How would you make breakfast?" he asked. "I'll just make you coffee because I'm nice."

"And I saved you from the boiler room."

"You're just gonna keep using that as a bargaining tool, aren't you?" he asked with a sigh.

"Probably. Let's also not forget how you most likely bruised my butt when you ran into and knocked me over," I said.

"Most likely?"

"Well, I haven't exactly checked out my own ass lately," I said.

"I'll do it for you," he said as we started walking down the stairs back into the mall part of the mall.

"Pfft."

"I'm a registered booty inspector."

"Not even if you paid me," I said. There ain't no way some *stranger* is gonna look at my booty.

"Well, have fun with that booty bruising."

"I will. And you can have fun making me coffee *and* breakfast now."

"Why do I have to make you breakfast now too?" he asked as we reached the bottom of the staircase.

"Because you tried to sneak a peek at my booty."

"I didn't try. I asked. There's a difference," Evan stated.

"What's the difference?"

"Well, one is pervy and creepy. The other is light-hearted and was meant to be taken as a joke, which isn't funny now that you made me explain it."

"I'm a joke killer. What can ya do, eh?" I teased him.

"Make you coffee, apparently," he said jokingly.

"You make good coffee."

"Right. Right. While I make the coffee, you go off and get a bunch of candles for us to have some light for when we make our beds," Evan stated.

"Candles? Isn't that a bit—"

"Cliché and romantic? Well, don't worry. Nothing remotely romantic or sexual can happen because this isn't our third date, nor is it a motel room on the night of prom."

"Yeah. Those are pretty clichéd."

"I promise you that there will be no romantic shenanigans by the candlelight tonight. Okay, Spencer?" he said. "Now go. Get us some candles. Oh, and a lighter."

"Well, romantic is okay. Sexual is not."

"I'm not gonna sit and write poems about the way your eyes sparkle in the candlelight," Evan said flatly.

"Dude, why not? My eyes are beautiful," I joked to him. Well, I was only kinda joking. My eyes *are* beautiful.

"They're sparkly green and gorgeous. That's as much as you're getting from me," Evan said, probably said it begrudgingly at best.

"Do you *really* think that?" I asked, nudging his arm.

"I actually do. You have really cool eyes." He swatted my arm away. "Now, can you go and find us those frigging candles?"

"Aye, aye, captain," I said, giving him a little salute, which made him chuckle a bit. He had such a cute little chuckle.

"Meet me at the game store, okay?" Evan said as I turned away from him to walk off.

"I think I can manage that. Wish me luck," I said, walking into the darkness, alone and with my trusty flashlight.

"Wait, why do you need luck?"

I turned back around. "All those cannibals lurking out there in the dark," I joked.

He scoffed, shook his head, and walked off towards the food court. Yeah, if I were him, I'd be sick of my shit by this point too.

I walked into the dark mall, shining my flashlight into the stores as I walked towards the way where I thought the hippie-ass store with candles and junk would be. I knew it was somewhere around where I was, but I can't remember perfectly, and the darkness didn't really help me all that much with finding it.

I finally did find the store though, the stupid hippie-ass store. I walked inside and sort of sighed in relief that there wasn't a gate in the way. I'd have been so pissed if I had to find a way to open the gate, or if I had to go and get Evan just to get the gate open. I grabbed a small wicker basket and filled it with a bunch of candles, most likely scented ones, but I wasn't paying attention to what candles I was grabbing. I also grabbed a handful of lighters from the convenience kiosk just outside the store. Time to go back to Evan.

I walked back towards the food court and saw the light from his flashlight, which helped me in knowing where he was. But then it dawned on me. This was a prime time for him to scare the shit out of me for earlier, y'know, the chainsaw thing.

"Evan?" I called out as I walked over to the coffee shop. I turned my flashlight off and put it into the basket I was carrying. I picked up his flashlight from the counter where he had left it. "You back there, Evan?" I asked into the darkness of the kitchen.

I didn't get any answers. I didn't expect to get any either. Where the hell did this kid go? I shrugged it off and walked towards the kitchen. May as well just get the scare over with.

"Why'd you take my flashlight?" Evan's voice asked from behind me.

I turned and shined the light on him. "Why'd you just leave it lying around?"

"I had to carry our coffee to the game store."

"That makes sense," I said, walking back out from behind the counter. "I was pretty sure that you were gonna scare me as payback for the chainsaw."

"Damn. I should've. It was the perfect opportunity," he groaned.

"Ha, you suck," I said, handing him his flashlight.

"You should be glad I didn't scare you."

"You wouldn't have been able to do better than my chainsaw," I gloated.

"That may be true, but I still could have scared you. Let's go back and try this again, okay?"

"No chance. You messed up your best chance at payback," I said with a smirk.

"Shit," he muttered. "Well, whatever. Let's just take the candles and go get our coffee and make us some beds."

"Agreed. Sleepy Spencer is sleepy."

"We could sleep in the superstore. They got beds in there," Evan suggested.

"Sure. I don't wanna sleep in a game store, so I guess that's a better option," I stated.

We walked back to the game store, which wasn't very far. We grabbed our coffees and left. Evan carried the flashlight and his coffee, and I carried my coffee and the basket of candles and lighters. I really don't know why I grabbed seven or so lighters when we only really needed one or two, but all well.

"Figures," I muttered as we walked up to the store that had a large metal gate covering the entrance.

"We'll get in. Chill," Evan stated, setting his coffee down on the ground and walking over to the side of the entrance, presumably looking for the handle or something.

I let out a sigh. "Let's just go sleep on the beanbag chairs in the hippie store."

"What the hell? No. We're gonna get mattresses."

"So then open the gate."

"Don't sass me. I'm thinking."

"Well, think faster. I'm getting tired and cranky."

"Then drink my coffee too. Maybe that'll pep you up a little bit," Evan suggested.

I scoffed at him and drank a fair bit of my coffee. "You better hope that this caffeine kicks in soon."

"Seriously. Just down your coffee and mine so that way you can stay awake," Evan stated.

"Why?"

"Sleep is for the weak," he replied.

"Then just go ahead and call me weak, I'm tired."

"Just wait here. I'm gonna go get a crowbar," Evan said, walking past me. He took the light with him, of course, so I had to set down the basket and turn on my flashlight so I could see. I hated standing in the dark. It made me feel, I don't know, vulnerable in a way. There's no telling what lies in the darkness unless you can see it.

"Hurry up," I called out to him.

"I'll try," he called back. He already got a pretty fair distance from me. I guess he really was at least hurrying.

I watched as his light beam got farther and farther away from me. I waited for a while. It took Evan a few minutes to walk to the store and back. I heard footsteps and turned to shine my light on Evan. "Look who decided to come back."

"I got the crowbar," he said, holding the metal bar.

"Bust this bitch open then," I told him as he walked by me and to the latch where the gate met the wall. It was one of those super big sliding gates, not one of the gates that you have to pull down.

"No, really? I thought sleeping on the tiles would be a better idea than going in and sleeping on real mattresses," Evan sassed me.

"Shut up." I pouted at him a little, but I doubt he even noticed.

Evan raised the crowbar and starting prying at the latch of the gate, trying to get it to pop open.

"Is it even locked though?" I asked.

"No. This gate needs to be fixed. It gets stuck like this an awful lot. I used to work here. I'm amazed that they haven't fixed it yet," Evan said as he strained to pry the gate open.

"You used to work here?" I asked.

"Yeah," he said, groaning as he pulled on the crowbar. "Why?"

"Well, I shop here all the time. I've never seen you here before."

"I had longer hair. You know, the shaggy skater hair."

"I don't even think I remember anyone like that. It's probably just me though. I'm bad with remembering faces," I said with a small shrug.

"This goddamn crowbar won't get stuck where it needs to get stuck," Evan shouted. Each push and pull was getting more and more aggressive and desperate with frustration, and it was kind of entertaining.

"Gimme," I said, walking over and taking the crowbar. I moved it down from where he had it and jimmied it into the latching thing. "Kick it," I commanded him, moving back from the crowbar.

"Um, okay," he said, doubtful that this would work. I was pretty doubtful too. He took a few steps back and gave it a jogging start. He kicked the crowbar, and with a loud metal creak, the latch bent open, causing the crowbar to drop with a clang to the floor. I pulled the gate over so it was wide enough for us to get through.

"Hell yeah!" I shouted.

"Lucky," Evan said, picking up the basket with the candles and walking inside the store.

"Yeah. You're just mad because I got it and *you* didn't," I teased, picking up our coffees and walking into the store after Evan.

"Shut up," Evan grumbled.

"Don't be sassy with me."

"Just follow me to the bedding section," Evan groaned. I think he's getting sleepy too.

"Yes, ma'am."

"Oh, you're just asking to get your ass kicked."

"I could 100% beat you up," I said, pushing him playfully. "Oh, hey, look. Beds." I pointed towards the section of the store that had all the beds. Some of these beds were actually very nice and looked quite comfy. Probably much better than whatever mattress I had at home that I've been using for years too.

"Over here. There's two beds that are already set up," Evan said, walking towards the area he just described.

"Thank God that we don't have to set up the mattresses ourselves."

"Lucky guess on my part. This is all new. When I worked here, we had the mattresses all lined up on shelves, well, sorta. But yeah, this saves us a fair bit of time," Evan stated. "And we can even sit on the floor between these two beds, so that's cool."

"The floor isn't comfy though," I whined, following close behind Evan.

He sighed. "We can get you a little pillow for you to sit down on so it's more comfortable for you."

"Fine. What are we gonna do, play cards or something?"

"I dunno. Maybe tomorrow morning we could."

"It's Christmas Day tomorrow," I noted.

"Oh, yeah. It is. Well, we better make sure to get lots of sleep so that Santa will come and visit us tonight," Evan said, laying down the basket next to one of the beds.

"Why do you get that one?" I asked, looking at his bed.

"I gave you the bigger one," he said, sitting down on the edge of the bed he chose. I turned and looked at the other bed, which was next to his bed, but we had a ten-foot space between the two beds.

"I guess it looks bigger... but I don't like big beds. I feel so alone," I said, walking over and sitting down on the edge of the bed. "At least the mattress feels all nice and comfy."

"Your ass has a wonderful comfort sensor," Evan joked, pulling some of the candles out of the basket. "Do you wanna go to sleep now, or do you wanna stay up and play cards? 'Cause I *could* go and get a deck of cards for us."

"Well, it's been a long day and I'm tired."

"Sleep it is," he said, putting the candles back into the basket.

"Goodnight, Evan," I said, slipping my shoes off and laying myself down onto the bed.

"Night, Spencer. If you need anything, just wake me."

"Will do."

{Chapter: **Nine**}

I awoke, pretty much expecting that yesterday had just been some weird dream, but it wasn't. I opened and rubbed the sleep out of my eyes and saw the high ceiling of the store above me. I really did just sleep in a mall, huh? Wow. That was the most bizarre thing I've done in a long-ass time.

I rolled over to see Evan's bed to check if he was in the bed. And there was a surprising lack of Evan in that bed. I sat up and looked around. There was zero trace of Evan's existence around here. Maybe I just hallucinated him because of the darkness last night.

"Evan?" I called out into the store, my voice slightly echoing around the empty aisles and shelves.

The only answer I got was the silence. The lights weren't even on, minus a battery-powered lamp on a little table in between Evan's bed and mine. I guess Evan really does exist, because I sure as hell didn't set up any lamps.

"Evan, why'd you leave this lamp here?" I called out. Again, not getting any answers from the empty store. I got up and picked up my shoes. I better go look for this idiot.

I walked over to the clothing section and dropped my shoes to the floor, and then I slipped out of my pants and shirt and put on a new set of clothes. I grabbed my clothes and tossed them on the bed I had slept on. I'll come back for them… if I remember.

I took off my socks and balled them up inside of my shoes. I hate wearing socks when I wake up. I don't know, I just like the feel of cold tile on my feet. It's refreshing.

I walked out of the store and looked around. Now, if I were Evan, where would I go first thing in the morning?

Food court.

I walked towards the direction of the food court, wondering why this douche canoe didn't just leave me a note or something. I walked into the food court and smelt pancakes. Evan was cooking pancakes? Well, he better be cooking me some pancakes as payment for leaving me alone in the store like that. I walked towards the smell, which was coming from that Thai food place we had gotten food from yesterday.

"Evan?" I shouted into the restaurant.

"Spencer?" he called back. Oh, thank God. I found him.

I walked behind the counter and into the kitchen, where I saw Evan with a few of those battery-powered lamps lighting up the stove he was using to cook food.

"There's the sleepyhead," he said, glancing over at me. He was cooking on the fire grill thing. Gas burners are outage-proof. Smart.

"Why didn't you wake me up?" I asked, setting my shoes down on the counter.

"I woke up before you and I thought that waking you up to breakfast would have been nice. I thought I woulda had more time than this," he stated. "You were out like a light when I left."

"Oh. Right. Well, it's the thought that counts."

"You like pancakes, right?" he asked.

I nodded. "Obviously. Who the hell doesn't like pancakes?"

"My ex-girlfriend."

"Wow. Why did you even date her?"

"Now that I think about it, I don't really know," Evan said jokingly. "I didn't know if you liked maple syrup or butter syrup, so I brought a bottle of both."

"I like maple syrup," I said.

"Good. We can put the stupid butter syrup back in the trash where it belongs."

"They look pretty good. Are you, like, a culinary student or something?" I asked him.

"No. I already told you I'm a business student," Evan said.

"Oh, yeah," I said, remembering when he had told me last night. "I'm bad with the remembering things sometimes."

"It's alright. I remembered that you said you were in college to become a porn star."

"I'm in an art and design class, asshole."

"I was just teasing you. Calm down," he said. "Grab a plate from beside me. The pancakes are almost ready."

I walked just past him and grabbed myself a plate from the stack of plates he had next to him. "Here," I said, handing him my plate.

He took the plate and put three pancakes down onto it. "Here," he mocked, handing me back the plate with the pancakes.

"Smells so good," I said, grabbing the bottle of maple syrup from the counter.

"You like simple things, don't you?"

"I like some simple things," I stated, walking towards the front counter. I grabbed a little plastic bag that had a fork and spoon in it as I walked out. "I'll see you out here." I walked over and sat at one of the tables that were lit up by the skylight. Saves us from using those lamps.

"Don't start without me," Evan said, rushing over with his own plate of pancakes in his hands.

"Wouldn't dream of it," I said as I ripped open the plastic bag on one of those little plastic cutlery sets and pulling out the fork from it.

Evan sat down in front of me and smiled. "Morning."

"Morning," I said. "Did you remember to get a fork for yourself?"

"Of course," he said, pulling the plastic-wrapped cutlery out of his pocket and opening it up. "Did you really think I would forget eating utensils?"

"I don't know. Yes."

"I'm shocked in your doubt in me," Evan said, taking the bottle of maple syrup and pouring some on his pancakes.

"Gimme," I said, grabbing at the syrup bottle. "I was about to use that, you thief."

"Were you?" he said, letting go of the bottle.

69

"I was."

He flashed me a smile as he started to eat a piece of his pancake.

"What are we gonna do after this?" I asked him, drizzling the syrup over my pancake stack.

"Well, it is Christmas today," Evan said, chewing some pancake as he spoke.

"Merry Christmas," I said.

"Mm, a merry Christmas to you too," he said.

"Should we get gifts for each other?"

"That sounds like a good idea, but you're just gonna get me socks or something, aren't you?"

I shook my head as I took a bite of pancake.

"Then what?"

I shrugged as I swallowed my food. "Whatcha want?"

"Xbox 360, Xbox 360," he said jokingly.

"I'll get you socks, and you'll friggin' enjoy them," I said, cutting up more of my pancakes.

"Well, I think getting each other gifts would be a pretty good idea," Evan stated. "I mean, we're locked in a mall, so we're surrounded by things that can be given as presents. We don't have to take anything home. It's more or less for the spirit of Christmas. Right?"

"I'll agree to actually getting gifts if you agree to wrapping them," I bargained.

"Why do we have to wrap them?"

"Ripping open the packaging on gifts is the best part of the gift. All that anticipation building up," I said, taking another bite of pancake. "Y'know?"

"I guess," he said with a shrug. "Can I just give you yours in a bag or something?"

"No," I said. "You have to wrap them nice and good, or else I won't give you the gifts I'm gonna get you."

"So we're really gonna do this?" he asked.

"Yes. Let's really get each other some gifts."

"Anything in particular that you want?"

"A boyfriend," I said with a playful wink to him.

"Already here," he said with a wink back. "But seriously, tell me three things you want. We'll get each other three things."

"I don't know. Get me whatever you think I'd want," I told him. "What do you want?"

"I have to tell you what to get me, but you won't just tell me what you want?" Evan asked, sounding a bit frustrated at me.

"Get me a book or something."

"I'm not getting you a book."

"Fine, jerk."

"We need to set some boundaries though," Evan stated.

"What do you mean?"

"Like, I'll get gifts for you from the bottom floor stores, and you can go upstairs to the second floor to get presents for me," Evan explained. "That way, we won't bump into each other and ruin the surprise."

"Where can I get wrapping paper upstairs?" I asked.

"They have an arts and crafts store on the second floor," Evan replied.

And I think we both got excited, because we started eating our pancakes hella quickly. We really wanted to finish eating so we could go gift "shopping" for each other.

"Ready to go?" I asked.

"Wait here for a minute," he said, swallowing the last of his pancakes.

"What? Why?" I asked as he got up from the table.

"I'm gonna get us flashlights," he stated. "The stores and shit will be dark 'cause the skylights can't light up the whole mall."

"Oh, smart idea. I'll wait here."

"No shit," he said as he started walking back towards the store we had slept in last night.

And so I waited. It took Evan at least five minutes to go to the store, get flashlights, and come back over to me. I watched as he walked over to me, he was playing with one of the flashlights, just clicking it on and off a few times. I stuck my hand out as he walked over, and he handed a flashlight to me, and I promptly flashed the light on and off while I aimed it at his face.

"Are you always this annoying?" he barked at me, swatting my hand and flashlight down to the table.

"Usually," I said, clicking the flashlight off. "Yeah."

"Well, get gone. I'm gonna go and search for some presents for you," Evan said.

"When and where are we gonna meet up when we're done?" I asked.

"We'll meet up in an hour back at our beds," Evan stated.

I nodded. "Okay, that sounds like a plan."

"Well, see you in about an hour or so."

I stood up from the table and sighed. "Time to go gift shopping again. Lame."

Evan laughed softly as he started to walk away. "Have fun."

"I'll try," I said, walking off in the other direction. I walked towards the stairs that led to the second floor and walked up them, duh. What else was I gonna do on the stairs?

I made it to the top of the stairs, barely winded, and looked around. I wondered what a dude like Evan would even want for a gift. I mean, he wears that beanie all the time from what I can tell, so I guess I could find him a new beanie. I think there's a hat store with a good beanie selection on the second floor somewhere.

I walked towards along the row of stores, flashing my flashlight into each of the stores to see what that store had in it, and so far, I couldn't see any beanies or tuques. I kept walking though, just hoping to find a hat store. And that's when I did see the hat store. It was just across from where I was, so I walked on over, shining my flashlight at the hats in the hat rack closest to the outside of the store.

I picked up a hat as I got there, it wasn't a beanie, it was a snapback, but at least I'm in the right store. I put the hat back and walked into the store.

I shone the light around the store. The walls were lined with hats. They had snapbacks, fitted hats, beanies, beanies with pompoms on top and flaps that covered your ears, and Santa hats, since it was Christmas and all.

I walked over to the beanie wall and looked it over, up and down, left and right, looking for a really cool beanie for Evan. I grabbed a few, but they were kinda nasty colours. And then I saw it. I saw a classic Mighty Ducks-coloured beanie with a pom-pom on the top of it. I pulled it down and looked it over. The green and purple and silver colours really meshed well with each other. I think Evan would like this one a lot. I thought it would suit him well.

I went over to the counter and dug around for a plastic bag that I could put the hat in. I grabbed another hat too. It was a similar one that had earflaps as well as the pompom on the top.

"Evan better like these," I grumbled to myself as I put the two hats into the little plastic bag. I walked out of the store and flashed the light down along the other stores. I think there might be a chocolates-only store up here. I could get Evan chocolate. He has to like chocolate. Everyone likes chocolate.

I walked around more, searching for that chocolate store. I eventually did find it, but only after walking around the main loop of the second floor a few times. It was right in the corner, tucked away. I walked over and looked through the half-closed gate and into the store. They had a lot of chocolate here, obviously.

I went over and looked at the Belgian chocolates display. I don't think Evan would really care what country's chocolates he's eating, but I got him a variety. I grabbed a box of Belgian chocolates first, followed by Swiss chocolates, and then I also got him some domestic chocolates. I think the box said that they were from a chocolate factory in Halifax or something.

"Shit. What else would this kid want?" I muttered into the empty mall as I walked out of the chocolates store. I walked around some more and looked at all the stores I passed by. They were all just clothing stores or stores for little kids or stores for girls. I mean, maybe I could get him a really sexy set of lingerie as a joke.

I walked around until I found a store that sold games and comics. I walked in and started looking around. I guessed that Evan would probably like some lame-ass board game. He seems like the kind of dude who might like to play a game of Monopoly based on different forms of bacon.

I went over to the counter and grabbed a bigger bag. The little bag from the hat store wasn't gonna be able to fit a board game on top of the three small boxes of chocolate and the two hats that were already in there. I put the smaller bag into the new bag I just got. "I should have just grabbed a big bag in the first place," I groaned, putting the bacon-themed Monopoly into the bag.

I walked back towards the hat store. The store that had gift wrap stuff in it was back over that way. I should have also taken the wrapping paper to go before I left that section of the mall. I can be dumb sometimes.

I walked into the store and grabbed some wrapping paper and tape. I was never any good at wrapping presents. I pride myself on being good at a lot of things, but wrapping presents was not one of my strong suits.

I sat down and tried my best to wrap the hats up. They ended up looking like a ball of poorly taped wrapping paper if anything. The boxes of chocolate and the board game were easier for me to wrap, but I still managed to make them too big on the ends and that made it crease all weird. Whatever. It would have to do.

I grabbed some little sticky bows and put them on each of the presents. It looked like I had gotten him five gifts now. I picked up the gifts after putting the bow on the last present.

I took the presents in my arms and carried them back down to our meeting area. I don't think I was more than a half an hour. I guess waiting for Evan to be done with his shopping is just a *great* way to pass the rest of the hour or so.

{Chapter: **Ten**}

After a half an hour of waiting by our "campsite," Evan finally re-turned with his arms full of poorly wrapped presents for me.

I was really curious as to what Evan got me. But I swear to God, if he got me a stuffed animal, I might punch him. Stuffed animals are such a cliché gift to give to a girl, in my opinion. It doesn't matter what occasion the gift is for. Stuffed animals are clichés.

"Hey, stranger," Evan said, walking over and laying the gifts down on his bed.

"I've been waiting here for quite some time," I told him, sitting up on my bed, as I had been just lying down for a little bit.

"Why didn't you come and get me?" Evan asked, sitting down across from me on the edge of his bed.

"I thought we had the agreement of not meeting up again until we met back here. I was just obeying the rules we set."

"Well, stop."

"Stop what?"

"Obeying the rules all the time," Evan stated.

"How 'bout I just punch you?"

"That'd be against the law."

"Laws are rules," I rebutted.

"Okay, but no breaking the law," he said with a sigh.

"Fine." I let out a sigh as I looked down to the floor and ruffled my hands through my yet-to-be-brushed hair. I liked it messy though. I guess leaving it messy sometimes is a good idea. I should do that more often.

"It's cute," Evan said.

"Hmm?" I mumbled, looking up at him. "What's cute?"

"You," he replied. "It's cute the way you run your fingers through your hair like that."

"Oh, shut up," I snapped at him.

"Sorry," he said, pouting slightly.

"Alright, so you wanna swap some Christmas presents now?" I asked him.

He shook his head. "It doesn't feel like Christmas right just yet."

"How do we make it feel like Christmas?" I asked.

"Easily," he said. "We have to go and find stockings and fill them with candy and gum and chocolate."

"And eggnog," I said. "It ain't Christmas without some eggnog."

"I'll get the eggnog. If it hasn't all gone bad though," Evan stated. "You go off and stuff a stocking for me."

I nodded, standing up. "Will do." I walked off toward the Christmassy section. Of course, the floor was pretty cold on my bare feet. I had taken my shoes and socks off because I like being comfortable and comfort isn't wearing socks. Socks are foot prisons. RT if you agree.

"Get yourself some socks too," Evan called after me.

I swear he's a mind reader. "Nope," I called back, rounding the corner and walking down a large aisle. Off to the Christmas decoration section for me.

As I walked, I realized that I hadn't brought a flashlight with me, which was a problem. It was pretty dark in this store. They didn't have any skylights or anything in here. I guess it's up to my eyes. I walked slowly, waiting for my eyes to adjust to the darkness.

After about a minute or so, I could see fairly decently. I made it to the Christmas section without stubbing my toe a third time and got a stocking to fill up for Evan.

Then I walked over to the chocolates and candy aisle, my favourite aisle, and started to pile random candies and chocolates into the stocking. It was too dark for me to be picky about what I give Evan in a stocking. I doubt he would be picky about what he got anyway.

I walked back over to the beds and sat on mine. Evan wasn't back yet though. He's a little slacker. I was tempted to just open the presents that Evan had brought back for me, but I fought off the temptation.

"You didn't bring a flashlight when you left, did ya?" Evan asked.

I looked over and watched him walking back over with a basket in one hand and a flashlight in the other. "No. I forgot."

"Idiot. Did you manage to get the stocking filled?"

"I did," I said with a pleased smile.

"Spencer's a little owl now," he joked, sitting down on his bed and laying the basket down on the floor between our beds.

I looked down and could see the eggnog as well as two cups in the basket. Evan was on the ball today.

"Wanna do the honours?" he asked, pushing the basket towards me with his foot.

"Of opening this bitch up and drinking its guts?" I asked, picking up the basket. "I'd love to."

"You need any help?" he asked as I picked up the carton.

"Listen, bitch, I can handle opening a carton of eggnog," I said, opening the carton up. "But thank you for the offer."

"Wow. Don't get sassy with me," Evan said, raising his hands as if he were surrendering to me.

"Sorry," I said, grabbing a cup from the basket and pouring some of the eggnog into it. I guess the fridges here have good seals because the eggnog was still pretty cold. I held out the cup to him. "Take it," I told him.

He groaned softly as he got off his bed and took the cup from me. "Thank you."

"Anytime," I said, grabbing the second cup from the basket.

"Hey, how come you got me five gifts?" Evan asked, motioning with his head towards the stack of gifts next to me on my bed. "We agreed on getting each other three gifts. Are you trying to make me look bad?"

"Well, three of them are the same gift, or at least, that's how I classified them as being."

"I bet they're different."

"Why would they be different?" I asked.

"You wanna look like the big shot here."

"Evan," I said. "It's just the two of us here. Who the hell would I be trying to impress? I don't even buy into the consumerism of Christmas."

"What do you mean?" Evan asked, sipping some of his eggnog.

"Well," I said, pouring some eggnog into the cup I had been holding, "Christmas used to be about sentiments and family and friends and other loved ones. And I guess it could still be that way if you want it to be, but I think companies only care about it because of the insane amounts of money that they make from it. And the kids like it for all the gifts. I just think that, as a society, we're kind of losing the meaning of Christmas and how Christmas should be."

Evan nodded in agreement as I set down the carton of eggnog. "Yeah. I see what you're saying."

"Yeah?"

"I said it to agree with you," Evan said. "I agree that Christmas has turned into a giant end of the year sale. It lasts all December too. We have Christmas sales and then Boxing Day sales. It's still nice to give gifts and all, but yeah, it's lost its meaning."

"I love Boxing Day sales though."

"Me too," Evan said. "It's the one time a year I can buy a surplus of shit I don't need and nobody will judge me on it or tell me that I'm spending too much money on something useless."

"I feel you on that," I said, sipping some eggnog. "I guess the consumerism isn't *all* bad then."

"I *love* consumerism on Halloween though."

"Why?" I asked.

Evan smirked a little. "Really? You can't think of why?"

"No?"

"All the Halloween candy that goes on sale in the week after Halloween. You can go get boxes of chocolate and candy for half off," Evan explained.

"I love the week after Halloween," I said, almost moaning at the thought of all that reduced-price chocolate. It's too bad that Halloween already passed this year.

"It really is the best week for getting diabetes," Evan joked.

"All this talk of chocolate makes me wanna go and just stuff my face with as much chocolate as I possibly can."

"We're stuck in a mall. You *can* eat all the chocolate you want."

"Totally didn't even think of that," I said flatly, astounded by my own dumbness.

"We can go get some after we swap presents," Evan stated.

I leaned over and grabbed the three boxes of chocolates I had gotten him. "Right. So take these and open them. They're all kinda the same thing," I told him, sliding the three boxes over to him with my foot.

"I don't know if I can open them now," he said.

"Why?" I asked.

He picked them up with a disgusted face. "Your bare feet touched them, yuck."

"What, are you four?" I asked, shooting him a blank stare.

"Yeah," he said as he laid two of the boxes down next to him on his bed.

"Well then."

He shook the box a little bit. "These are chocolates, aren't they?" he asked.

I looked down and sighed. "Yeah. They're chocolates."

"Are they any good?"

"How the hell would I know? I didn't sample any."

He ripped the wrapping paper off of the boxes, which was easy because of my horrible wrapping job. "Thank you for the chocolates, Spencer."

"Any time."

He picked up a poorly wrapped lump of something. "Here," he said, tossing it over to me.

"Is it socks?" I asked flatly.

"No," he said, looking away.

"It is socks." I sighed as I started to unwrap the clump of wrapping paper. Evan's wrapping skills make mine look hella good.

"I promise that it isn't socks," he said.

I ripped the rest of the wrapping paper off of the gift that was inside.

"They're slippers," he said as I pulled them out.

"They're rabbit slippers."

"I could not think of literally anything to get you. I'm sorry."

"It's okay. I like them. They're kinda cute," I told him.

He smiled soft. "Okay. If long as you like them, then I like them."

"I like them," I said, setting them next to me.

"Not enough to wear them," he said, huffing and crossing his arms like he was offended by me.

"Barefoot is better. Slippers and socks are foot prisons. Can't have that kind of negativity in my life."

"You're so weird," he said, shaking his head at me slightly.

"Just for that, you don't get any more presents."

"Ooh, I'm so scared," he joked.

I tossed him the bacon-themed Monopoly game. "Here, open it and shut your face-hole," I snapped.

"Is it more chocolate?" he asked, shaking it. "Are you trying to make me fat?"

"Yeah," I said bluntly.

He sighed, ripping the wrapping paper off the box. "Oh, hey. I've seen this in that game store," he said, looking at the box. "I've actually always wanted to buy this, but I never had the extra cash. Aw, now I get it for free."

"If we're allowed to keep it," I said.

"Meh. We'll be allowed."

"Yeah?"

"Yeah. We were stuck in here. We should get some consolation, right?" Evan stated, turning and picking up another one of the poorly wrapped presents he had for me. "Here you go," he said, sliding the present across the floor towards me.

"What is it?" I asked.

"It's something very special," he said.

"Oh," I said, picking it up.

I started unwrapping the wrapping paper. The wrapping was done a little better on this one, but still pretty badly. The two of us should not be allowed to wrap anything ever again.

I pulled out a DVD case. I looked it over and saw that it was the case for *The Vow*. Weird. Why'd he give me a chick flick?

"Can I tell you a secret?" he asked.

"Sure," I said, setting the movie down beside me.

"That's actually one of my favourite movies. That's why I got it for you. I didn't know any of your favourite movies, so I figured that you might like it because you're lame like me, right?"

"It's in my top ten," I said with a wink.

"Thank God."

"No. Thank you. You got me the one movie I think I don't own," I stated. "Even though owning physical copies of movies is going downhill because Netflix is a thing."

"Yeah," he said. "But sometimes, it's nice to plug in the old DVD player and watch the movie like the good old days."

"The good old days?"

"VHS sucked ass," Evan said flatly.

"VHS tapes were the best," I argued back.

"No. They had to be rewound and fast-forwarded and they didn't have special features and shit. Plus they would sometimes get stuck and all the tape inside would rip out. That sucked."

"But the authenticity."

"Nope," Evan stated. "Sorry. VHS tapes are forever banished from my life. DVDs and streaming for me."

"What about Blu-Ray?" I asked.

"Screw those too," he said.

"Only own a DVD player, huh?"

"I own a PlayStation. My DVD player broke."

"Lame," I teased. "So do you want your last gift now? Or would you rather just wait a little longer?"

He sighed. "I'll take it now. I bet this one will be the most disappointing one of all."

"Screw you," I said, throwing the hats at him, and of course they were both wrapped up in a clumpy ball of poorly taped together pieces of wrapping paper.

"Okay, *these* are definitely socks," he said, noticing that there was some fabric inside the ball of wrapping paper.

"They are not socks."

"Then I guess they're underwear."

"They are most certainly not underwear," I said.

"But I might need underwear," Evan said, unwrapping the present with a big rip of the paper.

"Sorry, that's a *you* problem," I told him.

He shrugged a little as one of the hats fell out and plopped to the floor. "You got me beanies!" he shouted, tossing aside the wrapping paper and holding the other hat in his hand.

"I thought you might enjoy some new hats," I said with a small smile.

"I love them," he said, picking up the hat that had fallen to the floor.

"Good," I said. "I don't wanna have to beat you up."

"You'd beat me up if I didn't enjoy these hats?" Evan asked.

"Yes."

He shook his head and chuckled softly at me. "Alrighty then," he said, sliding the last present towards me. "I got this one because I know you're a little nerd."

"A nerd?" I asked, picking it up.

"It's obviously a chemistry set," Evan joked as I started to unwrap the present.

"It's a book," I said, feeling the familiar papery sides of the hardcover book.

"We have a winner," Evan shouted, waving his arms in the air overdramatically.

"What book is it?" I asked, looking up to Evan as I tossed the wrapping paper to the pile on the floor.

"Look at the cover and find out, dumbass."

I looked down. Thank God for the lamps that light up our makeshift bedroom. I flipped the book over to see the cover. "*The Book Thief*," I read aloud.

"Yeah. I thought you might enjoy it," Evan said.

"The movie was good too," I said.

"You've read it before?" he asked.

I nodded. "It was on the list of books to read for my summative assignments in my senior English class."

"So you like it?"

"Love it," I said. "Books are a second home for me."

"How so?" Evan asked.

"Well," I said, pausing, "it's just that books are a way to grow and expand your mind. You can read about all these crazy adventures from the safety of your bed. You can write books and make stories out of nothing. It's pretty cool when you think about it. And this book deals with how books do that type of thing."

"So you should let me borrow that sometime," Evan said with a small smirk.

"You read?"

"Why do you say it as if I'm an illiterate dumbass?" he asked, glaring slightly at me.

"Because you *are* an illiterate dumbass?"

"So hurtful," he said, taking a sip of his eggnog.

I picked up mine too, having totally forgotten about the fact that I had poured myself a glass of eggnog. I sipped some as Evan sipped his. We connected stares and sort of had a sip-off. Within seconds, both of our cups were empty.

"It's a draw," Evan said, slowly setting the cup down on the floor.

"So be it," I said, setting mine down slowly as well.

"What should we go do now?" I asked with a sigh.

"I think we should go do some workout stuff. I feel like I need to do some physical activity so I don't get fat off these chocolates," Evan suggested.

"Physical activity? Like what?"

"Hmm," Evan said, pausing to think.

"Hockey?"

"Hockey." He nodded

"Hockey?"

He snickered. "Yes, hockey."

"Fine, but you have to be goalie."

"Fine by me," Evan said, standing up. "Put your slippers on. We have some work to do."

{Chapter: **Eleven**}

I followed Evan out of the store and towards the area of the mall lit up by the skylight. It was funny watching him walk around in the goalie equipment. The goalie pads made it so hard for him to carry a stick and a net at the same time, but I was too lazy to offer him any help. He's a big strong man. He can handle it.

"You really should have helped," Evan grumbled, dropping the net down in the big open clearing where the mall would have usually had a car giveaway thing placed. You know what I mean, how they have a car parked in the middle of the mall and you enter a raffle or some other bullshit like that? Well, the car wasn't here, so we had a nice big open area to play some ball hockey.

"I could have helped, but if I helped, would it have taught you the value of hard work?" I asked.

"You're an idiot," he said, fixing his mask. He had laid his beanie on top of the net so that he could wear a goalie mask instead, which was probably the safe choice.

"I am so not an idiot," I argued.

"Here," he said, rolling the little orange ball out towards me.

I dropped the blade of my stick to the floor to stop it from rolling any further. "You know you're gonna get scored on a whole lot, right?"

"I figured," he said with a shrug. "In fairness, I suck."

"I suck too, but I just figured that you're gonna suck a slight little bit more than I do."

"Shut up," he said, fixing the position of the net.

"You 'bout ready?" I asked.

He turned back to me and fiddled with his pads a little. "Yeah," he said as he finished checking them.

"Practice shots?" I asked.

He nodded as he took a goalie pose in the net.

I walked out in front of him and took a little wrist shot and he kicked it away. I chased it down and walked back over to take another shot. We did this for a few minutes until he had enough of it.

"Okay," Evan said, standing up. "Give me your best dekes."

"You sure?" I asked.

"Of course. I wanna see what you got," he said, and I could see that he was smirking under that mask.

I jogged in and did a little deke, but Evan made the easy pad save. I could almost hear him mocking me, but I was just getting started. I let him have a few more easy saves as I warmed up. I was a little rusty at the whole "hockey" thing right now.

"So, like, what do you feel like talking about?" I asked, snapping a shot that sailed passed his glove.

He groaned as he turned around. "I don't know. How about scoring?" he said, passing the ball back over to me.

"Scoring? You mean, like, how I just went top shelf on you?" I joked, bringing the ball to a stop.

"No," he said. "And that was a lucky shot."

"It was all skill," I stated, shooting the ball at him, which he kicked away with his left pad.

"You ain't got no skill in scoring," Evan taunted.

"Neither do you," I said. "Scoring goals or ladies."

"I can score ladies just fine," he said as I took a shot on him, which he gloved and tossed back out to me.

I gave him a dry, short laugh. "Yeah, right."

"You don't know me, man," he argued. "I got game."

"Stop trying to make me laugh so I miss the shot."

"I'm not trying to make you laugh," Evan said as I sent a shot flying towards him. He kicked it away. "I got the moves like Jagger."

"Just not with the ladies," I said, running over to get the ball.

"Why do you think I can't get the ladies?" Evan asked.

"Because, I don't know, you seem like the shy kind of dude," I said, taking a shot and scoring on him.

"Well, yeah, I guess so," he said with a shrug. "But it works in my favour."

"How?"

"Who doesn't like the shy kid, right?"

"I guess that's a good point," I said, slapping a shot toward him, which he stopped with his chest.

He tossed the ball back over to me. "Shy girls are the cutest. They always look away and smile and it's just so very cute."

"I guess I'm not cute then, eh?" I joked, walking in and deking around him to score.

He scooped the ball out of the net with a sigh. "Nah, but you're cute in a different way."

"Oh, but I am cute?" I asked, winking at him as he sent the ball back over my way.

"Well, yeah."

I smiled and felt a little blush rise to my cheeks. "Oh. Well, thank you, I guess, even if you sound a little unsure."

I'm not used to getting compliments, not even a little bit. I never get hit on or anything. It's also just weird to hear a stranger mention a compliment like that so nonchalantly.

"I mean it," he stated.

"Just 'cause you complimented me, it doesn't mean I'm gonna put out," I told him, shooting the ball at him again.

He gloved it and tossed it back to me. "I don't know about you, but it was a compliment, not an invitation into my bed."

"I'm just saying."

"Call me crazy, but I actually respect women and their choices."

"That's not crazy, that's just common sense," I corrected him.

"Exactly," he said, stopping a shot I aimed for the top shelf.

"Common sense and feminism," I said, chasing down and stopping the ball from rolling too far away.

"Not so much feminism."

"Why's that?"

"Feminism gets such a bad rep these days," Evan said. "I consider myself an egalitarian. Equality for everyone regardless of gender, age, race, culture, language, religion, you name it."

"Wait," I said. "How does feminism have a bad rep?"

"Think about how a lot of vocal feminists come across as these man-hating crazy people," Evan explained. "It makes the idea of feminism seem less like women getting equality and more like they're just wanting men to become the oppressed ones instead."

"Okay, fair point," I said. "But consider this, men aren't oppressed and, really, they never have been."

"I know that. But it's like these radical feminists forget that men have issues too. Actually, I'm pretty sure everyone forgets that men have issues. I think the media has done a right good job at making us believe that all men have to show no emotions except happy and angry. And it really doesn't help anything that when an issue arises, both genders start to play 'Who has it worse?' instead of trying to figure it out together to make that issue go away for everyone," Evan rambled. "It's stupid."

"Again, fair point," I said. "The media sexualizes and idealizes both genders to the point that we have to argue with each other over who has it worse when we should be arguing against the media for portraying beauty and emotions in a way that tries to control how we develop."

"Exactly. Femininity and masculinity are just manmade terms to try and force us to be a certain way," Evan preached. "Screw gender roles."

"Yes," I said. "If you're a 300-pound bodybuilder and you wanna pick flowers and drink virgin margaritas, do it. If you're a 100-pound girl that likes to wear dresses while you work on cars, good on you. I hate that we think we have a choice in other people's lives, and I hate it even more that we argue over things that don't affect us in the slightest.

"Like how people are against gay marriage?" Evan asked.

"Exactly that," I said. "It just boggles my mind that people have the audacity to tell people they can't be married because they don't approve of their love. That has to be the most absurd thing ever. It's not like two guys getting married means you have to go move in with them and see them make out and have sex all the time. It literally has zero effect on your life."

"It's even funnier when dudes who watch lesbian porn all the time start saying that gays shouldn't be allowed to get married."

"Yeah," I said, sliding the ball through Evan's legs. "People are stupid."

"Most people are, yeah."

"I just wish more people could realize that equality for all is the best way to be. I don't see what is so hard to understand about all of us being stuck here on this planet together as equals," I said.

"Yeah. At the end of the day, we're all human beings. It doesn't matter where you come from, what you identify as, what you practise, what you do for a living, where you live, what you like, the colour of your skin, the person you are, none of that matters, or at least, it shouldn't matter. At the end of the day, we're all just human beings trying to live our lives."

"Humans, pfft," I said, shooting at Evan again, which he stopped.

"Humans might be very intelligent, but we sure are dumb," he said, tossing the ball back out to me. "We can make such wonderful things, but yet we still do such stupid things to each other. Rape, murder, torture, child abuse, letting people starve, making fun of people based on things that they have no control over, ganging up on the weak, letting the rich get richer while punishing the poor for being poor, hating people based on stupid things that don't even matter. I feel like the list goes on forever."

"I never understood why people of different cultures get hated on by the others," I said.

"Me either," Evan said. "I always loved learning about other cultures. They were so cool *because* they were different than my own. Maybe some people are just scared of difference, and learning about other cultures and beliefs scares them or something."

I took a shot and Evan swatted it away, with his stick this time. "This is getting me all heated and riled up," I said, taking a deep breath as I chased the ball down.

"You're out of shape and you're not used to serious talks," Evan said, sitting down in front of the net.

"Shut up," I snapped. "I haven't taken a gym class since forever ago. And I didn't do any work in gym class anyway."

"No excuse, ma'am. It's up to you to keep up your physique."

"Shut up."

"And what is with you randomly falling asleep? You need to fix that too," Evan teased.

"It was once," I said. "It was just this once."

"I'm sure it was," Evan said as I walked over and sat next to him. He pulled his goalie mask off his head. His hair was all messy and spiked up now. "Why were you in the mall anyway?"

"Last-minute Christmas shopping."

"Where are the presents then?"

Good question. I guess I had lost track of what I did with most of those. "I think my friends took them home. I don't even remember," I said with a shrug. "Mm, yes, because I was trying to buy something for myself before the mall closed. Like an idiot."

Evan laughed softly. "D'you wanna grab us a water?" he asked, motioning towards a case of bottled water that we had brought over before we went back to get the net and sticks.

I sighed as I stood up. "Fine."

"Thank you."

I walked over and ripped the plastic wrapping and took two bottles of water out. I walked back over and tossed one of the bottles down to him. "Why were you in the mall?"

"I don't really wanna say," he said.

"Aw, why not? I told you my reason."

"Mine's shitty."

"I doubt it," I said.

"I meant that it's shitty for me," he said.

I poked nudged him with my elbow. "Come on, tell me. It really can't be that bad, can it?"

"You really wanna know?"

I nodded.

"No laughing or feeling sorry for me," he said.

I nodded again. "Got it."

"I got stood up," he said softly.

"Like—"

89

"Like a date, yes," he said, reading my mind. "I was supposed to meet her for a Christmas Eve dinner and she didn't show up."

"Do you think it was the weather?" I asked him.

"Nope."

"How do you know?"

"Because she was with you when I ran past you guys," he said.

"You had a date with Charlotte?" I asked.

He nodded. "Mm-hmm."

"Well, I'll have words with her."

"It's okay. I sorta figured that she wouldn't have shown up," Evan said, shrugging. How can he just not care about it? I would care a lot about it.

"She is kind of a bitch," I said, trying to comfort him a little.

"I thought she was your best friend?"

"No. My best friend is Mindy, but she's moving away though."

He nodded in understanding. "I'll be your new best friend. That's assuming there's an opening."

"I don't know," I said. "You're a little too lame for my liking." I shot him a small smile and wrapped an arm around his shoulders.

"We'd be the best of friends then," he stated. "You're lame, I'm lame. It'd be perfect."

"You make a very strong argument."

"I also make very good brownies," he said. "Okay, so maybe I don't make them per se, but I can buy really good brownies."

I chuckled softly. "You're an idiot. I like it."

"What do you wanna do now, friend?"

"No idea, friend," I said. "My feet hurt though. Massage them."

"Not gonna happen."

"They don't stink… that bad."

"Friends don't massage feet," Evan stated.

"Okay, Evan, you're my boyfriend. Massage my feet."

"It doesn't work that way. You can't just rope me into a relation-ship so you can have a personal masseuse," he said.

"Well… why not?"

"Because."

"Because why?" I asked.

"Just because."

"Fine. It's over then," I said firmly. "But for real, what should we do now?"

"We could go get into some trouble."

"And how do ya suppose we do that?" I asked.

"I don't know," he said. "I thought you might be able to help us in that department."

"I'm not a troublemaker though."

"Ah, then we are at a crossroads, because I am not a trouble-maker," he said.

"Mm, we should go eat more food."

"Fatass."

"I like to snack," I stated. "Let's go find and eat some pretzels."

"Okay, that actually sounds pretty good right now," he said, finally opening his water bottle.

I cracked open the lid on my water bottle too. I took a ridiculously long drink of water, drinking at least half of the water. I let out a loud sigh of relief. "Damn, water is so good."

"Agreed," Evan said, twisting the lid back on his water bottle.

"Come with me," I said, standing up. "We're gonna go and get some pretzels."

Evan groaned as he got up. "Alright."

"Don't be like that. You want the pretzels just as bad."

"Yeah, you're right. I kinda do."

I grabbed his arm and started tugging on it as I walked off in the direction of the superstore we had slept in.

"Easy on me," he whined. "I'm fragile."

"Sorry," I said, letting go off his arm. "I just *really* want pretzels now." I dropped off my hockey gloves and left them on the floor as we walked off. Evan did the same, except he tossed his back and they landed in the net. *Goal.*

{Chapter: **Twelve**}

Evan and I walked back to the store and over to our beds so we could swap our sweaty socks and running shoes for clean socks and our regular shoes.

Evan let out a loud sigh of relief. "So nice to be out of those sweaty socks," he said, collapsing backwards onto the bed after pulling the second sock on.

"Yeah," I said, sliding the sock up my foot. "I think we need to figure out a shower or bath though."

"Later," Evan said. "Let's just go do something fun for now."

"Like?"

"Get those pretzels that you wanted so badly," he suggested.

"I like the way you think," I said as he sat back up on his bed.

"Mm, let's go." He stood up and motioned for me to follow him as he turned and started walking away.

I got up and started to follow him. "Do you think they have flavoured ones?" I asked.

"I would assume so, yes."

"Okay, good. You can have the unsalted ones though. They're gross," I told him.

He scoffed. "You're gross."

"Stop acting five."

"I'm not acting," he said as we turned down the chip aisle. He clicked a flashlight on, which was weird, because I totally didn't think he even had anything in his hands when we started towards the chips aisle, but okay.

"Look," I said, pointing at the wall of chips. "Friends."

"If they're friends, you can't eat them, you sicko," Evan said, grabbing a bag of Doritos off the shelf.

"Friendship is letting each other eat each other."

"That isn't friendship, Spencer. That's sick."

"Shh."

"Grab some snacks," Evan said, kicking the lower part of the shelf that had all the pretzels on it.

"Don't kick them," I said, leaning down to pick up a bag of thin and salted pretzels.

"They can't feel pain."

"Well, you won't feel pain in a minute once I kill you, Mr. Sassy," I snapped as I stood back upright.

"Is that a threat?"

"It's a promise." I stood up on my toes a bit more to be closer to his height as I stared daggers into his eyes.

"I'm not scared of you," he said, pushing me backwards, and although it was a light push, I stumbled back quite a bit because of me being on my tiptoes.

I grabbed the shelf and knocked down a few bags of chips as I regained my balance. Evan had grabbed a hold on my wrist to help keep me from falling. "Thanks, asshole," I muttered to him.

"You got to learn how to stand properly," Evan teased.

"You got to learn how to not push people over into a shelf that has a bunch of bags of chips on it, ya dick," I sassed back to him.

"Fair point," he said, crouching down to pick up the chips. He tossed them one by one back onto the shelf.

I peeled the bag open and took out a pretzel. I looked it over and put it between my fingers and then flick-tossed it at Evan.

"Stop," he whined as it hit him and fell to the floor.

"Don't be a baby," I said. "It was little pretzels." I pulled out a few pretzels and shoved them into my face-hole.

"Maybe I got a cut," Evan said. "Pretzels hurt, y'know."

"Wuss," I said through a mouthful of food.

"I'll fight you," he threatened.

"I'd like to see you try."

"I'll beat you up."

"Once again," I said, "I'd like to see you try."

"We should go try on stupid outfits now," Evan said, walking past me.

"That was random, considering how we were talking about me kicking your ass, but yeah, let's go try on clothes," I said, following after him as he led me back out of the aisle.

"Your stupidity got me thinking about stupid stuff, like stupid outfits that would look hilarious on you," Evan sassed.

I scoffed at him. "Let's go dress like lame-ass hipsters and shit."

"You already are a hipster," he teased as we walked.

"I'll punch you." I shoved him from behind a little. "I'm not a hipster."

"I was just kidding around."

"Can we dress up as elves?" I asked, looking over to a display that had a bunch of Christmas-themed outfits.

"Do they have the little ears though?" Evan asked as we turned and started walking towards the elf costumes.

"I hope so," I said. And I meant it. I've always wanted to have cute little elf ears. I feel like they'd really complement the red hair. I'd be an elf princess. I'd have my own Disney movie made about me someday.

Evan's hand waved around my face, snapping me from my thoughts. "Earth to Spencer," he said.

"Sorry," I said. "I was just thinking about how dorky you'd look with elf ears and an elf outfit on."

"You mean how cute I'd look?" he teased.

"Nah. You would have to be cute first."

"Hurtful," he said, picking up a little green elf hat.

I smiled at him, sweetly but sarcastically. "You know I meant it as a compliment."

"That doesn't make sense."

"It doesn't have to," I said, picking up a pair of elf ears. "These should fit your ears. Put them on." I held them out to him.

He reluctantly grabbed them from my hand, sighing slightly as he did. He tried to put them on his ears, but they weren't sticking properly. "I think they're too small, you try them," he said, handing them back to me.

I took them with a groan. "Fine." I put them on my ears and he smiled.

"Y'know, they do fit me," he said, still smiling. "I just thought they'd look cuter on you."

"Smooth. But," I said, picking up another set of ears, "you still have to put a pair of elf ears on. *We're* gonna be elves."

"Yeah, yeah," he whined, grabbing the ears from me.

I watched him put them on. "See, you look cute too now."

"They feel weird."

"That weird feeling will wear off once you realize how majestic you really are."

"You're weird," he said, putting on the elf hat he had been holding in his hand since we had got to the display.

I smiled at him.

"What?"

"You're pretty," I said dopily.

He smiled a little. "Thanks."

"You're welcome," I said, grabbing a big white beard from the display. "But I'm gonna be an elfish Santa."

"Santa Clause doesn't have elf ears."

"That's why I said elfish," I said as I raised the little black elastic over my head. I swept my hair over top of it and fixed it so the moustache and beard lined up with my lips properly. I turned to face Evan after I had it set up. "How's it look?"

"You're missing this," he said, holding a Santa hat to me.

"Ah, yes," I said, taking it and putting it on. "*Le piece de résistance.*"

"Cutest. Santa. Ever."

"Thanks," I said, punching him lightly. "Get back to work. I don't pay you to sit around and do nothing."

"You don't pay me at all," Evan rebutted.

"Santa's basically a slave owner, huh?"

"I guess he is."

Evan shook his head and scoffed. "And here we were thinking he was the good guy."

"He's on his own naughty list."

"You're on my naughty list," Evan said flatly.

"Oh, behave," I said, impersonating Austin Powers' voice.

Evan started cackling, think hyena but also bullfrog.

"Why's that so funny to you?" I asked him, pouting a little because he wouldn't stop laughing, presumably at me.

"Your accent was hilarious," he said through a laugh. "And the face you made. Oh, my God."

"Stop laughing," I demanded.

"I'm sorry," he said, pressing a finger to his lips and stifling his laughter to a dull whisper.

"I'ma cut you, bitch," I said in a growly voice.

"Yeah. A redhead Santa is just *so* scary."

"That's it. You're on the naughty list."

"Oh, no. I can't be on the naughty list. Please let me make it up to you, San'a," he said, mimicking the voice of a saddened child.

"No, no, no!" I belted out in a deep, jolly voice.

"That was a spot-on impression," Evan said, giving me a small clapping applause.

"Thank you," I said, doing a curtsey. "I try my very best. I'll be here all week."

"Let's hope you aren't, actually."

"Yeah. It would suck if we were stuck in here for a week."

"It'd get lonely," Evan said.

"What?" I turned to him. "You have me to keep you company."

"Two people can be lonely together," he said, shaking his head slightly, as if I were to know something like that already.

"That sounds lovey-dovey," I said, furrowing my eyebrows slightly at him.

He nodded. "I know."

"Weird." I walked over to the display of elf stuff and swapped my Santa beard and hat for an elf hat. I turned back to Evan and smiled. "Cute, right?"

"Obviously," he said with a small, sweet smile. He had a really nice smile now that I took notice of it.

"So," I said, adjusting the elf hat. "What should we go dress up as next?"

"Hipsters?"

"Oh, my God! Yes! Duh."

"You sound so excited," Evan noted.

"I wanna dress like a hipster from Coachella," I said, smiling. "But! I'm keeping the elf ears on."

"Good. They make you look 1.7 times cuter," Evan said as he winked and walked past me.

"That's an oddly specific multiplier," I said as I followed him off deeper into the store.

"It's hard to multiply perfection."

"Mm, why are you being so flirtatious today? Did you do something bad to me? Is there gonna be some horrible surprise awaiting me at some point or something?"

"No," he replied. "I just grew the balls to say what I'm thinking."

"Thanks."

He stumbled a bit, tripping over his feet. Obviously, I had to giggle at that. Well, it was actually more of a squealing snort, think pig mixed with dying cow.

"Douchebag," he muttered as he regained his balance.

"You would have laughed if it were me," I snapped.

"But it wasn't you, it was me," he stated.

I rested a hand on his shoulder as we came to a stop. "But it's funnier when it happens to you. And you know that. Deep down... you know."

"Here," he said with a sigh. "Replace your hat with these."

I reached for the two thin headbands he was holding out. "Okay," I groaned. I took the hat off and tossed it at a display of T-shirts. I put the two headbands on my head. It felt weird to have headbands holding my hair down. I've never worn them before now.

"Cutie," he said, tossing me a pair of sunglasses.

"It's dark in here though," I whined, barely catching the glasses in my hands.

"Don't care," Evan said. "You need to look ultra hipster."

"Well, what are you gonna wear? If I have to look like a mega hipster, then you do too," I stated.

"I'll figure something out," he said, turning and walking away from me.

I started following his lead.

He turned around and gave me a weird look. "No. You stay here. This is the lady clothes section," he said, pointing beside us to the large section of clothes.

"So?"

"I'm gonna go get my hipster outfit on, and you stay here and pick your hipster outfit," Evan stated. "And put it on, duh."

"Fine," I groaned, turning and walking away from Evan.

"See you in a few," he said, walking off.

I watched as he walked off, leaving me all alone. What a jerk.

I walked over to the shirt section and searched for a "hipster" shirt. I eventually settled on an off-shoulder top with the skyline of New York on it. It looked pretty hipsterish to me.

I took off my sunglasses so I could see and remove my shirt, and then I stripped out of my current shirt and put this one on. It felt weird changing my shirt in the middle of a store like this, all well though The cameras are off anyway... I hope.

I waltzed on over to the leg clothing. I looked over the clothes they had. Jeans, jean shorts, skirts, and more jeans. I grabbed a pair of jean shorts, the raggedy ones. The ones that looked roughly cut off. I stripped out of my pants and was about to put on the shorts when I noticed a section of leggings.

I walked over and grabbed the first galaxy-patterned leggings I saw. This screams hipster, I think. I put them on and pulled the shorts over top of them. I walked over to one of the large mirrors and looked my outfit over. It looked very stereotypical hipster. And the sad thing is that it actually suits me to dress this way.

I walked over and got some ankle-high, combat-styled boots. They were black and had those straps and shit on them. They were comfortable too. I might have to just keep these. I looked myself over once more in the mirror. "Nice," I whispered to myself.

I took my time walking back to our little makeshift bedroom. I figured that's where he would have wanted me to wait for him. I sat on the edge of my bed and waited. It got boring really fast too. There's nothing to do in the dark.

"How hipster do you look?" Evan's voice called out from somewhere in the store.

"Very," I called back. At least, I think I did. Evan would have to decide on that.

"Does it look cute?"

"I does look cute, yes," I replied.

I heard his footsteps coming closer. I turned and saw Evan in a dark blue dress shirt with plaid patterning, suspenders for his khakis, a dark red bow tie, nerdy glasses that were obviously not for his vision, and of course he had his trademark beanie on. Still, he looked like a hipster. He looked like he was about to start writing a screenplay in the nearest coffee shop.

"You do look cute," he said, looking me over.

I laughed softly. "You look ridiculous."

"You just can't handle how antiestablishment I am," he said, walking over and sitting across from me on his bed.

"I guess you look alright," I said. "It's almost as if you were meant to be a super hipster."

"That would be a really lame superhero name."

"What? Super Hipster?"

He nodded.

"The Super Hipster, protecting coffee shops from bad screenplays and from becoming too mainstream," I joked.

"Shut up," Evan snapped.

"What do you wanna go do now?"

"I feel like I wanna go and play a board game or something."

"Yeah?" I asked. "Like what? What should we play?"

"I dunno," he replied.

I stood up from the bed and yawned and stretched a little. "How about we just go find a bunch and we'll decide then?"

"I'm hungry though," Evan said.

"We can go grill up some burgers or something and then find a game to play," I suggested to him.

"Sounds like a plan," he said, standing up. "Let's get going."

{Chapter: **Thirteen**}

I followed Evan as we walked to the food court. Evan kept flashing his flashlight at my face. It wasn't really dark enough where we were walking for him to actually need to use it to see. So I guess why not try to annoy me, right?

"Stop," I demanded for the seventh time.

"No," he said, still waving the light back and forth on my face. It's like he's trying to be the world's most annoying person.

"I'll spit on your burger," I threatened.

"Tasty," he said, rubbing his stomach.

"You're nasty."

"That was the joke. Thank you," he said flatly, disappointed in me ruining his joke. It's not like it was very funny anyway.

"Make it funnier next time," I sassed.

"You can make your own burger now."

I mustered up a few fake giggles. "It was *so* funny."

"Nope."

I groaned. "Please just make me a burger, dammit."

He stopped and looked up to think for a second. "No."

"You're a douche," I said with a sigh.

"I'll make you a burger," Evan said.

"What's the condition?"

"What do you mean?"

"Well," I said, "you're offering to make me a burger now, so what the hell do I have to agree to?"

"Nothing," he said. Why do I not believe that? I'm not buying it.

"Tell me," I pried.

"There's no fine print."

I sighed. "Okay, whatever you say."

"I was gonna make you a burger regardless," he said. "I'm just nice like that, ya know?"

"What board game do you wanna play, then?" I asked as he hopped over the counter of a random food outlet. I think it was a place that cooks burgers, which would be smart. It would save us from going to get burgers if they were already here.

"I don't know. Monopoly, Scrabble, Operation," he said as he fiddled with the large propane grill in the kitchen.

"Battleship," I suggested.

"I would whoop your ass," Evan chuckled back as he turned and walked towards the large freezer in the back of the store.

"You most certainly would not."

"Oh, yeah?" He turned back to me with a smirk. "I'm a Battleship master."

"Let's make a bet."

"I bet you the star on the top of the tree in the main atrium or whatever it's called," Evan said.

I cocked my head and knitted my brows. "What do you mean?"

"Well, whoever loses our game of Battleship has to climb up the tree and take down the big shimmering star that's on the top of the tree," Evan explained.

"We get to eat first though, right?" I asked.

He nodded.

I sighed in relief. "Thank God for that."

"Are you gonna want me to cook you some bacon for your burger?" Evan asked.

I nodded. "You better believe it."

Evan walked back to the grill with a stack of frozen patties and a package of bacon. "Thank God for industrial freezers. It's still so cold in there."

"Well, make them un-colded. I'm hungry," I whined at him.

"You're so weird," Evan said with a soft sigh as he peeled the wax paper from the burgers.

"Did I ever claim to be normal?"

He shrugged as he plopped the burgers onto the grill. "That's a fair point to make, weirdo."

"Hurry up."

"I *just* put the damn things on the grill," Evan snapped. "Are you blind or intentionally being annoying?"

"The latter."

"I kinda figured that, but it was also a rhetorical question."

"Yeah, but you knew I would answer it."

Man, he must really be annoyed with me by now. Being stuck around me for extended period of times would probably annoy anybody, to be honest.

He groaned. "I'm gonna beat you with this spatula."

"Try it," I taunted.

"Later. I'm cooking with it."

I walked into the kitchen area. "Couldn't stand leaning over the counter like that. It felt like someone was gonna come up from behind me and kill me or something," I said as I pulled a stool over to the grill.

"Whatever. No touching the food until it's cooked."

"I wasn't gonna," I said. "Jeez, calm down."

"Just making sure," he said. "Hey, get the onions and lettuce and all that other good stuff."

"You just told me not to touch the food until I was cooked?"

He groaned. "Just get the onions and lettuce and shit."

I sighed. "Fine." I got up and walked over to the prep station. I grabbed the small metal bin of buns and the one with lettuce, and then made another trip for the ones with onions and pickles in them.

"Thanks," Evan said as he started cooking some of the bacon.

"Oh, you're welcome," I said, sitting back on my little stool.

"You want a lot of bacon on your burger?" Evan asked.

"Obviously."

"We need cheese," he said, turning around and walking towards the prep area.

"Bacon cheeseburgers. Mm." My mouth is already watering.

He turned and came back over with a bunch of cheese slices. "Too bad they don't have mozzarella cheese here."

"We could go get some," I suggested.

He shook his head. "Nah, too lazy."

"Yeah, me too."

"Go get some," he said.

"Too lazy," I grumbled.

"Here," he said, putting a patty down on one of the bottom buns for me. "You can decorate your own burger."

"Sweet." I grabbed the burger and put a bunch of onions and pickles and lettuce on it. I topped it off with some cheese as Evan slid some cooked bacon my way. "Thanks. I almost forgot about the bacon I was so hungry."

"Rude. How dare you forget about the best part of the burger."

I finished the burger and put the top bun on top of it. I squished it down a little so it would be able to fit in my little-ass mouth.

"How is it?" Evan asked as he started to put together his burger.

I, of course, had a mouth that was full of burger and he could see that. Regardless, I mumbled, "It's good."

"I knew it would be," he said with a cocky little smirk.

"Well, it would be pretty hard to screw up a burger."

"You callin' me a bad cook? I slave over this nasty smelling propane stove making you a burger, and this is the thanks I get?" Evan rambled, feigning a deep emotional trauma.

I swallowed the food in my mouth and made a disgusted face. "You're a bad cook," I said, sticking my tongue out at him. "This burger is the worst thing I've ever tasted in my entire life. Yuck."

His smirk dropped as he gave me a very blank stare. "Really, Spencer?"

"Yeah. I changed my mind. This burger tastes like old man ass."

"That's nasty," he said, shooting me disgusted look.

"So is this burger," I sassed back.

"I hate you," he said with a pout as he turned back to his burger.

I took another bite of the burger. "I know."

"Stop talking with your mouth full."

"Make me," I mumbled through the food.

"You're such an asshole," Evan said with a sigh as he started eating his burger. "But I guess I'll forgive you."

"Why?"

"You're kind of cute, and you're a little funny."

I rolled my eyes and took another bite of my burger.

"I mean it," he said, reaffirming his previous statement.

"Sure you do."

He sighed. "I do."

"You're not gettin' any trapped-together sexual favours from me," I said through a mouthful of burger.

"I don't want any."

"Mm-hmm," I said, cocking an eyebrow at him as I bit down on the burger.

"I wish we had electricity. Fries would go so nicely with this burger," Evan said, letting out a sorrowful sigh about it. I didn't really want to be the person who had to tell him that fryers also use gas to heat the oil.

"I want a lollipop."

"That's random. Isn't there a candy store somewhere in the mall? We can go and get you one," Evan suggested.

"You're such a nice person. I'll wait right here. Get me a variety of flavours, please and thanks."

He shook his head at me. "I never said *I* was going to get you any lollipops."

"But, Evan," I whined.

"Spencer," he said firmly, turning to me so that he fully faced me. "No."

"But, Evan!" I whined louder.

"No, Spencer. No means no," he said, mocking me with his own whiny voice. It almost sounded like a little kid that was out of breath.

We finished the rest of our burgers in silence, mostly. It was nice to just hang out with someone like this. I don't know if I've said that already, but it still holds true.

"Time for Battleship?" Evan asked as he started cleaning up the mess we had made from making the burgers.

I let out a loud burp. "You betcha."

"You're so nasty."

"You want a root beer or something?" I asked, walking over to the fridge, not even acknowledging his remark about my burp.

"That'd be nice of you to get me one," he replied.

"They only have diet," I lied, opening the fridge.

"Gross."

"Just kidding," I said, grabbing two bottles of root beer and turning back to Evan. "Here, catch." I tossed his a bottle and he caught it.

"I almost had a heart attack, to be honest."

"I wouldn't have blamed you," I said, sitting on the stool and cracking open my bottle of root beer. "Diet pop is just nasty." I took a sip and sighed a deep sigh of contentment.

"Yeah, it taste like rotten milk."

"I don't wanna know how or why you know that," I said, stopping mid-sip to give him a grossed-out look.

He made a slightly horrified face, most likely aimed at himself. "I don't always make the best choices in life."

I started laughing a little, spitting up some of the root beer I was trying to drink.

"Shut up," he snapped.

"Sorry," I said, calming myself down. "It's just that the face you made was hilarious."

Evan pouted at me and then walked past me. "Let's go so I can kick your ass in Battleship, you little turd."

"Whatever you say, loser," I said, turning and hopping off the stool to follow him. I followed his lead out of the food court and back to our makeshift bedroom in the superstore.

"You wait here," he said as we reached our beds.

"You wait here," I mocked him.

He gave me a deadpanned look and just shook his head as he turned off to go find the board game section.

I waited on the edge of the bed, putting my socks on and then back off out of boredom. Without Wi-Fi, I get way too bored. Which is evident by the socks thing you just read. Come to think of it, I really don't know how this habit of putting socks on and then taking them off started. Weird.

"I found it!" Evan called out from the dimly lit store.

"Then get ready to have your ass handed to you," I called out.

"I'm actually getting ready to whoop your ass," Evan said as he walked over to me.

I breathed a heavy breath and started laughing in a really breathy way. "You think— No, no, no." I fell to the ground laughing to emphasize my point. "My dear boy, you're going down."

"Shut up," he grumbled as he sat down in front of me on the floor.

I crawled my way over to him and sat upright.

He pulled open the box and dumped everything onto the floor.

"Whoa! You're making a mess, buddy," I shouted at him.

He gave me a deadpan look. "Shut up."

"Don't lose any of those little red pieces. You're gonna need to mark off all the times I hit you," I said, sweeping up the little red and white pieces that marked off hits and misses.

Evan started sorting the ship pieces and then handed me a handful of light blue boats. "These are yours."

"Thanks," I said, taking them from him.

He handed me a playing board thing. "This is also yours."

I took it from him. "Once again, thanks."

"Let's battle, loser."

I started placing my ships down on the board. "You better not be stacking your boats in once place to cheat."

"I'm not," Evan stated. "We're gonna play fairly and without cheating. That's the agreement. That's what we're gonna stick to."

"Okay, you ready?" I asked as I placed my final ship down.

He hesitated a minute as he placed a ship. "Okay, now I'm ready."

"A1?" I asked.

He laughed. "Nope, you dummy."

"Well, you're stupid. I thought you might have put it in that little corner there."

"Well, I didn't," he said.

I sighed. "This isn't even that fun. I've lost all morale."

"Me too."

"War isn't fun. It's sad."

"Tragic," Evan noted, closing his playing board.

I closed mine too. I'm hungry again.

"You're a fatass," Evan said with a laugh.

"I wonder how hectic real ship battles get though," I said, turning and lying down on the floor.

Evan took a sharp breath has laid himself down next to me. "I'd assume they get pretty hectic. You know, life or death. Those type of situations would probably get really intense."

"War is scary."

"It is," Evan agreed. "Anything that causes destruction, injury, and death is usually scary. War, hurricanes, riots, missile strikes, tornadoes, lightning… All that shit."

"Hurricanes are pretty scary," I said.

"Blizzards are too."

I rolled over to face him. "Why would they be scary? We're not in a life-or-death situation right now."

"Well, think about it."

I paused for a moment to think, but I could not figure out why they would inherently be scary. Like, if it's snowing, just go inside.

"I'm assuming you can't think of why a blizzard would be scary?"

"No, I can't," I replied. "Tell me."

"Imagine being stuck in a blizzard. Cold. Alone. Hungry," Evan stated. "The only thing that you can see, for miles in any direction, is a blurry whiteness that stings your exposed skin."

"I see your point."

"Imagine wondering if the starvation or hypothermia would kill you first as you desperately search for shelter and food."

"Gettin' real dark over there, buddy."

"I was trying to emphasize my point, buddy," he sassed.

I smacked his shoulder. "Stop it."

"So, when do you wanna go make more food, you fatass?"

"I'm not a fatass," I said with a sigh. "You should have made those burgers more filling."

"So, should we have burritos this time?"

"You're making the food, so I don't really care."

He sat up and glared at me. "Why do I have to make the food? I'm not your personal chef."

"Literally, you are. You've made all the food so far," I stated.

"Well, shut up. Let's go make food and hang out on the roof."

"Ooh, I like that idea," I said, sitting upright. "Gotta take advantage of this opportunity. I doubt we'll ever be able to go up on the roof ever again."

"You said the before too."

"And now I'm talking about the grander picture," I told him. "Like, these few days will be the only time we get this opportunity. So why waste it?"

He smirked and shook his head at me. "If you say so."

{Chapter: **Fourteen**}

I got up and left Evan alone while I went off to the bathroom. It was weird, trying to pee in a dark public bathroom with just a flashlight. It just made everything feel like I was in the middle of a horror game. And, usually, the horror games where you have a flashlight are the ones where you die. Well, actually, you die in most horror games either way. At least a few times.

After successfully avoiding death via monster in a dark room, I made it back to our little makeshift bedroom. Evan was sitting on the bed waiting for me. He'd make a good butler. He cooks on command and is very good at waiting.

"There you are," he said, standing up and stretching out his limbs.

"I know. I was a little too long, but it was a long pee."

"That's probably TMI," he said, walking over to meet me before I reached our beds.

I shrugged as we turned to walk out of the store. "The bathroom makes me feel like I'm in a horror game."

"I know, right?" he said. "It's frickin' creepy in those bathrooms. They're dark and the flashlight adds to the creepy factor."

"We need to do something about this whole not-having-power thing," I grumbled.

"I agree. It's starting to get a little cold. If it gets any colder, we're gonna have to cuddle to stay warm." He shot me a wink.

I punched him in the arm. "Keep dreaming."

"I'd have to start dreaming first," he sassed back.

"Well, start dreaming and maybe I'll cuddle you if it was a dream, you see? That was the point I was trying to make."

He gave me a weird look.

I sighed. "You know what I mean. Let's just go and make those burritos you promised me, okay?"

"Fine."

I flashed the light at his face and he glared at me. "You can punch me. It's okay. I'll allow it."

"I really do want to sometimes," he whined.

I pushed him again. "Come on. Fight me, nerd."

"I'm not gonna do that," he stated.

"Why not?"

He smirked at me. "Let's be honest here. I would kick your ass."

"Haven't we gone over this?"

"Yeah," he said, shrugging. "I'd still kick your ass."

"Ha!" I bellowed. "Okay."

"I'm spitting in your food for real this time," he said with a sigh as we started to get close to the food court.

"Please don't," I said, pushing his forward.

"Stop pushing me, got damn," he whined as he tripped over his feet a little.

I chucked. "You're really just gonna let me beat you up?"

"All you're doing is pushing me," he stated. "It's not beating me up. It's annoying as hell though."

"I'm gonna push you off the roof too," I told him.

"Bitch," Evan said as he coughed.

I pushed him again. "At least try to make it sound like you're covering an insult with a cough."

"I wanted to make sure that you would hear it."

"Oh, I heard ya loud and clear."

Evan smiled and walked over towards the burrito place. "Good."

I sighed and started following him. "You know how to make burritos, right?" I asked him.

"It's not that hard," he replied.

I sighed. "No, but like, do you know how to fold them and shit?"

He shrugged. "I'm sure I'll figure that out when the time comes."

"Oh, come on. I don't wanna be eating a bean and beef salad in a tortilla bowl. Make them right or I will actually beat you up."

"What's with all the threats?"

"I'm hungry," I whined.

Evan let out a groan. "If you stop insulting me and threatening me and being physically violent towards me, I will make you a really good burrito."

"Burritos," I said, correcting him. He has to find a way to make up for making wimpy-ass burgers.

"How many do you want?"

I paused for a moment and looked away as if I were having some deep and profound moment of thought. "I'm thinking five or six."

"You're a legitimate fatass," Evan said, laughing a little as he hopped over the counter and into the burrito place. Too lazy to look up and figure out the name of it.

"Want a flashlight?" I asked, pulling a second flashlight from my pocket.

"I'd enjoy a flashlight, yes," Evan said, turning to me.

I put the flashlight down on the counter. "Is that all, sir?"

"The joke would have been funnier if you were on this side and I was on that side," Evan stated.

I sighed. "Way to kill the joke, asshole."

"I know you love me," he said with a wink as he turned on the flashlight.

"I do not," I snapped.

"Not yet."

"You're really cocky."

"No," he said. "I'm really loveable."

I shrugged. "Not really."

"But," he said, turning and giving me a pouty face. "I'm just so cute. Look at this wittle face."

"Keep dreaming."

"I must be dreaming. No one's ever been this sassy to me before in real life," Evan said, turning back to the grill.

"We need to fix the power at some point. It seriously is getting chilly in here."

"Like I said, we could cuddle for warmth."

"No," I snapped. "It's like I said, keep dreaming."

Evan sighed. "I'm slacking on the beef in your burrito."

I climbed over the counter and into the kitchen. I walked over to him and pushed him again. "Fight me then, nerd."

"Stop it," he whined, stumbling a little. "I will seriously cook your food in my piss. You're so annoying."

"Sorry," I said, hopping up on one of the prep counters.

He sighed and started gathering up ingredients. "You're a real douche. Get down from there."

I smiled at him. "I know. And, no."

"Here." Evan handed me a piece of tortilla. "Snack on this until I finish making our burritos," he said, rolling the R.

"Yay," I said, grabbing the piece of tortilla from him. I took a bite and spit it out. "Never mind. Plain tortilla is just gross."

"I slaved over a hot stove all day to make you that tortilla," Evan said, pretending to be offended… again.

I tossed the tortilla back at him and it hit him in the side of his face. It fell to the countertop and he picked it up and threw it back at me.

I smacked it in midair, causing it to go way across the kitchen. "Gonna have to be quicker than that."

Evan sighed again. "Okay." He went back to prepping everything.

I watched him closely. I didn't want him to get any cheap shots on me.

"Stop staring at me," he said, turning to me.

I stuck my tongue out at him. "Boo. I wasn't even staring at you. I was staring at the beef you're cooking."

"Do you want me to add bacon to these too?"

I nodded.

"Okay. You're still kind of cool at least." He walked over to the freezer and pulled out a pack of bacon. He tossed a few strips onto the grill.

I took a deep breath as the smells of bacon filled the air. "Ah, the wonderful sizzle of heavenly strips of deliciousness. Don't you just love it, Evan? Don't you? Don't you just love our heavenly ambrosia that is bacon? Can you smell that? Mmm."

"Stop that."

"Stop what?" I asked.

"Having an orgasm over bacon."

I hopped down from the counter and rested a hand on his back. "You just do not get it. Bacon... It's more than just a food. It's a life-style. It's a way of thinking."

"It's not a very healthy one then."

"Shut up. I will take my heart attack with pride."

"Better take your heart meds with pride too," he joked.

I sighed. "I'm not. I'm an Olympic athlete, clearly."

"Yeah," he said, looking over at me. "Okay."

"I am," I said, pouting at him.

Evan scoffed. "I bet you couldn't even do twenty push-ups."

I raised an eyebrow at him. "Challenge accepted."

"This'll be good," he said, turning to watch me as I walked to the middle of the kitchen floor.

I left my flashlight on the counter and got down to the ground.

"Waiting," Evan said, flashing the light from his flashlight around me a few times.

"Okay, Mr. Impatient. I'm getting to it," I groaned, getting into a push-up position.

"Come on," he whined. "You have to do twenty."

"I know," I grumbled, doing a push-up. "That's one."

"Do another," he said. I could hear the amusement in his voice.

I tried to do another one, but I couldn't push myself back up. I heard Evan stifle back some laughter. "Okay," I groaned, standing back up. "Why don't you do twenty push-ups, then?"

"Two reasons. One, I never claimed to be an Olympic athlete, and two, I'm cooking your food, so I don't really think you would appreciate my hands on the nasty kitchen floor and then all in your food," Evan stated, turning back to the grill.

"That's such a cop out." I walked back over to the counter and hopped back up. "I'm exhausted."

"You didn't even do two push-ups. Come on now."

"Lotta energy, ya know?"

He scoffed again. "You're an idiot."

"Admittedly."

"You just admit to being an idiot?"

"Well, it's been instilled in me."

He rolled his eyes and smirked at me. "Is that partially my fault too now?"

I laughed softly. "Maybe."

"Here," he said, handing me a burrito. "Eat this and be happy about it. It took a lot of effort to make this stupid thing."

I pushed it away. "No, no, no, no. You have to wrap it in paper, put it in a bag, and then we're gonna go to the roof."

"Frick. Fine," he grumbled. "Go get our coats."

"Fine," I said, hopping from the counter and grabbing my flashlight. "I'm not gonna be happy about it though."

"That's more than okay with me."

I hopped back over the counter and into the food court. I clicked the flashlight on and walked on back to the store. I grabbed our coats from our beds and went back to the food court.

Evan walked over to me as he saw me coming over. "'Bout time."

"Shut up," I said, tossing his coat to him.

Evan walked ahead of me and led us up the stairs and to the third floor. "Come on, you slowpoke."

"Shut up," I whined, trying to keep up to him. "My legs is smaller than yours."

"Not really a good excuse," he said, holding the door to the roof stairwell open for me.

I grabbed the bag of burritos from him. "Be nice or I won't share my food with you."

"Bitch, please," he said, following me up the stairs. "I made the food. You have to be nice."

"Doesn't mean I'm gonna share with you," I said, stopping at the door. "Before you come out, make sure the water bottle is propped to keep the door open."

"Right," Evan said, grabbing the big-ass water bottle from beside the door to slide it in place so we won't get locked out.

I walked out into the cold winter air and took a deep breath. It was so pretty now that the clouds have mostly gone away. The moon shone brightly in the sky and all the little flecks of snow that were falling all around us looked like little twinkling stars.

"Nice out tonight," Evan said, walking up beside me. His breathing puffed out around his face.

I looked around and then to him. "Yeah, not very windy and not too cold. It's a pretty nice night to be stuck in a snowed-in mall, wouldn't you think so?"

"I keep forgetting that we're actually, like, *stuck* in here."

"Wanna go try to dig out of the snow to get a reminder?"

"No, I'm good. Snow is cold and I'd like to stay warm," Evan replied. "Thanks for the offer though."

I laughed and pushed him softly. "That's what I thought, bitch." I pulled a burrito out of the bag and handed it to him. "Now eat up before I change my mind."

He took the burrito from me and smiled. "Thank you, sir. I'll be a good boy now, sir. I'll make sure I do all my chores."

"Okay. Well, for one, I'm not a sir, and for two, you don't live in some strict orphanage that's run by me."

"Maybe I do," Evan said as he unwrapped his burrito. "It certainly would make for an interesting twist to our story if you were actually running an empty mall as an orphanage."

"You're right, but that would be *too* interesting. Also, these burritos are surprisingly well prepared," I said, opening a burrito of my own. "Did you work at a taco place or something before?"

"No. I just love tacos and burritos and pitas. I make them all the time at home."

I took a bite of the burrito. It was actually very good for a shitty burrito. "I bet your family enjoys when you cook dinner."

"I don't actually get to cook for anyone," Evan said as he walked over to the edge of the little wall. He rested his elbows on the wall as he took a bite of his burrito. "Like, ever."

"Not even a girlfriend or friends or younger sibling?" I asked.

"Pfft. Girls. You're funny," he said as I walked over and leaned on the wall with him. "Nobody asks me to cook for them. Maybe that's why I don't really mind cooking for you. I don't know. Cooking is fun, and cooking for people is even more fun because they get to enjoy food I made. I just don't get to cook for people."

"Nice. I'm gonna employ you to be my personal chef. I can't pay you with money, would you accept sass as payment?"

"Nope," he said, winking at me.

I sighed. "Okay, I'll blow you once a week."

"Twice a week and you'll have yourself a deal."

I clicked my flashlight off, put it in my pocket, and stuck my hand out to Evan. "Shake my hand and let's make it official."

Evan shook his head. "I'm not gonna prostitute my cooking services for sex."

"I was willing to actually prostitute my actual self for your cooking services. You're a teen boy. You're supposed to like head."

"I also have morals," he said. "If I accepted sex as payment, how would I ever be able to make money to afford the food and ingredients that I'd be cooking?"

"I'll get rich."

"How?"

"I'd win the lottery," I stated.

"Why are you trying to blow me for food?"

"I'm not," I shouted. "I just like the food you make and I want you to make me food after we get out of here. I have friends. I'll hook you up. We'll crowdfund you."

"You're really too lazy to cook for yourself, huh?"

I shook my head. "It's not that. It's just that I don't like to cook. I also suck. You're way better. Please cook for me."

"Shut up."

"Be my personal Gordon Ramsay."

"I'm gonna push you off the roof in a minute."

I laughed and shook my head. "You're really getting fed up with me, huh?"

He nodded.

"Am sorry. I'll do better," I told him.

"No, you won't," he said.

"Yeah," I said, taking a big bite of the burrito. "You're right."

"Stop talking with food in your mouth," Evan whined. "Ain't you ever learnt any manners?"

"Shut your face," I snapped back.

"Shut it for me."

I took the opportunity and smacked his face. "Did that do it?"

He turned to me and gave me a death stare.

"Love you," I said, winking.

"You're lucky that I'm too busy eating to beat you up for that," he barked back.

I smiled at him. "Yeah, yeah. I'm sure that's the reason you won't fight back." I pushed him lightly as he went to take another bite from his burrito.

He sighed and pushed my burrito up into my face and smushed it around a little. "Eat up."

{Chapter: **Fifteen**}

The door slammed shut behind us as we walked back into the mall from outside on the roof. It got so cold out there after a little while.

"My face is still so cold," Evan said, rubbing his hands on his cheeks in a valiant effort to warm them up.

I pushed him lightly so it would make him go down the stairs quicker. "Rub your face later, weirdo." I just wanted to get back to somewhere warm. All this cold air was a bit too much for me right now.

"Hey, you hear that?"

I stopped behind him and listened. "Just a low whirring sound."

"Exactly," Evan said. "The backup generators must have finally kicked in or something."

"We have power?" I asked.

"We might," he replied. "I think the stores on the bottom floor will have power. I guess that's good that our beds are on that floor then, right?"

"Yes. I need warmth. Let's move the mattresses to a smaller store," I suggested. "It'll preserve the heat even more or whatever."

"I will help you move them, but I am *not* moving them by myself," Evan stated.

I let out a loud, bear-like groan. "I *hate* you."

"You have arms and legs, you're totally capable of moving a mattress with me," Evan stated.

"But I'm just a weak little girl."

He shook his head and laughed slightly. "Girls aren't weak."

"I am."

He shot me a quick smirk. "Time to build you some muscle."

"Gah, I hate you."

Evan opened the door back into the third floor of the mall and smiled. "I know you do, Spencer. I know you do."

"I mean, I don't really hate you," I stated. "It's just that you… well, you have cooties."

"What, are you five?" Evan asked as we walked into the hallway.

"Bitch, I might be," I said, pushing him. It must be really annoying for him that I keep pushing and punching him, but whatever, that's what I'm here for.

"You know what we should do?"

I sighed. "What should we do?"

"I don't know."

"Man, I feel like I ask that an awful lot though," I mumbled.

"You kinda do, yeah. But, I don't know, maybe we should go use one of the hot tubs. There's a hot tub store on the bottom floor. We could totally go do it," Evan suggested.

"Swimsuits and Spencers do not mix," I stated.

Evan sighed. "C'mon. Let's go hot tubbin'."

"Love to, but I'm wearing jeans and a sweater."

"But—"

"No buts," I stated firmly. "I'm not very self-body positive."

Evan rested a hand on my shoulder as we reached the stairs back down to the mall. "You're a beautiful little flower, Spencer."

"Shut up," I muttered swatting his hand away from me.

"I refuse."

I shook my head and walked away from him. "Not gonna do it." I heard him let out a sigh as I kept walking down the stairs. I led the way back to the first floor and then all the way back to the superstore where our makeshift bedroom was.

Maybe that's something wrong with me that I don't like wearing swimsuits, but I don't exactly compare to Instagram models.

"Stop being so quiet," Evan said as we reached the beds. "It's weird and it's creeping me the frick out."

"Sorry," I said, jumping onto my bed and stretching out.

"Get up. We're gonna move the mattresses and go get into a hot tub. Come on."

I groaned. "But I don't wanna move. I'm so damn comfortable right now."

"But... hot tub," Evan whined, making a sad, pouty face.

"I dislike my midriff."

"Your what?"

"Midriff."

"No," Evan said. "I know what you said, I was just waiting for you to say it like a normal person would say it."

"My stomach?"

"Better."

I sat up and shook my head. "Me and my midriff are gonna stay fully clothed."

"Come on," Evan whined. "Just get in a swimsuit and we'll get in a hot tub and we'll get a bottle of wine and it'll be lots of fun."

"Mm, I don't know," I said. "Sounds a little too romantic."

"It'll be completely platonic."

"Yeah?"

"Yeah, of course," he replied. "We'll get rose petals to float in the water and we'll light candles and have slow music playing in the background. It'll be completely platonic."

"Shut up," I barked.

"Just go hot tubbing with me for a little bit."

I sighed and stood up. "Let's move the beds first."

"You better be helping me."

"Well, we have to start moving them for me to help you. I would also prefer we move them to a store closer to the food court. Just putting in my request."

Evan chuckled softly. "Fatass."

"Shut up," I barked.

"So grouchy."

"You keep calling me a fatass," I stated.

"And you keep pushing me," Evan rebutted.

I stood up and walked over to him and pushed him again. "I do not know what it is that you are referring to, my good sir."

"You're lucky you're cute," he mumbled.

"Heard that," I said with a wink.

He smirked. "You were meant to." He turned and lifted his mattress up from the one corner. "Now, can you help me with the other side? We need to get this sumbitch to the game store."

"That's gonna be weird when the employees come back," I said, walking over to the other side of the bed.

Evan gave me a confused look. "What's going to be weird? Do you mean that two mattresses being in a gaming store isn't a normal thing to see?"

"It's totally normal," I said. "You know, if your name is Evan and your IQ is lower than the temperature right now."

"Celsius or Fahrenheit?" Evan asked as we lifted the mattress up.

"Pretty sure it's cold enough outside that they'd both be in the negative. So does it really matter?" I groaned as I lifted my end of the mattress. I really hope my mattress is lighter than his. This thing is heavy for a mattress.

"You look like you're having a hard time."

"Shut up. I don't need your smugness and attitude. Okay?"

"Sorry."

"I just have a heart condition," I said. "No biggie."

Evan dropped the mattress at his feet. "Are you serious?"

"Dude," I groaned. "We're halfway to the fricking store and you're gonna just drop the goddamn mattress?"

"You said you—"

"I was messing around with you. Can you just pick up your end and let's get this thing over there?"

"Bossy," Evan muttered as he picked up the mattress.

"Don't make me go get the chainsaw again," I threatened.

Evan shot me a blank stare. "Okay, okay."

"I'll actually use it on you this time too, so be careful."

"I'm still gonna get you back for that," Evan stated. "And you're never gonna see it coming."

"Drop it. Let's go get the other bed," I said as we got into the store.

Evan flipped the mattress over to the open part of the store and pushed it to the back so my mattress would have room. "Let's go get yours."

"Or we could share?" I said, nudging him in the ribs playfully.

"Not even if my life depended on it," Evan said, walking out of the store.

I followed him out. "Hurtful."

"That was the point, sweetheart."

"Yeah, yeah."

Evan led the way back to the store. "You're still gonna go hot tubbing with me, right?"

"You're mean. Why would I wanna do anything with you?"

He paused for a minute. "You want to have more cool stuff to tell your friends?"

"I'll consider it," I told him. "For now, let's just focus on getting my shit to the shit where your shit is."

"Okay," Evan said.

I smirked at him as we lifted the mattress.

"Why are you smirking?" he asked.

"Oh, just thinking about how badly you want me."

"I don't."

"Mm-hmm," I taunted him.

"Chill your fucking ego, mate."

"Well, I never said *how* you want me," I said. "Maybe I just meant how badly you want me as a friend."

"Would it be a bad thing if I did want you as a friend?" he asked.

I shook my head. "No. It'd be kinda nice to hear that, actually."

"I'm not gonna say it."

"Come on," I begged. "Say it. I'll go hot tubbing with you if you say it."

"Fine," he groaned as we exited the store with the mattress. "I really want you to be my friend, Spencer."

"I'd like to think we're pals already though," I stated.

"Why's that?"

"Well, with the time we've spent in here, and if you don't go and mess it all up, I'd say that we've made a pretty good connection," I told him.

"I guess so. So let's get this mattress business over with so we can go hot tub."

I laughed. "Agreed, agreed. Might give me time to start agreeing to get into the hot tub."

"Works for me," Evan said as he led us into the game store. "Okay, drop it there." He nodded towards the area next to where his bed was.

"You don't say," I teased him.

Evan dropped his end of the mattress. "Don't be a dick."

"I'm not being a dick," I said, dropping my end of the mattress with an exaggerated thud.

"You're being sassy." He pushed the mattress into place.

"Sassy is my second nature."

"I can tell," Evan said with a sigh.

I sighed and looked at our new bedroom. "This feels so much more cramped than our old sleeping place."

"Yeah, but it'll be warmer once the heat kicks back in," Evan stated.

"What about lights?"

"They'll be dim," Evan replied. "That's just how the mall works. It has to conserve power, so it's heat and dim lights and minimal outlet power to the bottom floor only. This mall sucks, I know. Cut it some slack. It's older than time."

"Yeah, okay," I said." But you know what sucks even more? The fact that you wanna use what little power we have on a hot tub session."

"It wouldn't be a waste," Evan argued. "Hot tubs are the shit."

"I would have to agree."

"You would," he said, with a small smirk forming on his face.

"I mean hot tubs, they're okay, but Jacuzzis are where it's at," I stated.

"What's the difference?"

"I'm not sure, to be honest."

"I think one is a brand name, the other is just the actual name of the item," I stated.

He shrugged. "Either way."

"Either way, Spencer's right."

He scoffed. "Ain't that the truth."

I rolled my eyes. "Alright. Should we go get some swimsuits, then?" I asked reluctantly.

Evan nodded. "I hope they have ugly floral-patterned shorts for me."

"Why would you ever want such a thing?"

"Because it would be funny."

"Mm, yeah, I don't know about that."

He walked out of the store. "Come on, let's go get you a cute bikini or something."

"It'll have to be made out of kittens to make me even the slightest bit cute."

"Stop being so negative towards yourself," Evan barked as he led us back towards the superstore. "You're a very attractive young lady. And I mean that. As a friend of course."

"Thanks," I said, blushing a little. I don't know why, I wasn't really attracted to Evan, so me blushing was purely because I'm not very used to compliments. "I just don't see myself that way. And you should know, I got a little chub."

"A little chub is cute though," Evan stated. "In my professional opinion, at least."

I sighed. "I wish I had a flat stomach."

"You basically do," he said. "It's just got a little extra on it, whoop dee fricking do."

"But still."

"But still nothing. There's nothing wrong with you or the other fricking billion girls who think they aren't good enough," Evan shouted. "I swear, this goddamn media with its shallow ideas of conventional beauty."

I walked closer to him and rested a hand on his shoulder. "The world needs more people like you."

"Shh," he said, swatting my hand away. "Let's go and get us some swim gear."

I followed him inside and toward the swimwear section. "Should I go to the girls' section then?"

He turned to me and sighed. "Well, unless you wanted to wear a speedo?" he asked, nodding toward a display of speedos.

"Yeah, those are all yours, buddy," I said, turning around and heading towards the lady swimwear.

I perused the aisles of clothes. Perused. That's a neat word. Anyway, I kept looking around until I found a two-piece that I liked enough to wear. It was red, so I figured it would suit me because, I mean, I am a ginger after all. Red is the colour of my people.

"Did you find something?" Evan called out from somewhere in the boys' section.

"I did," I yelled back.

"Where are the dressing rooms at in this place now?" Evan shouted. "I haven't been back here in a while."

"Come here," I called back to him, walking towards where his voice sounded like it was coming from.

Evan walked over to me and I flashed my flashlight on him to see him with a pair of floral-patterned shorts slung over his shoulder. "Like the pattern?"

I shook my head. "Ugly as hell."

"Pfft," he said, walking past me and taking my flashlight. "At least it'll keep you from looking."

"Why are you taking my light?" I barked. "You have your own."

"Battery's dead."

I let out a groan. "That doesn't mean you just get to take my frickin' flashlight."

"Yeah, it do."

I walked quickly to catch up to Evan. I grabbed the flashlight back from his hand. "I'll just take that back. Thanks."

"Dick," he grumbled.

"It wasn't yours to begin with."

"It's not exactly yours either," he noted.

I paused for a minute. "Um, well… Okay, so you got me there."

"Gimme it," he whined.

I extended my hand and pulled it away as he tried to grab the flashlight from me. I winked at him. "Try harder."

"You're a jerk," Evan whined.

I smirked at him. "Get your own flashlight, you tool."

"Batteries are too far and the other flashlights are all the way back in the game store."

"You brought them there already?" I asked.

Evan nodded. "Of course. Gotta move the essentials to our fancy, new crib."

"When did you do that?"

"A while ago. Don't question it."

I sighed. "Whatever. Let's go get into our swimsuits." I nodded toward the change rooms ahead of us.

"Ahh, yeah. Let's do that," Evan said, walking over to the front desk. He grabbed a key and tossed it to me.

"Thanks," I said as he grabbed a key for himself.

I watched Evan walk over to one of the rooms. I looked at the key and walked over to the room it was assigned. I unlocked the door and then opened it and went inside. I set the flashlight down on the little bench so it lit up the small room as best as it could.

I slipped out of all my clothes and put on the bikini. It's an odd thing to wear a bikini in the middle of December though. I put my shirt and pants back on over the bikini and then grabbed the flashlight. I balled my bra and underwear up and quickly found a bag for them. I stuck them in the bag and by that time, Evan came out of his room with swim trunks and his shirt on.

"I love your bikini," Evan joked as he walked over to me.

I pushed him for the millionth time in the past day. "Shut up. Now, let's go see if you can get this hot tub working."

"Trust me," he said, turning and leading the way towards the exit of the store. "I'm a professional hot tub repairman. I got this."

"You're not any kind of repairman, so I'm definitely looking forward to this."

"Shush."

"Do you think full-body electrocution hurts, or does your heart just *stop*?" I teased him.

"I don't know. When you get electrocuted in ten minutes, let me know with a Ouija board, okay?"

"I'll be sure to get right on that."

{Chapter: **Sixteen**}

I watched as Evan fiddled around with the hot tub. He had actually gotten the backup power to work in this store, so kudos to him for that. But the real test was if he could get one of the display hot tubs in working order.

Evan stood up and turned to me. "I think I got it."

"It's either you got it or you didn't," I told him.

"Well," he said, walking around the hot tub and pressing some buttons and shit. "It should be whirring to life right *now*." His smirk faded to a slight frown.

"It's doing a thing," I said, pointing to the water as it began to bubble slightly.

He looked down and then raised his eyebrows in amazement or something. "Oh, the jets weren't turned up." He twisted a knob on the hot tub and then it whirred and stirred and bubbled to life.

"You did it!" I said. And then I remembered that we had to now get into the hot tub and spend time in it. "I mean… you did it," I said, more sombrely this time.

"Just give it a few seconds to warm up," Evan told me. "It's still a little cold."

"A cold hot tub… how peculiar."

Evan shook his head. "You're an idiot, Spencer."

I stuck my tongue out at him, because I couldn't push him right now as he was on the other side of the hot tub. "You're a jerk, Evan."

"Fight me. One-vee-one me in the hot tub."

"Not likely."

"So it's not unlikely either?"

"What?"

"Exactly," he said, nodding slightly.

"You're a strange young man," I stated.

"Yeah, I know." He nodded. "Now, let's get in. It'll be warm enough and it'll get hot soon."

"Ladies first," I said, lifting my arm to motion to the hot tub, as if to tell him to get in.

"So get in," he said, kicking his shoes off.

"After you."

"You're a wimp," he said with a sigh as he lifted off his shirt.

"Nice no-pack."

"There's a faint sixer," he said, sounding a little bit hurt.

I nodded. "Really faint."

"Shut up," Evan barked, stepping into the hot tub. "Okay, it's nice and warm."

"And bubbly?"

"Why are you asking that? You can see."

"Not very well," I stated. "Hold on." I turned and walked out of the store and across the mall. I went into another store and grabbed some candles. I walked back and dug a lighter from my pocket.

"Why you got candles?" Evan asked, looking over to me.

"It's too dark and these flashlights aren't lighting up the room enough for me."

Evan nodded. "Gotcha."

I set up some candles as close to the hot tub as I could, and then I went back around and lit them all up. I've been keeping a lighter in my jeans for lighting candles. The hot tub was illuminated in a dimly flickering light, dancing on the turbulent water of the hot tub.

"These jets are really nice, bruh," Evan said.

"Yeah, yeah," I said, walking over to the hot tub.

Evan sighed. "We should have gotten Doritos or something. I got the craving for some snacks."

I shrugged as I undid my zipper for my jeans. "That's your problem, not mine."

"I'll go get some," he said, getting out of the hot tub. "I'll get towels while I'm gone too," he said, looking around and realizing that we didn't have any towels for when we got out. "I don't know how we forgot towels."

"Have fun," I said, slipping out of my jeans.

"Will do," he yelled back to me as he jogged away.

I shook my head. Evan's such a loser. I kicked my jeans over to where the bag with my bra and underwear was. I peeled my shirt off and tossed it over there to cap off the small pile of clothes I had.

I climbed over the edge of the hot tub and sort of just plopped down into water with a pretty excessive splash of water. I accidentally swallowed a little bit, which caused me to start coughing.

After I finished dying of pneumonia and sat back in the hot tub, rubbing at my throat. "Coughing up water hurts," I grumbled.

"I would imagine so," Evan's voice chimed as he walked over.

I turned to see him walking over with two big bags full of snacks and drinks for us to eat. He also had some towels draped over his shoulders. That was fast.

"I mean, what? I didn't just choke on water while getting into a hot tub. Psht, you're crazy," I stated.

"I heard you from outside the store," Evan said, dropping the bags on the side of the hot tub.

"I'm so sorry my coughing disturbed you," I said as he climbed back into the hot tub.

He shrugged. "They didn't disturb me."

"Ooh, hey, did you get the good kind of Doritos?"

"They're all good kinds," Evan said, reaching over to the bags. He tossed me a bag of the regular Doritos, you know, the nacho cheese ones. "Make sure you wipe your hands on the towel. I don't think we need any soggy Doritos in the bag."

"Yeah, yeah, so toss me a towel then."

Evan handed me a towel and I put it next to me.

"This is nice," I said, drying my hands off and opening the bag. I set them on the side of the hot tub so the bag wouldn't be floating around in the water all intrusive and shit.

"So, what now?" Evan asked.

I shrugged as I stuffed some chips into my mouth. "You decide. This was your idea."

"Don't talk with a mouth full of chips. You're gonna get crumbs all in the water," Evan whined.

"Oh, shut up," I barked.

He smirked at me. "Nah."

"This is so odd," I said, looking around as I grabbed more chips from the bag next to me.

Evan cocked his eyebrow at me. "What do you mean?"

"Like, look around. Look how romantic this is. We're in a hot tub, in the dark, and surrounded by candles."

"Hmm, if we weren't about to bang, I'd agree with you."

"Shut up," I barked. "I just mean that it's so weird. Even those little coffee breaks on the roof were vaguely romantic."

"I guess you kind of have a point here," Evan said. "We should have been knee deep in teen romance by now. What gives?"

"What gives is that I don't wanna date someone I barely know."

"Well, we've been in here with just each other for a while. I'd like to think we've made it past the awkward stage," Evan stated.

"Okay, but you're still a stranger."

"My favourite animals are cats," Evan told me.

I cocked my eyebrow a little. "That was random."

"I don't wanna be a stranger to you, Spencer," Evan stated. "You're a really cool girl, and I don't wanna not have a friendship with you once we get out of here."

"Okay. Keep going," I told him.

"Um, well, I also wanna move to Vancouver some—"

"I meant about how cool I am," I snapped, interrupting him.

"Oh." He pouted at me. "Well, you're cute and funny and smart and I like your company. You're not a total asshole to me like a lot of other people, even though you constantly tease and push and harass me, so I really appreciate that, and you and I would very much enjoy continuing our unlikely friendship when we finally get out of this place."

"Wait. Why have we not tried a payphone yet? Are there any left here?" I asked. "Those would work to call out, right?"

"The mall removed all the payphones last month. The only payphones are outside by the bus terminal."

"Oh, yeah. *Outside.*"

Evan nodded. "We're stuck until someone comes to dig out the mall. Probably a few days."

"Let's just dig ourselves out."

Evan shook his head. "I'm not digging myself out of all that ice and snow. We've been through this."

"You're just lazy," I muttered.

"I thought we agreed to just enjoy ourselves in here. When do you think we'll ever have an entire mall to ourselves, ya know?"

"I know," I said with a sigh. "I just miss Netflix and my bed."

"I know those feels, man. I know those feels."

"Yeah. Netflix is my family," I said, probably sounding a little whiny. "And my family is my family too."

Evan sighed. "This hot tub is pretty amazing though. The world outside will be there waiting for us whenever we get out of this mall, Spencer. Don't you worry."

"I'm glad you convinced me to get in this hot tub, to be honest."

Evan smiled slyly. "You're welcome."

"It's nice and hot, hot, hot. Me so on fire, feeling hot, hot, hot."

"Stop."

I smiled slightly. "If you wanna be my friend, you're gonna have to learn to put up with me and all my shit."

"You're probably really annoying when you get comfortable with people. Aren't you?"

I nodded. "You better believe it."

"Did I make a mistake?"

I nodded.

"Well, shit," he muttered.

I grabbed some chips and shovelled them into my face-hole. "But I'm also very cool. So you're either missing out on me or putting up with me. Either way, there's a bad side and a good side, so…"

"I think I can put up with you being annoying."

"Are you annoying?"

"No."

"I beg to differ."

"I'm not," Evan said, raising his hand to his chest and the other one straight upward into the air. "Scout's honour."

I shook my head. "You're a tool."

"But I'm your tool now, Spencer," he said, moving over and resting a hand on my shoulder. He looked me dead in the eyes. "I'm your tool."

"I'm taking you back for a refund."

"You can't. No refunds," Evan stated as he moved back to where he was sitting before. "I'm a final sale."

"That's okay. They made dumpsters for a reason."

"That's cold."

I shrugged. "The water was too hot, so I had to cool it down."

"When are we gonna get out?"

"Preferably never." I shrugged once more. "This kinda all feels so surreal though," I stated.

"Well, we are just characters, so…"

"But still."

"And it is a fiction novel," Evan noted.

"Whatever," I said with a sigh. "Anyway, what should we do when we get out?"

"No idea. Maybe we just never get out."

I let out a slight groan. "I can't believe that we're in a mall and have limitless things to do, and yet we still can't think of something amazing."

"We're lame."

"We're *so* lame."

Evan reached over to the bag of goodies he had brought with him. "You want a soda? A pop? A fizzy drink? I got root beer, cola, and ginger ale."

"Toss me a root beer," I said.

He handed me a root beer from the bag, taking one for himself as well. "I was actually kidding though. I only brought root beer."

"Well, I'm not gonna complain about that," I told him, cracking the tab of the root beer can open.

"We should go do some Go Fish for, like, five minutes," Evan suggested. "You know, before we get tired of it and then go find something else to do."

"Let's talk about space, bruh."

Evan cocked an eyebrow at me. "Bruh. That was way out of left-field, don't cha think?"

I pouted a little. "Stars are cool."

"Did you ever have a telescope as a kid?"

I shook my head. "I've always wanted one though."

"Why do you like stars so much?"

I shrugged. "I don't really know. It's just something about the endless starry skies that calm me down. I love knowing that there are other things out there that we'll never be able to see. The universe is so huge and we're so little."

"That was so deep," Evan said, looking at me like I was a crazy person. I don't blame him though. I mean, I don't think he was expecting that answer from me.

I nodded. "I love space, man. Space is the coolest."

"I can agree to that."

And then we talked about space, and then the moon, and then about how the moon has saved us from asteroids, and then about dying from asteroids, and then we talked about Armageddon, and then we talked about other movies. And we managed to munch through a fair bit of those snacks he had brought for us. And then my fingers started getting all wrinkly.

"Hey, bud," I said, interrupting Evan's sentence.

"Yeah?"

"Can we get the hell out now? My fingertips are starting to look like little pink raisins."

"Yeah, my hands are looking too much like an old man's hands right now," Evan said with a little laugh.

I got up out of the water and stepped over the edge to get out.

"Whoa."

I turned to Evan and shot him a look. "What?"

"Your bum. It's very nice," he said.

I turned away quickly to avoid him making fun of the blush rising to me cheeks. "You shut the hell up about my butt. Friends shouldn't be checking out other friends' bums, by the way, Evan. Not very platonic of you."

"Eh, it was just an observation."

"Observe yourself shutting up," I snapped, grabbing a towel and wrapping it around my wet body. I grabbed a second towel and dried the bottom half of my hair. It was really weird having the top half of my head being dry and then my hair on the bottom being wet. Could have been avoided if I were smarter and just out my hair up in a bun or something, but as I've demonstrated so far, I am not the sharpest tool in the shed.

"Let's go off to the wonderful land of our beds," Evan said, climbing over the hot tub and getting out.

"Nice bum," I joked, grabbing the bag of my clothes.

"Oh, shut up," he snapped back, flinging the towel around his shoulders.

I smiled back at him. "It's weird, right?"

"A little bit, dang. But thanks. I do my squats."

"Weirdo," I said, wrapping my hair up in a towel, mostly to avoid having wet hair tickling my back like they were the hands of a pervy Poseidon.

Evan shrugged. "You go set up a game of Go Fish for us to play. I'm gonna go make us a tea."

"What if I don't like tea?"

Evan started laughing. "Everyone likes tea. Try again."

"Fair enough," I said, walking towards the exit.

"Hey," Evan shouted at me.

I swivelled on my heel to face him. "Yo."

"Take this bag of leftover snacks and drank back to the beds."

"Fine," I whined, walking over and taking the bag from him. "Have fun turning off the hot tub."

"Will do," he said, turning it off. "Oh, that was just so exhilarating. I wanna do it again."

"Shut up." I walked out of the store. "See ya back at the beds."

And that's exactly what I did. I walked to the game store where we had our beds set up and then I got our card game set up while I waited for Evan to come back with our bedtime teas.

Evan took a long-ass time, in my opinion anyway, to get back with the tea, but it was very good tea, so I forgave him for taking too long. And then we played Go Fish until we started to get to tired too sit up properly.

Evan was the first to lie down, and I followed his lead, turning off the lights as I did. And we lied in our beds talking about space some more, about all the endless and vast blackness in a light-filled sky.

And then we both slowly just faded our way to sleep. It was nice. It was relaxing. It was just a really nice way to end the day, I thought. It seemed like we had a good time in the hot tubs, better than I thought we would. Evan and I really connected.

{Chapter: **Seventeen**}

I rubbed my eyes and yawned as I slowly stirred awake. I rolled over and saw Evan still fast asleep in his bed. What a little cutie. He was snoring softly and curled up into his blankets.

I sat up and stretched out my arms and yawned again, you know, for good measure. I looked around, not expecting to see anything different. It was the same old gaming store as the night before. We were still in the same mall. I was really starting to lose hope in the idea that this was just a really long and elaborate dream.

I stood up and swapped the pyjama pants I had put on for a pair of fresh jeans. I changed my drool-stained shirt, joke, and put on a button-up plaid shirt. I forgot to get a new clean bra to change into, so all well. That can wait till later.

I tiptoed out of the store, as to not wake Evan because that'd be pretty rude of me. I made my way over to the store that Evan had our little makeshift coffee station set up. I walked around the counter and into the kitchen. I grabbed a pot and filled it with water from the tap. I put the pot of water on the stove thing and then flicked it on as to boil the pot of water. I grabbed one of the cups Evan had laid out beside the stove.

I dumped some sugar and instant coffee mix into the cup. Should be noted that I hate instant coffee, but it's the best I had, so it had to work. I hopped up onto the counter and sat there while I waited for my water to boil. After a minute or two, I prepped a coffee for Evan too, because I think it would be nice to repay him a little for how nice he was to me lately.

I probably should have brought a flashlight with me. I could barely see in the kitchen. The light from the skylight wasn't cutting it, but I'm too lazy too walk all the way back to the store to get a flashlight.

After an eternity, the pot of water was finally bubbling and boiled. I *carefully* spilled water all over the place as I filled the cups. I stirred them up and cleaned up the countertop. I walked to the freezer and grabbed some cream.

We had to put it in there because the freezer was still cold and the fridges weren't very cold anymore. Though with power returning in slow bursts to the food court, they might work again soon. I stirred some cream into our coffees and finished cleaning up.

I clicked the stove off and grabbed our coffees. I walked back out and around the counter and then I walked back to the gaming store. Little Evan was still asleep, aw, how cute.

I set the two cups of coffee down next to my bed and then I jumped onto Evan and started shaking him rather violently. "Wake up, bitch!" I shouted at him.

He startled himself awake. "Get off me," he shouted, pushing me off the mattress and to the floor.

I landed on my butt with a softly loud thud. "Ouch. You're pretty strong for a jerk."

"Why the hell did you wake me up like that?" he said, sitting up and reaching over for his shirt.

"I made us coffee," I said, reaching over and dragging the two cups of coffee over to me.

Evan sighed as he put his shirt on. "Well, I guess you're not the worst person in the world then." He held his hand out to me.

I handed the coffee to him and watched as he sipped the coffee and immediately made a scowl as he burnt his tongue.

I smiled at his stupidity. "It's hot and fresh, by the way."

"Mm, yep, just like me," Evan said, winking at me and setting the cup down next to his bed.

I shook my head. "Not even a little bit." Even though that was kind of a lie. He was starting to get a little hotter with each passing day, and that's probably a bad thing for our friendship. "Anyways... what are we gonna do today?" I asked.

He shrugged. "Let's go to the hardware store and dick around or something," Evan suggested. "No chainsaws though."

"Did you pee yourself a little when I scared you, or..."

"No... I peed myself a lot," Evan said. "Good thing I always wear adult diapers."

I smirked and took a sip of my coffee. "Good."

"You're creepy," Evan said, yawning and stretching out his arms.

I nodded. "So, what exactly do you want to do in said hardware store?"

"I don't know. Let's just mess around with stuff," he replied.

"Like?"

Evan shrugged. "We can paint something."

"Can I paint you?"

"Good idea," Evan said, looking at me like I just solved one of those unsolved math problems. "We can paint each other."

"Uh, no. I said that I would paint you," I said quickly, trying to get out of being splattered with paint.

"Let me paint you," Evan said, puffing his lower lip out and making the cutest little pouty face that he could.

I shook my head. "I don't wanna be covered in paint, dude."

"But I'll be covered in paint too," he noted.

"Don't care. It's me that doesn't want to be covered in paint," I told him. "And the desire to stay not covered in paint beats the desire to cover you in paint."

Evan shook his head out of frustration. "I'll cook for you some more."

"You'll have to do better than that, bud. Also don't you just use food to tempt me. That's my weakness and it's not fair. If you wanna paint me, you have to make me some jam. Homemade jam."

Evan sighed loudly. "If I promise to try to make some homemade raspberry jam for you, will you have a paint fight with me?"

"Hmm," I said, raising a finger to my chin to pretend like I was thinking. "Fine. But this raspberry jam better be amazing."

"It will be," Evan stated. "Alright, let's go." He stood from his bed and stretched out. He somehow managed to not spill his coffee while he stretched.

I stumbled my way to my feet and stretched out as he started walking out of the store. "Eh, wait up," I said, running after him, trying to not spill my coffee.

"You might wanna go change into your swimsuit," Evan said, turning to me.

I cocked my eyebrow at him. "Why would I do that?"

"Unless you want me to paint all of your clothes?"

"Oh," I said. "I thought we were gonna just get naked and do this, but hey, swimsuits are a good idea." I winked at him as if to tell him he missed his chance at seeing me suit up in my birthday suit.

"Can I retract that previous statement and replace it with your idea?"

I shook my head. "Nah. You messed up."

"Fine." He let out a sigh. "You stay here and get changed and then I'll go off to the hardware store and get paint ready and get into some shorts and we'll have a paint fight."

"Alright, get going," I barked at him. "I wanna get changed before I change my mind about doing this."

"Mm-hmm," he said, turned and walking off. "Try not to take too long."

I didn't bother responding. I just walked back inside the game store and set my coffee down on a display table that had a handheld gaming devices set up around it for you to try out to see if you wanted it to buy or not.

I grabbed my swimsuit from the little plastic baggy that I was using as a makeshift dresser of sorts. I slipped out of my clothes, pretty much all at once. It was actually pretty impressive. I kicked my clothes over onto my bed and put my swimsuit on. I was too tired to really care about putting anything back on top of it. I don't wanna risk having everything get covered in paint anyway.

I felt very exposed. Being in nothing but a swimsuit in the middle of a mall was a very strange feeling. And the cold tile floor I was walking on wasn't the best feeling for my bare feet either. I walked away from the game store and towards the hardware store. I was really hoping that Evan wouldn't be bare pickle by the time I got there. That would be just a little weird and awkward.

I walked into the hardware store and looked around. I noticed that all, or most, of the lights were on. I guess Evan got them working again. "Hello?" I called out.

"Over here, snookums," Evan yelled back.

I followed the sound of the voice to the paint section. "I see you got the lights working."

He was setting down two cans of paint as I walked into the aisle. He looked up and smirked. "I see you need to work on your tan."

"I'm a *ginger*. Pale is a *lifestyle*," I snapped back.

"I never said I didn't like it," he said with a wink. "And it doesn't matter anyways. You'll be covered in paint soon enough."

"So will you, pancake nipples," I said, taking a shot at him for being shirtless.

He scoffed. "My nipples are cute." He climbed up a ladder and reached for two more cans of paint.

"Why are you going up there for paint?" I asked. "There's all this paint here," I said, motioning to the bottom shelves.

"Yeah," Evan said, climbing down, "but the ones on the bottom are more expensive and they're the dual stuff."

"So?"

"I don't even think basic paint is good for your skin, so I mean, let's try to minimize our damages here," Evan said, adding the two new cans to the stack of cans he had amassed.

I shrugged. "Well, that's a fair point to make, I guess."

"Can you get two little paint can openers?"

"Where they at?"

Evan pointed behind me. "Walk that way, turn right at the end of the aisle, and then they should be somewhere around there."

I sighed. "Fine." I turned on my bare heels and walked off to find the paint can opener. I followed his direction, and sure enough, I found the paint can openers. I grabbed one, because that boy is dumb as hell if he thinks I'm gonna help him open any paint cans. I walked back over to Evan and dropped the paint can opener beside the bundle of paint cans.

"Why didn't you get two?" he asked, looking over to me.

I shrugged. "I'm lazy. I don't wanna open all these paint cans."

"Spencer," Evan groaned, picking up the opener.

"You made fun of my lack of a tan."

"I merely suggested that you might need a tan. It was a light-hearted comment on the beauty of your paleness."

I shook my head. "Sorry, too distraught to open paint cans."

"I hate you so much," he mumbled as he sat down next to the heap of paint cans.

I sat down across from him, "I know you do."

"Shh," he said, cracking open the lid of the first paint can. "I'm working."

"Slowly."

"That's 'cause you don't wanna help," he snapped back.

I shrugged. "You should learn to be nicer to gingers. We're rare and we should be treasured. We might go extinct someday."

"Humanity will forever miss your curly hair, bright eyes, and paleness, you beautiful freckled angels," Evan said as he cracked the second paint can open.

I grabbed the first can and peeled the lid off the rest of the way, carefully avoiding any spillage of paint. "The floor is cold on my bum."

"No shit."

"I shoulda had sweatpants," I whined. "My bum and legs are cold. Why are tiles so cold? Why do tiles hate humans?"

Evan shrugged. "Why do humans hate tiles?"

I shrugged. "Why do human tiles hate?"

"Stop," he said, sliding me the two paint cans. "Open these."

"Only if you hurry your ass up and get the rest of those cans opened," I ordered him, taking the first of the two paint cans he slid to me. I ripped the lid off and then did the same to the next. "You have a good eye for colours."

"Because blue, red, and yellow are such great colours?"

I nodded.

And then we really went to work on getting all these paint cans open. Should have gotten two massive paint cans instead of a dozen small ones. We got it down to having 13 open cans and we only had a few left and then I noticed Evan grabbing for a can of black paint.

"No black paint."

"Why?" he asked, letting go of the black can of paint.

I stared at Evan for a few seconds, just so he knew how dumb he was. "Black paint will be the hardest to get off. Speaking of, how are we even gonna get the paint off?"

"I dunno," Evan said, shrugging. "We'll think of something."

"Open the last red," I said, motioning to the last can of paint that wasn't black paint. I took advantage of him being distracted and I dunked my hand into a can of green paint and splattered him with it.

"Spencer!" he shouted. I had clearly taken him by surprise.

I smirked at him. "Yes?"

"What the hell was that for?" he asked.

"Paint fight, dummy," I told him, standing up and grabbing a paintbrush from the wall of brushes behind me. "*En garde.*"

Evan stood up and grabbed a full can of paint from the floor.

"Evan, don't do it," I said, backing away from him while grabbing my own bucket of paint from the floor.

"Don't do what, Spencer?" His eyes shined with a shimmer of evil intention. I knew what was coming.

I closed my eyes and jumped to the side as a huge wave of yellow paint came splashing towards me. I felt it splash all over my right side and right leg. I wasted no time in tossing a splash of red paint back at him. It got all over his arm and shoulder.

"You asked for it now," Evan said, grabbing a nearby brush.

We dunked our brushes at the same time and we then had ourselves a rousing a swordfight with them. He got me good a few times, streaking red paint over the yellow paint, and I got him pretty good with some yellow paint to cover the red.

By the time we were done throwing paint at each other, we were completely covered, nearly. Our faces were speckled with paint, not entirely covered though. It was down to the last little bit of paint. His red brush versus my freshly green brush.

We ran towards each other and did that thing where we both hold each other's brushes back, kinda like how they do with knives in movies and stuff.

"You can kill me, but you can never kill my spirit," I growled.

"You killed my father! And I vow that I will have my revenge!"

"I had sex with your brother!"

"Jokes on you, I had sex with yours."

"What?" I asked.

He shrugged. "I was getting sick of being so serious."

"Just let me get another swipe at you and we can call it quits," I said, still trying to catch my breath from all the running around.

Evan shook his head. "Never," he muttered, equally out of breath.

And then, we started ferociously pushing each other's brush hands back, and then we remembered how much wet paint was on the floor. Of course, we only remembered that because we slipped and toppled over with him landing on me and me landing back-first on the floor.

He groaned and looked up to my face. "Hmm, you have nice eyes. You know that?"

"Yeah? Do I?"

"Yeah," he said.

"You're kinda crushing me," I grumbled.

He shifted his weight so it was mostly lifted from me. "Sorry."

"It's okay," I said with a soft laugh. "You're warming me up."

"Is that the Spencer way of telling me to get up?"

I shook my head. "Nah."

Evan pushed some hair out of my face and then I realized that this was the closest the two of us had ever gotten, physically speaking. I watched as his pale blue eyes scanned over my face.

"You're staring," I noted.

"Sorry."

I blushed a little from that. Not entirely sure why. "It's okay," I whispered back.

"We should, um…"

"Get up?"

He nodded. "Yeah, that's what I meant to say."

I smirked at him. "Did I just leave you speechless?"

He smiled softly back at me as he pushed himself off of me. "In your dreams."

{Chapter: **Eighteen**}

I watched as Evan walked away from me, past the counter, and into the staff room in the back of the hardware store. I had made him go find me some water. The paint fight made me hella thirsty.

He walked back out a few moments later, holding two water bottles in his hands. "Boom," he said, raising them up in the air.

"I need," I said, sounding remarkably froglike from the thirst.

Evan handed me a bottle. "You can use it to wash off with too."

I shook my head as I cracked it open. "I'll bathe in the hot tub."

Evan shook his head and sighed as I drank from my water.

"What?" I asked.

"You're not washing paint off in a hot tub."

"Evan."

He raised a finger at me to shush me. "We can use the fountain. It'll probably be just as refreshing as a pool on a summer's day."

"You want us to bathe…"

He nodded. "That is correct."

"In a fountain?"

He nodded again. "Yes, ma'am."

"Why?"

"Seems like a good idea," he said, shrugging as he started to walk on by me. "Well, are you gonna come with?"

I turned and started walking with him. "You know, there's paint all up in my hair right now."

"Oh, I know," he said with a smirk tugging at his lips.

"Go get some good-ass shampoo for us."

"I will," he said. "You're dripping with paint still." He pointed to my leg.

There was still quite a lot of paint running and dripping down my back, butt, and legs. I shrugged. "Whatever"

"You're gonna have to clean up all this paint you're tracking through the mall," Evan said, shaking his head at me.

"No, I won't. They have janitors for a reason," I told him. "Now get gone. Make sure you get soap for us too."

Evan nodded and walked a different route than me. I just kept walking along towards the fountain. I walked over and sat on the ledge, waiting for Evan to find his way back over to me.

It must have been a good half an hour before he came back. Any wet paint that was left on me was long dried when I saw him walking over from down the mall.

He kicked a bar of soap towards me. "Get clean."

I picked up the soap after it hit the side of the fountain. "It smells weird," I said, opening the box and pulling the soap out.

"Well, yeah." He sat down next to me and put down a shampoo bottle in between us.

I picked it up and opened it up. "Smells kinda nice, I guess."

"It's a little girly for my liking, but I can deal with it."

"You only got the one?" I asked.

He nodded. "I got this one for you, isn't that enough?"

"You're sassy today," I said. "I like it."

Evan shrugged. "Gotta try to keep my sass levels up to par with yours, y'know?"

"So, how is this going down?" I asked, turning to stare at the water in the fountain. "Do we just hop in and roll around?"

"If you want to."

"Will you wash my back?"

He shook his head. "I'd rather watch you suffer with trying to get that one spot that you can't fully reach."

"You're a goddamn jerk."

Evan smiled. "Yeah. Probably."

I swung around my legs around and dipped my feet in the water. "Okay, well, at least this water is kinda warm."

"Yeah?" he asked, leaning over and putting his hand in. "Hmm. I thought it was gonna be a lot colder than this."

"Are you complaining?" I asked, standing up in the water. I started walking around a little to get used to the water. The water was just under my knees at the edge, but it got deeper the closer I walked inward.

"No," Evan said, swinging his legs over and following me into the fountain. "Where exactly are you walking to?"

"The fountain part," I said, pointing to the water falling from the higher part of the fountain. "It's like a shower. You feel?"

"Ah. You little smartass."

"I try."

Evan walked over and dunked his head under the little waterfall. "This *is* kinda nice though."

I walked over and dunked my head underneath the water, letting it wash through my hair. I ran my hands through my hair and forced some of the dried paint out, with a wince of slight pain of course.

"Hey," Evan said.

I took a step back and swept my all my wet hair to the side. "Yo?"

Evan was looking down at my side. "What's that from?" he asked, pointing to my side now.

I looked down to what he was pointing at, I mean, I knew what he was pointing at. "Oh, that." I said, making sure he was pointing at my scar. "Well, that's from a shark."

"I call bullshit," he said flatly. "What's it really from?"

"Appendectomy."

"Ooh, local anaesthesia?"

I winked. "You better believe it."

"You're such a badass."

"Well, I think I was a badass for not crying my ass off in the emergency room."

Evan nodded. "Yeah. I guess not crying would make you slightly more badass."

"You got any scars?" I asked, looking him over.

He shook his head. "Not any really visible ones. Also, you can stop looking for them now."

"Nah, I just needed an excuse to check out that ass."

Evan shook his head again, but it was more pitiful this time. "Why do you have this allure to you that makes me want to stay friends with you?"

"My freckles."

"You have one freckle for every soul you've stolen, huh?" he asked, winking.

I leaned down and splashed water at him. "Better watch it or your soul will be my next meal."

"I don't think I've ever seen a ginger with wet hair until now."

"I don't think I've ever seen a shirtless boy with a wet happy trail until right now."

He sighed. "You can't just do that."

"Do what?"

"You can't just say what I said but replace it with your own observation based on what I'm doing or wearing… or not wearing."

"Why can't I?"

"Just shush," Evan said, sighing lightly. "So, how old were you when you had to get your appendix ripped out?"

"It was two years ago," I replied.

"So you were sixteen. You couldn't just say you were sixteen?" Evan asked.

I shook my head.

He sighed as he looked down. "My nipples are perky."

I saw him crack a smile at himself. He's such a dork.

I walked over to the ledge and grabbed the bottle of shampoo. "I need to get this paint out of my hair now."

He ruffled his hand through his hair, sending little dried chips of paint flying out around him like a colourful dandruff shower. "I feel you on that one."

I started wading my way back over to him. "This is the longest I've seen you without your beanie on."

He shrugged. "Yeah. Don't get used to it."

"Paint pulled out some of your hair," I said, noticing some pieces of hair in the paint chips.

147

"Yeah. I just have really weak hair," he said, shrugging. "Genetics, ya know? What can ya do?"

"Mm, fair enough," I said, squirting out some shampoo on my hand. I tossed the bottle to him and started to lather up my hair in fruity shampoo. I kept it quick. I rinsed and repeated though.

"At least my hair smells like summer fruits now," Evan said, tossing the shampoo bottle far out of the fountain.

"You suck at throwing."

"Shut up. The intoxicating aroma of fruit has taken me prisoner and rendered all my muscle movements completely useless."

I shook my head. "Nah, you just throw like a little girl."

"Fight me IRL, nerd," Evan snapped, turning to me.

I pushed Evan for the billionth time. "Let's go."

He pushed me back. "Swing first."

I shoved him back as hard as I could, which meant that he went stumbling backwards and onto his ass in the water. I laughed at him as he struggled to get himself back to his feet.

"You're such an ass," he grumbled.

"Hey, look up," I said, looking up at the overhead skylight.

Evan peered up too. "Damn, looks like a fair bit of snow has piled up on top of us, huh?"

"Yep."

"We should probably go shovel that or something," he suggested.

I walked underneath the waterfall and sat down. "Maybe later."

Evan followed and sat next to me. "This is kind of nice."

"What is?" I asked, turning to him.

"This," he said, opening his arms and motioning to the water falling all around and in front of us. "We're sitting in the water and enjoying a fountain falling around us. It's nice. It's kind of calming too. This is a once-in-a-lifetime experience right here."

"I guess you do have a point there."

"Don't I always have a point?"

"No."

He raised a finger to my lips. "Shh."

I smacked his hand away. "You're a dork."

"I am not."

"Are too."

"Do you want me to make you food later? 'Cause if so, you better stop calling me names," Evan said.

"Okay. You say that, but I have this thing called *cute girl* syndrome, and it makes you do whatever I say."

"No."

I scoffed. "You know you like my freckles. You said so yourself."

"Well, freckles are what makes you so cute."

I smirked. "So make me food later, you dork."

"Stop calling me a dork."

"Why should I?"

Evan turned to me and sighed. "Bish, do you want me to give you a matching scar on your other side?"

I shook my head.

"Then stop calling me a dork," he commanded.

"Whatever you say… nerd."

He sighed. "Okay. What do you want for food?"

"Well, can you work some magic and get the deep fryers working?" I asked. "You know, the gas-powered fryers."

"Oh." His eyes widened and he realized how dumb he was earlier. "Wow, okay, I'm dumb. We could have had fries this whole time too. Wow. Whatever. What do you want right now?"

"I want chicken."

Evan nodded. "I can do that. Like, a chicken burger or just a 20-piece bucket of chicken?"

"The second one," I replied. "The 20 pieces of chicken."

Evan grabbed a handful of my hair and swept it across my face so it covered my eyes.

I smacked his hand away. "What the hell are you doing?"

"I don't know. I was bored."

I pushed the hair out of my face and scowled at him slightly. "We should go dry off. I'm starting to get old people hands again."

Evan stood up and walked out from under the fountain. I watched his blurred silhouette walk away to the edge of the fountain.

I sighed. I knew I had to get up now too, but I was just so comfortable sitting here against the inner part of the fountain. I really didn't wanna move.

"You coming?" he called back to me.

I stood up with a slight groaning noise. "Yeah, yeah." I walked out from under the fountain, savouring the last little splash of overhead water.

"Oh, God. The paleness," Evan joked, shielding his eyes.

"Oh, piss off."

He smirked. "Go get dried off and into some dry clothes."

"I call dibs on changing in the game store." I stepped out of the fountain and onto the mall floor, dripping water all over place.

"Fine by me," he said as we started back towards the game store.

"It's nice to have cleaned up."

"Yeah. I smell nice again," Evan said, smiling softly.

I laughed a little. "Again? You would have had to smell nice to begin with."

"Shut up."

I pushed Evan again and walked into the store. I grabbed my bag of clothes and a towel and walked toward the back room.

"Where are you going?" Evan asked.

I turned around and pointed my thumb over my shoulder at the back room. "Gonna go change back there. Unless you got a problem with that?"

"Okay, well, don't get murdered."

I turned back around and continued walking to the back room. "I'll do my best to avoid that."

Evan grabbed his stuff and walked out of the game store. I pushed open the door and clicked the light on. Thank God that backup power is a thing that happened. It was dim, but I could still see well enough.

I stripped out of my swimsuit, and I do mean stripped. I can't be the only one who sometimes does erotic dances while getting out of clothes. Maybe I am... I guess I'm just weird then. *Whatever.* Don't patronize me. Don't judge me.

I dried off and then I slipped into my dry clothes. It felt so nice to be not wet or covered in paint. My jeans felt nice and warm. I walked back out and grabbed a Minecraft Creeper sweater. It was designed in the pattern of a Creeper. It was kinda nice. I was just cold and needed something to keep me nice and cozy and this was the first big comfy sweater I saw.

I hung my wet swimsuit up on a rack and walked out of the store. I figured Evan would be in the food court, so I walked over and saw him over at the chicken place, all the way on the other side of the food court from where I was. Sigh.

I walked over and watched him mess around with the deep fryer for a good 30 seconds or so. "Having fun?" I finally piped up.

"Loads," he said, quickly glancing to see me. "Nice sweater."

I looked down and smiled softly. "Thanks. I think it's very comfy."

"It shows off your figure in a very, um, soft and vivacious way."

"Thanks?"

"Anytime," Evan said, winking at me. "So how much chicken am I cooking? Also… are we wanting fries with it?"

"Who the hell wouldn't want fries with their fried chicken?"

"Fair point," Evan said. "I just wanted to be sure."

"I'm bored. What can I go do while you cook? Hmm."

Evan sighed. "Just go play Go Fish by yourself."

I shook my head. "That's dumb. I'm gonna go back to the store and get my phone."

"Are you gonna charge it and get us out of here?"

I shook my head. "Like we said before, we won't get another chance to enjoy an entire mall to ourselves. We may as well just enjoy it until someone comes to rescue us."

"Agreed," Evan said, smiling slightly.

"I'm gonna still go get my phone. I don't really wanna leave it behind anywhere and risk losing it."

"Hurry back," Evan said as I turned and started walking away.

I walked off to the store I had fallen asleep in and grabbed my phone. I had left it there with my other stuff for easy remembering. I slipped my phone into my pocket and grabbed the rest of my stuff. I walked back to the game store and put everything in the plastic bag I had kept my other clothes in.

I guess it's time to go back to Evan and get some food.

{Chapter: **Nineteen**}

I walked my way back over to the food court, still wearing my cozy sweater. I don't think I ever wanna take this thing off. It's so soft and comfy and warm and I now love it to death and back.

"There she is," Evan said as he saw me walking over.

"Here I am!" I shouted, sitting at a table close by.

Evan walked over to me with two buckets. "I made food."

"I can see that." I took a deep sniff of the intoxicating chicken smells emanating from the buckets. "And I can smell that."

He placed a bucket down in front of me. "Chicken and fries."

I looked and saw that he used one of those three-section buckets. In one section, he had filled it with fries. Another section was filled with drumsticks. The last section was filled with popcorn chicken.

I smiled widely at the food in front of us. "Bruh. I can already feel my arteries clenching. I love it."

"Eat up," Evan said, sitting down across from me at the table. "We gotta get our energy levels up before we go shovel the roof."

"Why do we even need to though?"

"So we can still hang out up there," he replied, popping a piece of popcorn chicken into his mouth. "Mm, hold up. I'm gonna grab us some dipping sauces."

"Smart idea," I said as he got up and walked back to the kitchen.

He walked to the chicken place and then back over to me with a small bag in his hand. "I got some macaroni salad too. It was still pretty cold, so I figured we may as well feast." He sat back down across from me.

"I love the macaroni *salad*."

"Why did you emphasize salad so much?"

I shrugged. "It's not really a salad."

"Sure it is. It's got vegetables... I think."

"Whatever," I said.

Evan stuck his tongue out at me so I smacked him. "Ouch," he yelped. "You're a jerk."

I nodded. "I knew that already, but uh, thanks for reaffirming it for me."

"Pfft." He dipped a piece of popcorn chicken in some plum sauce. "You're a real dork." He popped the chicken in his mouth as I kicked him from under the table. His hand shot up and he flipped me off. *Ooh, I'm so scared.*

"Let's hurry up and eat," I said, ripping open a couple sauces.

And then we did just that. We ate most of the bucket of food. Well, I mean, I did. I was starved. I'm always starved. I should probably go to a doctor about that. Maybe get on a healthier diet. Maybe I should exercise. Nah. You know what, if it ain't broke, don't fix it.

We finished our meal and I watched as Evan cleaned up for us. I think I'll really like having him as a friend. He takes care of me so well. I don't even have to lift a finger around him. All I have to do is be my regular self and he seems to be more than content with it.

"Better go get your coat," Evan said as he came back over to the table after throwing away our garbage. "We got a rooftop hangout to clear off."

I let out a loud groan, one very similar to a dying horse. "I don't want to. That sounds like a lot of work."

"It probably will be. You get our coats from the superstore, and I'll go grab some shovels from the hardware store," Evan stated. "Also... gloves. Gloves would help us a lot with shovelling. I don't really want to get frostbite."

"Gloves would for sure be good," I said, standing up from the table. "I guess we better go get 'er done."

Evan nodded. "Just meet me at the stairs and we'll get going." He walked off and I followed behind him.

I watched him walk away as I went into the game store. I put my shoes back on and then walked out. I headed back to the superstore and got our coats and two pairs of gloves for the two of us. I walked back out and made my way to the third floor. And then I waited.

I waited for a few minutes until I saw Evan walk around the far corner and start walking over to me. "'Bout time!" I shouted to him.

He flipped me off again while sneering at me. "I had to find the good shovels and not those plastic shitty ones that'll break after two minutes."

"Okay, well, not gonna diss that logic." I followed his lead up to the small stairway that leads to the roof.

"Ladies first," Evan said, pushing the door open.

"It's so cold," I said, stepping into the stairwell.

"No shit," Evan said. "The heat's not gonna stay in a concrete staircase like this."

I started up the stairs. Thank God for coats. "At least the cold is *kinda* refreshing."

"Is that what you take away from this?"

"Yeah. Gotta look on the bright side."

"Go outside. I need to prop the door," Evan grumbled as we reached the top of the stairs.

I pushed the door open. "You jerk." I walked out on the roof and under the sky. All the sky was bright and greyish white. It wasn't too windy and there was a soft snowfall calmly fluttering all around us.

"Damn. What a view," Evan said, walking out behind me.

I held my hand out as some snow fell onto it. "Yeah. It's really pretty." I turned to him to grab the shovel.

He passed me the shovel and caught eyes with me. "I meant you," he said, smirking at me.

"Simmer down," I said, cocking an eyebrow at him.

He put his finger up to his lips. "Shh. I'll do what I want."

I narrowed my gaze at him. "I *will* push you off this roof," I threatened threateningly.

Evan scoffed. "I'll be surprised if you'll even push any snow off the roof. You're lazy as hell."

"Am not," I argued.

He rolled his eyes slightly. "Right. Okay. You can't even make your own food. I've been doing *all* the cooking."

"You're a good cook. We've been through this."

"Well, I had to revisit it just to prove that you're lazy as hell. Okay?"

"Fair point," I said. "I just dislike doing things. I like being lazy. It's comfy and warm to stay inside all day."

"Read a lot?"

I nodded. "It's always nice to have books handy for when there's power outages or when I just get sick of watching my favourites shows over and over again on Netflix."

"If the power goes out, how you gonna read? You need light to read."

I sighed. "I guess candles and flashlights don't exist then."

"Oh," he said, pausing a moment. "You got me there."

"I know I did," I said, pushing some snow away from me.

There was so much snow up here. I didn't wanna shovel this. I mean, there was a little area without too much snow. We could just hang out right there and not have to shovel any of this shit. But there was no way Evan would let that happen.

Evan started pushing snow towards where I pushed my snow. "This will be the first pile."

"How many piles are we gonna make?"

"Probably just this one. I just wanna clear off the area by the door and stuff." Evan started pushing some more snow with the shovel.

I watched as he shovelled little by little. All his little puffs of breath poofing out around him as he bent over and pushed the snow along.

He turned to me after a minute or so and just gazed at me. "Are you gonna help, or…?"

"I like watching you," I replied, plopping my shovel down onto the roof and pushing some snow at his feet.

"You're creepy," he said, shaking his head. "Well, look, if you're not gonna shovel, at least get out of the way."

"Works for me," I said, walking over to the small concrete barrier wall. I brushed the snow off of the wall and hopped up. I set the shovel down beside me and watched Evan as he started shovelling again. I watched his little puffs of breath vapour floating around his face. They were getting a little bigger as he kept going.

He turned to me and shook his head. "Am I amusing to watch or something?"

"Just watching your breaths, to be honest."

"That's... kinda weird."

"No. It's kinda calming."

He gave me a weird look. "Like... how though?"

"I don't know," I barked. "It's just relaxing to watch them puff out and then, *poof*, they're gone."

"Mm, okay, then."

I smiled softly. "Yeah. I know. I'm weird as hell. I get it. But it's just part of my charm."

"Gonna need a massage later," Evan groaned, getting back to the shovelling job that I had shovelled onto him. Get it? 'Cause he's shovelling and I let him do it all because I'm lazy?

"Um. Okay, let's make a deal," I said. "If you do a good job shovelling and also if you're nice to me, I'll give you a *transcendent* back massage."

"Ever since I met you, I've always been nice to you," Evan stated. "And I'm the only one shovelling, so you already owe me a massage by that logic." He paused for a second. "I mean, like, if you're okay with doing that."

"Can we use lotion that smells like cucumbers or something?"

Evan let out a groan. "Yeah."

"You're the best."

He used his shovel to toss a small amount of snow at me. "*You're* the best."

I let the plume of snow he tossed at me float down around me. I love powdery snow for this reason. It doesn't clump together like half-melted snow. It just explodes in a glittery mist. It's pretty calming when it's not blowing in your face in high winds.

"My feet are a little cold," Evan groaned

"You shoulda got boots."

"Go get me some?" he asked.

"Are you serious?"

He nodded. "There's a lot of snow. It's cold. I'm not gonna finish for a while. I need something warmer than tattered skate shoes."

"Fine," I said, hopping down from the wall. I walked over to the door and then turned back to Evan. "What size boot are you?"

"Ten or eleven," he said with a shrug. "Just bring back two pairs and whatever one fits me, fits me."

"Okay."

And with that I walked back into the mall. I made my way as slowly but quickly as I could to the superstore. Basically, I just walked at a normal pace. I wasn't really in a rush to get back into the cold, but then at the same time, Evan could really use some warm boots since he's so determined to shovel.

I grabbed two pairs of boots. They were the exact same boots, but one was a bigger size, just like he specified.

I carried both of the boxes back up to the roof and tossed them at Evan. "There you go, bud."

"Oh, frick, thank you." He dropped the shovel and walked over to me. He took one of the boxes from me and took the boots out. "Size eleven better fit," he grumbled, pulling his shoe off and slipping the boot on.

"So?" I asked.

He looked up and nodded. "She fits," he said. He swapped feet and pulled the other shoe off.

I tossed the other pair of boots off to the side and took his shoes from the ground. I laid them just inside the door. "Now you can do all the shovelling again. Woo!"

"Yeah." He laughed a little as he went back to his shovelling. "Woo."

"I hear the sarcasm in your voice," I said, starting to ball up a little bit of snow.

He looked up at me. "You better not be planning on throwing that at me."

"Why not?"

"I'll push you off the roof."

I pouted at him. "But, Evan." I tried my best to sound as upset about it as I could. I mean, like, I can't be too mean to Evan. He is the one shovelling for us.

"We can have a snowball fight some other time."

"Tonight?" I asked.

Evan sighed. "Maybe. Okay? Just let me get finished with this shovelling first or we won't have room for the snowball fight."

"Okay, Mr. Sassy."

"I'm not sassy. I just wanna get this done."

I sighed. "Whatever."

He glared at me. "I mean, hey, if you would rather come and do this while I sit up there and judge you, be my guest."

"You know what, I'm good here."

"That's what I thought," he said, winking a little at me.

I turned and looked out over at the town. It was completely dead. There was zero movement. No cars or people. Usually, the mall and area around here would be crowded around this time of year. There would be a full parking lot and cars driving all over and people walking everywhere. They'd all have coffees or hot cocoas in their hands and be talking and laughing, but not today.

Today, the city was empty. The city was sleeping under a thick blanket. It was all so weird to see a city so quiet and dead. It was like *Silent Hill* out here. It was that eerie and quiet. The only sounds I could hear were the sounds of Evan's footsteps and his shovel scraping on the roof as he cleared away the snow.

"Quiet today, huh?" Evan said, as if he were reading my mind or something.

"Yeah," I said, turning back to him. "Absurdly quiet."

"Weird. I'm not used to it. Start doing noise things."

I shot him a weird look. "Noise things?"

"Yeah, y'know, like, make noises and stuff."

"No."

Evan looked up at me and pouted. "But, Spencer. Baby. Why?"

"I'm going inside," I said, hopping down from the half wall.

"Don't leave me."

"You're falling in love with me. I can't have that."

Evan laughed. "Because I called you baby?"

I shrugged. "I just needed an excuse to go inside."

"Oh." He nodded and winked. "Got ya. But… uh, please stay outside with me."

"Will you massage *my* back?" I asked.

"I will consider it after you massage mine later."

"Fine, fine." I walked back over to the barrier wall and hopped back up to my spot. It was still kinda warm from my butt, so that was kind of a good thing.

Evan grumbled something and then said, "I'm really gonna need a back massage right away. I'm sore as heck. Shovelling is not good for the back of a dying kid."

"You're dying?" I asked, snapping my focus over to him.

Evan looked over and stood straight up. "Well, sure. I mean, aren't we all just dying at different speeds? Isn't that what being alive is all about?"

I couldn't tell, but it felt like something wasn't right with how he phrases that thought. "Right, I mean, yeah. I get it."

"In some grand poetic way, we're all terminal and dying. We just die at different speeds."

And with that, he returned to shovelling. And I returned to watching him shovel, watching each puff of breath as it appeared and vanished.

{Chapter: **Twenty**}

I watched as Evan cleared the last little bit of snow from the area he was concerned about. He came over and grabbed my shovel from beside me on the barrier wall where I had left it. I probably shoulda helped him shovel, but nah. I like being lazy. Don't judge me. You're probably lazier.

"I'm just gonna leave these out here so we can use them again if we need to. Good idea or no?" Evan asked.

I shrugged. "It's up to you dude. I don't really care either way."

"I'll just leave them up here in case we need them later or something then. Thanks for your input."

I followed him over to the door. "Yeah. Sounds like a good idea. I probably won't help you shovel later though."

"There'll only be a little bit of snow later, so it won't be so bad."

"Will you teach me how to shovel?"

He scoffed and shook his head at me. "Yeah, sure thing," he said, opening the door for me. "Just get inside, would you?"

"Fine," I muttered, stepping past him and into the stairwell. It was a lot warmer in here than outside, so I guess I shouldn't really complain.

Evan shut the door behind us and took his boots off. "Finally get to get out of these damn boots."

"I thought they were warm?"

He nodded. "They were. They're also uncomfortable. They're not broken in or anything. They're all stiff and shit."

"You're stiff and shit."

"What?" he asked, cracking a smile and laughing slightly.

I shrugged. "I don't know."

"You're the strangest person I've ever met," Evan stated. "And I've met some pretty crazy weirdos."

"Yeah, okay, that's old news. So, about that dying thing you said earlier."

"Is it really bothering you?" he asked. "Sorry for getting so morbid. Just forget I even said anything."

"It's just that… Never mind. Forget that *I* said anything," I said.

He glared at me a little. "You sure?"

"Yeah," I said, nodding softly. "Let's just go. I owe you a back massage now."

"Oh, yeah. You do, don't you?" he said as we started off down the stairs.

I sighed. "That's what I literally just said to you. You need to grow a pair of ears, you deaf walrus."

Evan led the way back to our beds. Of course, I made him go off to make us fresh coffee first. I was cold and still a little sleepy, so I needed some coffee. Can't rub a back well if I don't have caffeine in my veins. I waited on his bed for him to come back with our two coffees.

He walked over and held the cup out to me.

I took a sip of the coffee after taking it from Evan. "It's good."

"No shit. I made it," he said, smirking slightly.

I scoffed. "You're getting too cocky for my liking."

"I'm not here for you to like me though."

"Touché."

He winked and sat down next to me on his bed. "You wanna get the cucumber-smelling lotion?" he asked, nodding towards my bed.

I looked over and noticed that I had left the lotion on my bed when I moved to sit on his bed. Oops. "Yeah." I groaned as I got up. I swear that teenagers shouldn't feel this achy and tired from getting off a mattress.

"Don't break a hip."

I flipped him off. "Shut up." I grabbed the bottle of lotion. The smell of cucumber was stronger than I expected, but I don't mean that in a bad way. Also, I don't think you ever really notice the smell of a cucumber until you notice it.

"Do I have to take my shirt off?" Evan asked as I sat back down next to him.

I nodded. "How else am I gonna get all up in your back? And do you really want this lotion all in your shirt? Well, I guess you could just change shirts, but still."

"Yeah, yeah," he mumbled, lifting his shirt up and pulling it over the top of his head.

"Not like you weren't shirtless with me just a little while ago."

"Yeah, but that was different."

"It wasn't. I was rubbing paint on you then."

Evan sighed. "Yeah. And now you're rubbing lotion on me, and that makes it much more sensual."

"Sexual?"

He chuckled softly as he laid himself down. "I said sensual, dumbass."

"Stop being mean to me," I whined, climbing onto his back.

"Why are you sitting on me?"

"So I can massage your back properly. Stop whining."

Evan scoffed, turning his head to the side to get comfy. "You know you only weigh, like, three pounds, right?"

"I'm well aware. It's most likely due to the fact that I'm short as shit. I don't know, man. Biology does weird things."

Evan chuckled a little, which caused his body to shake a little under me.

"No laughing," I barked. "Your whole body shakes."

"Sorry," Evan said. "I'll just stay quiet."

I shook my head. "Okay, *dumbass*, I said you couldn't laugh. I still wanna talk to you."

"That's so sweet of you."

"I try," I said, opening the bottle of lotion. "This is probably going to be a little bit cold at first. Just remember that you just got your fair warning."

"Oh, yay," Evan said flatly, amusing the idea of having something cold poured onto his back.

I squirted… ;) … some lotion onto his back. He shuddered from the sudden cold fingers of Satan tickling his skin. Yes, that's the metaphor I'm going with.

"Hurry and rub it in already," Evan whined. "It's cold."

I sighed. "I gave you a fair warning that it was gonna be cold. You should have braced yourself for this."

"But, oh, my God, it's *so* cold."

I rolled up the sleeves of my sweater and then I started rubbing the lotion across his back. "Is it getting any better now?"

"Yeah," he replied, suddenly sounding much more calm. "Your hands are really small and also really warm. They're like little fairy hands or something."

"Do me a favour and don't say I have fairy hands," I said, starting to put more pressure into the rubbing motions.

Evan yawned. "This is actually so nice. I haven't had a massage in ages and you're doing a really good job."

"Just don't fall asleep on me, okay?"

"Well, I'm technically under you, but okay."

I smacked the back of his head softly. "Don't be a smartass."

"You are still so goddamn mean even when you're being nice. You're giving my heart the most awkward half chub right now."

"The hell?"

He shrugged. "I don't know. You just confuse me with your passive-aggressive kindness."

"It's part of my charm."

"Charm. Is that what we're calling it now?"

I laughed a little, leaning in and rubbing Evan's shoulders more. "Yeah. I'm saying my passive-aggressive kindness is my charm."

"You make no sense sometimes."

"I think you mean that I make no sense most of the time, to be honest. Or really ever."

Evan nodded. "Yeah, that's for sure what I meant."

"Your back is so soft now. You're welcome for that."

He nodded again. "It was soft before too. I take care of my shit."

"No, you don't. Your skin was all dry and shit."

"It was not," he argued.

I sighed a little. "Okay then. How hot do you take your showers?"

"Pretty much comparable to the surface of the sun."

"Okay, well, hot water dries your skin out."

"It does?"

I nodded. "It does."

"Shit. I should probably tone down the temperature of my showers then, huh?"

I shrugged. "I mean, it's probably a smart idea, y'know, if you care about having nice skin."

He shrugged slightly. "Or I could just get you to do this every three days or something. I think I like my idea better."

"There's no way I'm doing this every three days," I told him. "Unlike your lame ass, I have a life and better things to do."

"Why not?" he asked. "I'll pay you."

"How will you pay me?" I asked as I started doing that twisty fist thing along his back.

He paused for a moment. "Um. Hmm."

"Can't think of anything?" I teased.

"I'll pay you with gum. I got some good flavours."

I couldn't help but laugh a little at that. "You're such an idiot. I don't really chew gum that often, so I don't know if that's really beneficial on my part. Is there anything else you can offer that will *sweeten* the deal for me?"

"I can also offer you one big jawbreaker each week?"

I raised a hand and stroked my nonexistent beard. "Hmm, yes, this intrigues me. Tell me, Evan, how big are these jawbreakers?"

"Big," he replied.

I lowered my hand and continued his back massage. "I'll think about it. I'ma need some serious payment if you expect me to put up with you *and* give you a massage every three days."

"I will give you head."

"And I will pass on that."

Evan chuckled softly. "Oh, Spencer, you're funny. Head are these candies that come in different head shaped containers. They're based on the favourite flavours of whoever's head it's modelled after. I wasn't offering to blow you."

"Oh…"

"You got a dirty little mind."

I sighed. "Yeah. I just haven't heard of that brand of candy before. I'll take your whole stock though."

"Yeah, they're pretty new still, so that's probably why. They're really good though."

"Get me some and we'll work something out."

Evan smiled. "Gotcha."

I kept on massaging, caressing, and fondling his back. Sorry, too much? You get the point. I did it for around an hour, and then my hands go way too tired. Seriously though, kudos to the professional massagers that do this for hours and hours every day.

I rolled off Evan and laid myself down beside him. "I'm done. My hands are too tired to go on."

"It was really relaxing though, he said.

I rolled over to face him. "Thank you. I tried to do my very best for you."

He smiled. "Yeah. I kinda wanna nap right now."

I shook my head. "I refuse to let you. Let's go get you a new shirt to wear."

"I don't wanna move though."

"Too bad, get up," I said, sitting up and then tugging on his arm.

Evan let out a loud groan. "I hate that I like you."

"Yeah, I get that a lot." I grabbed his arm, dragging him off the bed in one fluid motion.

"You're strong for such a small girl."

I shrugged. "Pilates, bitch."

Evan sat up on the floor. "Okay, well, I'm awake now."

I stretched out my arms and nodded. "That was the general idea of dragging you onto the floor. Yes. I am a genius."

"I think you're just an idiot with some dumb ideas that just seem to work in your favour," Evan grumbled as he stood up.

"Okay, well, you're just pissy because I won't let you take a nap."

He nodded. "I was so relaxed. I just wanted to snuggle up with a cute girl and take a nap."

"Well, if you had worded it like that, but also in the form of a question, I might have considered that."

"Well, maybe later then," Evan said, yawning. "Let's go get me a weird shirt or something. Maybe we can get you a weird shirt too."

I looked down at the hoodie I was still wearing. "I don't wanna take this off. It's comfy and it's warm and it smells nice."

"Fine," Evan said, pouting a little. "I'm still getting you a shirt and you better wear at some point.

I nodded. "I will."

"Let's go," Evan said, walking out of the store.

I followed his lead as we walked down a few stores to the first clothing store that didn't have a metal grating closed over it. "This place? Really?"

He shrugged. "Why not?"

"Fair enough." I followed him into the store. "They have boxing gloves here."

"They do," Evan said, walking over to the light switches.

"Oh, God, the light. It hurts my eyes."

Evan turned and gave me a slight scowl. "You're an idiot."

"That has got to be the fortieth time you've told me that."

He shrugged. "I guess it's been true forty times."

"Dumbass."

Evan pushed me lightly as I walked past him. "Stop being so rude to me, you jerk."

"Put on some of these gloves, pretty boy," I snapped, turning around to face him.

He looked over at the rack of boxing gloves. "For real?"

I nodded. "Yeah. Fight me. It's Boxing Day after all."

"I guess it is. All well," he said. "Your funeral." He grabbed some boxing gloves for himself. He then grabbed another pair of gloves and tossed them to me.

I caught them and, man, they were heavier than I thought they'd be. "Take it easy on me though. I'm half your size."

"Now you wanna bring up your size?"

"Yeah. Boxing might hurt. And I don't like being hurt."

Evan let out a slight sigh. "Okay, fine. Let's go."

"Hold on." I set down the gloves on the display next to me. I peeled off my sweater so I was just in my light T-shirt. "I wanted it to feel more authentic," I said, shrugging as I put my boxing gloves on.

"Whatever. You're still going down, loser," Evan taunted.

I raised my hands to the typical boxer position. "You feelin' lucky, punk?"

"Swing first."

"Why?" I asked.

"I feel uncomfortable throwing the first punch."

I shrugged. "No hitting below the belt though, okay?"

"And no titty shots."

"Right," I said.

Evan put his hands up too. "Ding, ding."

"Lamest bell sound ever," I said, throwing a punch towards him.

He swung back and I quickly dodged it. "At least I tried to make a bell sound," he stated.

"Boohoo," I said, throwing a punch toward his face, which he blocked with ease.

He swung a few quick punches at me, one of which landed on my ribs and knocked me back a little.

"Dick," I grumbled, throwing a few punches back at him the minute he pulled his glove back.

I kept throwing a quick flurry of punches, causing Evan to need to step backwards to avoid getting a steady barrage of fists to the face. This means I'm winning, right? I'll be honest. I have zero idea how boxing even works.

"You're pretty quick with your fists," Evan said, blocking a few punches and then tossing one back.

I shrugged as I threw a punch back. "I try my best."

He shook his head as he knocked my hand away. "I doubt that."

"I do!" I barked, getting a cheap shot in on his cheek.

He shot a quick punch back at me. "That last one actually kinda hurt a little."

"Gimme your lunch money, nerd," I said, throwing another quick flurry of punches at him.

Evan lost his balance and started to trip, so what does this idiot do? He grabs my wrist with both of his gloved hands so I would fall over with him.

The two of us collapsed over into a clothing display. The clothes went all over the place as the rack collapsed and fell over. This caused the two of us to quickly glance at each other and then burst out laughing. I took advantage of him being distracted to get one last shot in.

I climbed onto him and sat on his chest. "One. Two. Three. I win."

"We were boxing, not wrestling," he said with a soft chuckle.

"I still win."

He smiled at me and nodded. "I'll give this one to you since you caused me to fall over into the clothing rack."

"Told you I was gonna win," I said, trying to catch my breath, as well as trying to stop smiling from the ridiculousness that had just went down. Get it? Went down? 'Cause we fell over?

"So what now?" Evan asked.

I shrugged. "We could get more food. We could get you that shirt that we came here for."

"I kinda like both of those options."

"I like the idea someone had about getting food."

Evan laughed and shook his head. "For such a small girl, you always wanna eat."

"I'm really efficient at burning energy. Sue me."

"Get off me first," he said, pushing me over.

I stood up and looked at the mess we had made. It was pretty bad. I'm pretty sure clothing racks aren't supposed to metaphorically explode like this one just did. The clothes went all over. Oh, well, I'm not gonna be the one cleaning that shit up.

{23:59}

{Chapter: **Twenty-One**}

Evan struggled to pull himself up from the huge mess of clothes he was lying on. I helped him regain his balance once he was standing up straight. He looked around and seemed a little bewildered by the mess around us.

"I'm not cleaning this up," he said flatly.

I shrugged. "I sort of assumed that neither of us were gonna bother cleaning it up. We're just leaving everything for the janitors and stuff."

"Right. So, how about we go and get some food?" Evan asked, turning to me, straightening out his pants.

I nodded. "But you need a shirt first." I walked over and grabbed my hoodie from the display I had left it on. I swung the sweater around my back and then over my head. "Okay, now for you," I said, looking around the mess of clothes for anything that popped out and caught my eye.

"I don't know. I'm not seeing anything I like here," Evan said, looking at the mess of clothes.

I walked over a picked up a plain black T-shirt. "Here," I said, tossing it to him. "I think that'll do just fine. I'm hungry and I want food. I don't have the time to stick around while you debate shirt options."

"Yeah, you do," he said, tossing the black shirt away.

I sighed. "You suck."

"This was *your* idea, dumbass."

"I always reserve the right to change my ideas once I realize I have more important stuff to do. Or in the rare case it was a stupid idea. Which never happens."

Evan nodded disapprovingly. "Mm-hmm, unless the important stuff to do is dig us out of the mall, I'm not so sure it's any more important that looking for a cool shirt."

"These shirts all suck," I whined.

Evan nodded. "I agree."

"What if we got you a matching hoodie?" I suggested.

He turned and looked me over. "I guess."

"Wow," I said, turning to him. "Could you sound any less enthused by it?"

"I could try."

"Please don't," I said, walking by Evan and out of the store.

Evan followed me out. "What if they don't even have my size?"

"They will," I said as Evan led the way back to the game store.

"Do they have zip-ups?"

"Just pullovers," I told him. "Which is the opposite of you."

"What?"

"'Cause you're a pushover. Get it?"

Evan forced a laugh. "That was terrible."

I walked into the store, ignoring Evan's remark about my pun. My puns were fine. They were firm and round and I do my squats. Get it? Instead of buns I said puns. Like, as in my butt? No? Okay.

"You're not offended, are you?"

I shrugged. "My puns aren't for everyone. I guess they're just meant for the cool kids, which would make you a big ol' lame-o."

"Okay." Evan walked past me. "You're the lame-o here, bub."

I pushed him toward the rack of sweaters. "You."

"Stop pushing me. Uh, my God," he whined.

"Say my puns are funny."

"No."

I pouted at him fiercely. And I'm talking some serious pouting here. "Hate you."

Evan shook his head and smirked. "Whatever. How does this sweater look?" Evan asked, holding up a black sweater to himself.

I looked him over and nodded. "I think it suits you pretty well. The blandness of that sweater really brings out the colour in your, um… freckles?"

"That has to be the most awkward compliment I've ever received in my entire life, but thank you… I think."

I shrugged. "I think your freckles are cute."

"I don't even have that many. I'm not like you, all covered in freckles," Evan said, pulling the hoodie over his head.

"Okay, well, I'm covered in freckles because I'm a ginger. Haven't we gone over this? My freckles are cute."

"I never said they weren't."

I walked over to my bed and jumped on it, plopping down with a soft thud. I rolled over to lie on my stomach, 'cause why not. "I'm so done with you."

"Love you too, buds," Evan said, walking over and sitting next to me on the bed.

"I said I was done with you."

"And I said that I loved you too, buds."

I sighed. "Make me food, please."

"Right, food. We were gonna get food," Evan said, laying himself down onto my back.

"Get off, fatass," I grumbled.

I could feel him shake his head. "Nah, this is comfy."

"Your back is bent over me. There's no way this is comfy."

"But you're thin and small and warm, so it's not actually that un-comfortable on my back. Plus, the mattress sinks in a little."

"Well, I'm small. Get off me."

Evan scoffed. "You used to be cool, man."

"I'm not a body pillow."

Evan cocked his eyebrow. "Aren't you?"

"Okay, well, I'm not a mattress. That's what I meant. Piss off. Let's go get food," I whined, rolling off the other side of the mattress. I plopped, like, 5 inches to the ground and landed with a little thud on the floor. I stood up and yawned. "I guess that's a good enough nap then."

"You can sleep later, Spencer," Evan stated.

"I wanna sleep now," I whined.

Wow, I bet I look and sound like a total baby right now. Maybe I should get a onesie and start crying for my mom, which I admittedly did want to do. I missed being home. It was starting to get annoying that the mall was still forgotten about by society. I've been in here for so long now that I think I might be starting to go mad.

Evan sighed and walked out of the store. He does a lot of sighing at me. I mean, I'm not that bad, am I? Whatever. I followed him out of the store and over to the food court.

"See anything appetizing?" Evan asked.

I shrugged. "I dunno."

"Okay, you want food. Pick something."

"You pick."

"Are we really gonna do this whole first-date thing?"

I looked over to him. "What thing?"

"The thing where you tell me to pick, and then as soon as I do, you turn it down because you aren't in the mood for that?"

I shook my head.

"Tacos?" he asked.

I went to open my mouth and realized that I was about to do that first-date thing and turn down the tacos. Now I was juxtaposed between eating a food I don't want to or being a cliché. Damn, what a predicament I've found myself in.

He turned to me. "It's a no, isn't it?"

I nodded slowly.

He groaned. "I'm gonna go make us some more stir-fry, and you're gonna deal with it."

"Fine. That sounds lovely. Maybe if you had picked that as the first food you wanted to make."

"Maybe if you had just told me you wanted stir-fry," Evan snapped back, walking toward the stir-fry place.

"I don't know. I think I want some fries."

"Later," Evan muttered flatly.

I took a deep breath. "Fine."

Evan walked into the kitchen of the Thai food place and I went and took a seat at one of the tables close to it. I watched as Evan cooked and did kitchen things in the back. And by that, I watched as he tried to figure out what we wanted to eat.

This might sound a bit creepy or whatever, but I really liked watching Evan do these humdrum tasks. It was calming for me, calming to just know he was doing things, and things for me at that. I'm weird, I know. Get off my back, okay?

"Hey," Evan called out from the kitchen, "do you want me to make yours really spicy or just a little bit spicy?"

"Well, how spicy is really spicy?"

He shrugged. "Somewhere between burning your tongue and making your nose bleed."

"Well, I don't want that," I told him. "Just give me some medium spiciness."

"You wanna go run to the superstore place and get us some more Doritos for later?" he asked.

I groaned. "Evan, I *just* sat down."

He gave me the most *I hate you right now* face I've ever seen. "I am cooking food for you. Please go get us snack foods for later."

"Oh, my God, fine." I got up out of the chair, making my displeasure evident from my shuffled steps as I walked off.

"Be happy you get food."

"I'll be happy when I'm dead," I whined back at him. I would have flipped him off, but by this point, I had already passed by the wall that separated the two food things in between us, and he was probably focused on doing kitchen things anyway.

I walked off down the mall. I think this walk would be more enjoyable if I had an MP3 player or something. Oh, well, what can ya do? I took my time walking. I looked at all the stores I was walking past. It was still so creepy being in a mall *almost* alone.

I walked into the store and walked over to the checkouts to grab a few bags. As I grabbed some bags, I noticed that the phone was flipped off the receiver. I walked to the next checkout and it was the same thing. I checked the phones at the customer service desk, same thing with them.

Evan must have tried to use them to call for help. But I'm guessing they don't work. All the phone lines in the area must be down from the storm.

I shrugged it off and walked to the snack foods aisle. I grabbed some bags of Doritos and a bag of ripple cuts with some chip dip. I carried the bags of chips back to the food court.

"Evan," I called out after getting close to the kitchen.

"Yes?" he called back, walking over.

I reached into the bag and pulled out the chip dip. "Put this in the fridge for later. The fridge works now, right?"

"Well, barely, but it's better than nothing." He walked over and took the chip dip from me. "French onion, my fave."

"It better be," I said, laying the bags on the counter. "Also, did you try to use the phones in the store?"

He nodded as he opened the fridge and put the chip dip in it. "I did. I thought we wanted to get out of here, not live here forever."

"Well, did you get a hold of anyone?"

He shook his head. "I did not. The phone lines are all down on account of the raging white hurricane outside."

"Shit."

"But on the plus side, I finished cooking the food."

"That was pretty quick," I stated.

He shrugged. "It's stir-fry and you were gone a bit longer than you probably think you were."

"Whatever. Let's eat," I said.

And then that's what we did. We sat and ate the stir-fry. It was good. Evan's skills as a cook were getting better. Maybe he's trying to be a secret chef or something, and I would be totally okay with that if I can taste test his food. I mean, like, he's a good cook.

After we ate, I helped him clean up. It was the least I could do. He has been doing so much for me lately, and don't take my sarcasm as me taking it for granted. I was extremely grateful and lucky and happy to have been stuck in here with a cute guy that cooks for me and isn't a total douche canoe.

"Spencer," Evan said, snapping his fingers in front of my face.

I looked up at him quickly. "Yeah?"

"Did you want any pie? I don't remember if you said yes or not."

I nodded. "Pie is nice."

He set down a plate in front of me. On the plate, a piece of apple pie gently rested. Just kicking back, ready to be eaten.

I took a bite of the apple pie, and holy shit. "It's still so warm and good. What did you do, grill it?"

Evan shook his head. "I baked it."

"How?"

"How does anyone make a pie?" he asked. "They just do." He took a seat across from me at our little table and he started eating his slice of pie too.

I shrugged it off and kept eating the pie. It was insanely good. I'm starting to think Evan is just bullshitting me on this. There's no way he can be able to cook all these things.

"Hey, Evan."

"Yeah?"

"Where'd you learn to cook?"

He shrugged. "I just cook a lot."

"Yeah, you told me. I just mean where did you learn to cook *this* well?" I asked him.

He smiled shyly and shook his head a little. "It's not that great. You're giving me a lot more credit than I deserve."

"You deserve all the credit."

"I don't," he said, "but thank you."

I smiled softly at him. "Any time." And I meant it.

We sat and ate our pie in a mostly silent fashion. The only sounds were the clicking of plastic forks on glass plates.

I guess this silent dessert means we've transcended the need to talk to each other now. We can just sit in silence with each other and still feel like we're together and having a good time. I guess we both just genuinely enjoy the other's presence.

I can't speak for him though, but personally, I loved his presence. It was calming in the way that the rest of the world sorta just spiralled slightly away from wherever we were when he was close to me or talking to me or looking at me.

Oh, shit. Is this what catching feelings really feels like? Feeling a little dizzy and weak in the knees and feeling a slight tickle in your stomach, like a pang of nervousness when you have nothing to be nervous for? No. Evan's a friend. I can't go catching feelings just because he's nice to me and cooks for me and is just an all-around good dude. *Spencer, don't be dumb.*

"You look like something's bothering you."

"It's nothing," I lied.

He gave me a look, a look like he knew I was lying, to myself and to him. "Okay. Well, I'm here if you wanna open up."

"It's not anything important," I told him, shrugging. "I'm just worried about school stuff."

"It's the holidays, Spencer," Evan stated. "Even honour students need to take a break from everything. Try to let it all go for a while, okay?"

I nodded softly. "Okay."

{Chapter: **Twenty-Two**}

I waited for Evan to come back from the kitchen. He had gone to put the plates in the sink so they could be cleaned at some point. I personally would have just left the plates on the table. I'm also an ass.

"All done," Evan said, walking back over to me.

I smiled a little. "Good. What now?"

"We bang."

"No."

He shrugged slightly. "It was worth a try."

"Right, anyway… let's go find a Bible because your ass very clearly needs Jesus."

"No, you," he grumbled back at me.

I stood up from the table and stretched out a little. "I think I need some air."

"Roof again?" he suggested.

I nodded. "Let's make hot cocoa first though. Can't watch the snow fall without a nice hot cup of cocoa."

"It looks like the skies are clearing up even more though," Evan said, looking over to the skylight.

I looked over and saw the moon poking out from behind some clouds. "Hmm, well, nothing like enjoying a moon-filled sky with a hot cup of cocoa."

"I'll make the cocoa," Evan said. "You go get us our coats."

"Deal." I walked off and left Evan to tend to the hot cocoa. I walked into the game store and grabbed our coats. This is becoming like my personal chore now. I put my coat on and walked back to Evan with his coat in my hand. I tossed it at him; he didn't catch it.

"Spencer."

"Evan."

He sighed, leaning down to pick up his coat. "Thank you for getting my coat."

"Oh, any time," I replied, hopping up on a table to wait for him to finish getting our hot cocoas made.

Evan walked into the kitchen to check the water. "It's almost boiled," he stated.

"Okay, well, can you tell it to hurry up?"

"Yeah, sure thing," he said, turning to the kettle. "Hey, can you hurry up and boil faster, please?"

"Cutie."

"Me?" Evan asked, turning to me.

I nodded. "Yes, you."

"Why?"

"You actually just asked a kettle to boil faster for me."

He shrugged. "I thought it'd be funny, not cute."

"Eh, it was a little bit of both."

He shook his head as the kettle started doing that high-pitched whistle. "It's boiled," he proclaimed, taking it off the stove and pouring the boiling water into two rather large cups.

"Those are big cups."

"Well, do you not want a lot of hot cocoa?"

"No, I do," I said. "Fill 'er up."

He smiled slightly. "That's what I thought."

I sighed. "Okay, let's go."

He walked over to me and handed me the extra-large cup of hot cocoa. I guess I really shouldn't be complaining. An extra-large cup of anything is pretty good. Coffee, tea, hot cocoa, chicken noodle soup.

We walked up the stairs and up to the third floor. We opened the door and walked up to the roof door. Evan pulled it open for me and

I stepped out onto the roof, which looked so much different at night. The skies were no longer grey, but rather, they were sprinkled with stars. The moon shone bright as the centrepiece to the tapestry of the star-studded skies around it.

"Beautiful," I said, looking up.

"Yes, you are," he said.

I turned back to see him smiling up at me as he positioned the water jug in the doorway. "Shh," I said, quickly turning away to hide any blush that would be rising to my pale cheeks.

"It is really beautiful out here tonight though," he said, standing up next to me.

"It really is."

He walked over to the barrier wall that was separating us from the icy depths below. Okay, it was just the icy parking lot, but icy depths sounds cooler, more poetic.

"Don't fall off the roof," I said, walking over to him.

"I could jump down there," Evan said, looking over the wall to the snow-coated parking lot below.

I shook my head. "Nope."

"I could. There's a good seven feet of snow packed up close to all the walls. All that snow would cushion my fall."

"It's probably half ice by now. You'd definitely not be okay," I told him.

He shrugged. "I'm not gonna do it. I'm just saying I could."

"Well, you can do anything. Like, you could kill me, but you won't," I said.

"You're still stuck in here with me, so let's not get your hopes up on that one."

I scowled at him slightly. "As I was saying, jerk, just because you can or could do something, doesn't mean you should do it."

"Mm, I agree," Evan said. "I think choice is what makes us so evil. We have the ability to choose to hurt others or not."

"Getting too deep," I said,

"Sorry, I'll pull out a little."

I couldn't help but cough up a half-assed laugh at that joke.

Evan gave me a stern-looking pout. I don't think he was very happy that I had laughed like that at his joke.

"Hey. Look at the moon."

Evan looked up with me at the big grey moon. "It looks bigger than it should."

"And brighter."

"It looks brighter because the city lights aren't drowning out the light. It's the same effect that happens when you go out to the country."

"Ooh, you're so smart," I said teasingly. "I already knew that."

"I was just making sure. Dang."

I smiled softly. "You're a dork."

"I heard that," he said, glancing over at me.

"You were supposed to."

"So."

"So." I exhaled sharply, watching a plume of breath float out around my face. "It's nice that it's not windy."

"Don't jinx it," Evan stated.

I shrugged. "It's just nice out tonight."

"Not too cold, not too warm. Just right. It's the Goldilocks of winter nights."

"Yeah, exactly," I said, cracking a smile at his metaphor.

"I bet you we could make an ice rink up here."

"I bet you we could," I said.

"You're supposed to bet against my bet," Evan whined. "Do you even know how bets work?"

"Do you?" I asked. "I'm not betting against something I think we could do. That's stupid."

"You're stupid," he said, pouting toward the dark city streets.

"Rude," I said, punching his arm.

"Ow." He rubbed his arm where I hit it. "Oh, that hurt so bad."

"You're just *so* good at pretending to be hurt," I teased.

He shrugged. "I didn't wanna *bruise* your ego."

"Nice pun."

"I try."

I punched him again. "I'm trying to bruise more than your ego."

"You're lucky I don't bruise easily."

I chuckled softly. "And you're lucky I'm not really hitting you that hard."

He turned to his other side for a few seconds and then swung around and threw a handful of snow into my face. "Oops," he said with a faked sweet smile.

"You are the biggest dick," I yelped at him, furiously fanning my shirt and coat to get the snow out. "Although it's ironic that you're such a big dick because you probably have such a little one."

He gave me a displeased look. "That's just a low blow, Spencer."

"I know," I said, turning away from him to gather up my own handful of snow. "So is this," I said, jolting around and tossing the snow at his face.

He jumped back pretty quickly, but I still got his face covered in snow. And it obviously went down his shirt by the high-pitched yelping he made while flapping his coat and shirt all over the place.

"Don't mess with me, bro. I'll mess you up," I said, feeling proud that I got Evan back so good.

"Snow is so goddamn cold," he said, finally coming back over to me after getting the snow out. "Why is it so cold, Spencer? Why?"

I shrugged. "Beats me, dude."

"You gotta know. You're smart."

"I don't know. Snow is cold because it's frozen water droplets," I told him. "I hope that answers your question. Now shut up."

"Remember how I said I could jump off?" Evan asked.

I nodded. "I remember this happening moments ago. Yes."

"Well, could you?"

I feigned slightly, resting a hand over my heart. "How dare you suggest such a thing!"

Evan smiled and shook his head. "This girl, man. I swear." he said off to the side, as if he were talking to someone else.

"I'm a treasure."

He smirked and looked over at me. "Never said you weren't."

"Smooth," I said, looking over the barrier wall and sipping my hot cocoa. It was finally not boiling hot anymore, so it was actually drinkable. Thank God. I was thirsty.

Evan slurped loudly from his cup. "This tastes so rich."

"I know," I said, taking another sip from my cup. "I can almost taste the privilege of this cup of hot cocoa."

"I can taste its father's bank account."

"Where's the lie though?" I joked.

Evan took a long and annoyingly loud sip from his hot cocoa. As he drank, I smacked him in the arm for being so obnoxiously loud.

He turned to me, hot cocoa dripping from his chin. "What the hell, man?"

I shrugged. "You were being annoying."

"I was enjoying my cup of hot cocoa, you dick."

"Loudly and with a ridiculous amount of slurping," I barked. "You sounded like a kid trying to get the last three drops of pop from the bottom of the Big Gulp."

"Shove off," he whined, taking a much quieter sip from his cup now that I hit him once already.

I turned around and hopped up onto the barrier wall. There was no snow on it since I cleared it earlier. Good thinking, Spencer. Thanks, Spencer.

"Don't fall," Evan advised.

"Wasn't planning on it, but it's better than being near you."

"That's hurtful," Evan said, pouting while he slowly raised the cup to his lips to take another sip. "The hot cocoa helps. It warms my broken heart."

"You're a wuss."

"I'm just sensitive," Evan barked.

I took a long sip of hot cocoa, getting most of it. "Ahh." I watched a plume of breathe float out around me. "Hot cocoa makes me loco."

"I can see," he said, taking a long drink from his cup.

I turned around from the barrier wall and walked out into the middle of the roof. "I kinda wanna make an ice rink up here. I think it would be cool. We could skate under the stars and crap."

"Oh, boy, can we?" Evan said with the fakest enthusiasm as he walked over towards me.

"You're being a real jerk. I can hear all your fake enthusiasm."

"Can you?" he asked, walking up to me. He looked me dead in the eye. "Good."

I pouted and then slightly scowled at him. "Do you not know how to skate or something? Why so hostile to the idea of an ice rink?"

"Well, why make an ice rink when there's already an ice rink up here?" he asked, motioning past me and over to a section of the roof.

"What?" I asked, turning to see what he was motioning towards.

"The roof has a little dip that makes for a nice little pond to form in the winter time."

"How do you know that?" I asked, turning back to face him. "Have you taken other girls up here before?"

"My friends and I came up here a lot when we were kids."

"Really?"

Evan nodded. "My friend's brother was a security guard. He would let us come up here to skate on the roof. He would help us build up big snow banks around the rink so we wouldn't fall too close to the edge of the roof."

"Wow. You had some cool friends."

"Well, it was his brother, but yeah, I did," Evan said.

"Wanna go get me some skates?"

Evan smiled and nodded. "Yeah. I'll go do that. Size five, right?"

I nodded. "Something like that, yeah."

He turned and walked off, leaving me on the roof by myself. It was a little unnerving to be alone on the roof. The skies did help ease my nerves a little though. Something about all those stars just made me feel safe and relaxed.

I walked over to the part of the roof that Evan was talking about. For some reason, there was next to no snow here. I noticed the dull sheen of a slippery surface as I walked over. It really was a little ice rink. I wonder if the architects behind this mall did this on purpose. Then again, it could have just been a happy accident that happened from years of pressure slowly pushing the middle part of the roof in.

I started walking across the ice. I felt my feet start slipping underneath me, so I quickly jumped back off the ice. Skates were made for a reason.

After what felt like a good hour, I heard Evan's footsteps on the snow as he trekked back over to me.

He held up a pair of skates. "I got 'em."

"Gimme, gimme, gimme," I said, walking over to him.

He raised them up as high as he could and gave me a stern look. It was almost a fatherly scowl. "Manners, misses."

"May I please have the skates, Evan?" I grumbled begrudgingly, rolling my eyes slightly.

"Ooh, and she uses proper grammar. The English teachers of the world would be proud." He lowered the skates and held them out.

I grabbed the skates from him. They were all white and had the little ninja star at the end. I let out a sigh. "You got me figure skates?"

"The girls' hockey skates were up way high, and me and sharp metals don't get along," he said, leaning against a wall so he could take off his shoes and replace them with his skates.

I groaned. "Goddammit. Fine. I'll deal with lame figure skating skates. Whatever." I walked over to the barrier wall and cleared it off. I hopped up and slipped out of my shoes and into my skates.

"Do they fit?" Evan asked, looking over to me after he had tied up his skates.

I nodded, waving my feet around in front of me. "Like a glove."

"I have an eye for things like that."

I pushed down from the wall and waddled over to Evan. "Okay, you go first." I nodded towards the ice rink.

"Why do I have to go first?"

"Because if there's a patch not covered in ice, I want you to wipe out on it first. Duh. Don't be stupid."

He shook his head and walked away. "Lucky you're cute," I heard him mutter as he walked in front of me.

"I heard that," I whispered to him. And though I couldn't see his face, I knew it probably had one of those cute little dude blushes.

Evan walked out on this ice and started skating a little. He turned to me and motioned for me to join him. "Come on. The ice is fine."

I stepped out and skated over to him. "Ooh, I can still skate."

"It's not something that you really forget to do. It's like riding a bike, y'know?"

I shrugged. "You might."

"I might?"

"Yeah, you might forget."

He scoffed at me and started skating around. "Can you do any cool tricks?" he asked, turning back to me after he had skated a dozen feet away.

I shook my head. "I don't wanna break any bones."

"Ah, I see," he said, nodding slightly. He motioned for me to come over. "Come and skate with me, loser. I don't wanna be out here skating alone."

I skated over to him and he raised a hand. I gave him an odd look. He rolled his eyes a little and snapped his fingers until I grabbed a hold of his hand.

He tugged my hand a little as he skated slowly forwards. "Come on. Let's do some laps."

I sighed and skated beside him. "Why are you holding my hand though?"

"Because that's what you do when you go skating with a girl you like," Evan said.

"You like me, huh?" I asked, nudging his ribs a little as we rounded a corner. We were skating pretty slowly, but it was relaxing. It was pretty nice. The stars, the breeze from skating, the not-falling-on-my-face. It was all pretty good.

"I never said that."

"I think I heard you say you liked me," I said. I really wish he wouldn't just bullshit with me on this.

He shrugged. "Slip of the tongue."

And then, absent-mindedly, I said, "I'll slip you the tongue." My eyes widened when I caught on to what I said.

Evan snapped his gaze over to me, which caused him to not watch where we were going, and then... *whomp*. We ran straight into a snow bank and I toppled over onto him as we fell.

I looked down at him to see him laughing about it, snow all over his face. "What's so funny?"

"I thought you were gonna slip me the tongue," he said, winking at me.

"It was a slip of the tongue. It was a bad comeback."

"I'll say," he said. "But it *was* still funny enough to send us barrelling over into this here snow bank."

"Yeah, but I didn't mean to say it."

"I think you did."

I pouted a little. "I didn't."

"Spencer."

I looked up a little and caught eyes with him. "Yeah?"

He raised a hand and brushed the hair away from my face and then left it on my cheek, which was nice because his hand was warm. "I meant to say it."

I cocked an eyebrow in confusion. "Huh?"

He shook his head a little and pulled my head down. And then some weird instinct kicked in and I closed my eyes. And at this point, I was expecting him to push me off and laugh that we were about to kiss, but no, that didn't happen.

Instead, my lips met with his. And it was fireworks. It gave me a tingling feeling that started from my lips and exploded like the fourth of July all through my face. And I know it's cliché, but it's the truth.

And here I thought we were just gonna be friends.

{Chapter: **Twenty-Three**}

I woke up, as one does, and stretched out. I let out a loud yawn as I rubbed my eyes and sat up. I looked over to see Evan still conked out on his bed. What a cutie.

I stood up and stretched out again, for good measure and whatnot. I debated on whether or not I should put pants on or not. I didn't see a point. Evan's seen me in a bikini, and underwear is not really any different from that. I did put on my hoodie though. It was too comfy to not put it on.

I tried not to make too much noise as I left the game store. I didn't want to wake Evan up just yet. The game store was carpeted and so when my bare feet hit the tiled floors of the mall, it sent shivers up my legs and back.

"Goddamn tiles," I muttered as I started waddling my way over to the food court. I went to where we had our coffee station set up and started boiling some water.

While the water was boiling, I got two cups and put hot cocoa mix into them. I walked over to the next store over and grabbed myself a three-day-old chocolate doughnut. I needed some kind of food. I was currently hungered as shit. I sat on the counter and ate my doughnut as the water boiled. The doughnut was quite stale, but I suppose it's *still* a doughnut, so it's still pretty okay.

Once it was finished, I filled the cups and mixed them up really well so there wouldn't be any clumps of unmixed hot cocoa mix.

I cleaned up the mess I had made and walked the two cups back into the game store where Evan was still asleep. I must have been gone ten minutes though, so I didn't have high hopes that he would magically be wide awake. I sat down on my bed and sighed slightly. I'm kinda bored without Evan to pester or push around.

"I'm sorry for kissing you last night," he mumbled.

I looked over to him and saw him half asleep, lying on his side. "It's okay," I told him.

"It was totally uncool. We had agreed not to do just that, but I blame the stars for being so damn pretty."

"Evan," I snapped. "It's fine. I actually think I kinda liked it."

"Score," he said with a sleepy smile stretching across his face.

"By the way, I made you a hot chocolate," I told him.

He perked up slightly and looked over to me. "You're the greatest human being ever."

"Thanks."

"You know you kinda taste like strawberries, by the way," he said, raising his hand for me to put his cup of hot cocoa into it.

I handed him his cup and gave him a questioning look. "I do?"

He nodded. "It was a pleasant surprise."

"Why, what did you think I would taste like?"

"Sass and coffee."

I smiled softly. "I'd have preferred it if you had said that instead."

"What about me?"

"Dick," I said, winking at him.

"I hate you."

"Love you too, buddy."

He let out a sleepy groan. "I'm sorry for intentionally falling over last night to kiss you though."

"You what?" I asked. "You did it on purpose?"

He nodded. "I thought about how I would do it and I figured that was the best time to do it. You just slipped up and I figured I should take advantage of that and make you fall on top of me."

"Should I be mad that you intentionally tripped us, or should I be flattered that you tried so hard just to kiss me?"

"It was the stars," Evan said. "But you should feel flattered."

"Anyway," I said, trying to swap the subject because talking about kissing Evan made me want to kiss him again, and we just can't have that.

"Still surprised that you don't have a boyfriend."

"Why's that?" I asked, sipping some hot cocoa.

He shrugged a little. "I don't know. It's just that when I see a smart and beautiful girl, I expect her to be with some smart and good-looking dude, y'know?"

"Nah. I put too much time into my schooling and stuff," I said. "I never really had that much time for boys or dating. I mean, I do now, but I don't really have any experience. And from what I know, boys my age are looking for girls that wanna hit it and quit it."

"I'm a boy your age?" Evan raised a hand and pointed back down to himself.

"Yeah, but you suck for other reasons."

He scowled at me. "You suck."

"Look, pal, it was a kiss. Let's not get ahead of ourselves here."

"I just mean that not all boys our age are like that," Evan stated. "I know some guys who have only been with one girl, and some that still are. One of my friends has been with his girlfriend since they were in grade seven."

"That's a long time."

"Yeah, no shit," he said. "And it was hard for them to survive high school because there were all these new people and jealousy almost tore them apart, but they stuck it out. I'm just trying to say that some people will work things out, some people will wait, and that some people are worth waiting for. It's like fishing."

"Did you just compare dating to fishing?"

Evan nodded. "That's what I did, yes."

"Well, I guess I'm still trying to find my Nemo."

"I'll be your Nemo."

"Well, since none of your visible limbs are short, I'm gonna assume it's the one I can't see."

"Low blow, Spencer. Low blow."

I smiled and winked at him.

"You're so mean to me," he said with a sigh.

"Yeah," I said as we both then took a sip of our hot cocoa. "So, remember when you had that little metaphor or whatever about dying at different speeds? What exactly did you mean by that?"

"Nothing. I just meant that people die at different times. It's not anything profound," he said.

"No, no, no, no. You're goddamn lying to me. I know you are," I barked at him. "Tell me the truth."

"How do you know if I'm lying?"

I sighed. "You tug at the corner of your lip when you lie."

"Shit," he muttered.

"Tell me."

He shook his head. "It's nothing."

"Evan!"

"Spencer, please," he pleaded as he sat up in his bed, as if to try to take a stand against me prying at him.

I narrowed my eyes at him. "Evan, just tell me what you goddamn meant by it. Please."

"I'm most likely dying, Spencer," he said with a low voice. "Are you happy now that you know?"

I dropped any smugness, anger, or happiness from my face and looked at him in shock. "You're what?"

"Dying, Spencer. Dying. I said dying."

"What?"

"Spencer, don't make me spell it out for you."

I looked down. "I'm sorry."

"Sorry for what?"

"I don't know," I said, looking back up to him.

Evan sighed, put his head down, and rubbed his temples a little. "This is why I haven't told anyone."

"What do you mean?"

"People treat you different when they find out you have cancer, Spencer. You might not notice or think about it, but they do."

"I just… I'm sorry. This is a lot to take in," I said.

"No shit," Evan said. "I only found out a little while ago myself."

"Nobody else knows?" I asked.

He shook his head and looked up. "I haven't found the guts to tell anyone. So when I go for chemo or an appointment, I just lie and say I'm hanging out with friends or going to a group study or something. I don't want to be looked at like I'm wounded."

"Is the treatment... working?" I asked.

He shrugged. "It's still too early in the treatment to be able to tell for sure. I should know by my next appointment though."

"Evan, I'm sorry for making you tell me that if you weren't ready to talk about it or anything," I said, feeling like a mega jerk.

"It's fine. It feels a little better knowing that someone knows."

I got up and walked over to his bed and hugged him. "I'm here for you."

"I can see that. And before you ask about the hair, I got lucky with chemo. These drugs don't cause me to lose my hair. And before you wonder, yes, the chemo is why I started wearing beanies all the time."

"You're not wearing a beanie right now," I said, running my fingers through his hair.

"Well, to my credit, I *was just* asleep."

I smacked the back of his head. "Don't get sassy."

"Sorry."

"So when you said the thing about dying, you meant what exactly?"

Evan wrapped an arm around me and pulled me into a hug real close and looked me in the eyes. "We're all dying at different speeds; I'm just dying a little faster."

I leaned over and kissed him on the cheek. "You're not dying anytime soon, bud. I get you for the next 50 years, and if you think you're dying before that 50 years is up, you got another thing coming to you. I need you around to cook for me."

"If the treatment isn't gonna work, I've only got a few years left, Spencer," he stated. "And there's nothing you can do about that. It's life. Sometimes people die."

"Well, for however long you're alive, you're gonna be my bitch and I'm gonna be the best human being for you."

Evan smiled and kissed me on the cheek. "Thank you."

"For?"

"This," he said. "Giving me faith that not everything has to change because of some stupid disease."

"Nothing needs to change," I said. "Well, okay, one thing will change. You're gonna take me to your chemo and stuff so I can keep you company. We can buy coffees and bring Monopoly so I can kick your ass at it."

He smiled again, but this time a tear came to his eye.

I wiped away a few tears as they spilled out of his eye. "Why are you crying?"

"Because getting trapped inside this mall is the single best thing that's ever happened in my life. And also because you are one of the most amazing people I have ever met in my life."

I smiled and hugged him tightly. "Thank you. I try."

"Seriously, Spencer," he said, turning his head to look at me.

"Shh, shh," I said, raising my hand to his face and pressing my index finger to his lips. "I'm just gonna hug you some more."

He laughed a little. "Okay," he said, hugging me tightly.

"Okay, but, like, we talked about my lack of boyfriends, but what about you?"

"What about me?"

"Any big, glaring errors in your girlfriend history or anything?"

He shook his head. "Nah. All my exes and me and decently okay breakups."

"That's good," I said. "Having baggage sucks."

"It does, yeah."

"You, uh, you hittin' any of that?" I asked jokingly, nudging his ribs playfully.

He smiled and nodded. "You know it."

"Me too."

"I thought you didn't have time for boys?"

I shrugged. "We weren't dating."

"Is there a story you're itching to get off your chest?" he asked.

I smiled at him. "You're so smart."

"I know," Evan said with a wink. "Okay, lemme hear it."

"Well, I figured that I owe you one secret that nobody else really knows since you told me about the cancer thing."

"Right. Makes sense, I guess. Alright, once again, lemme hear it."

"Okay, so it happened during the summer, I had this best friend who was a dude, okay," I told him. "And we were both virgins at the time, and we were sitting around one night talking about college and all that junk and we both agreed that since we were so close throughout life, we should just do it with each other so it's not awkward or anything with some random from college."

"It was still awkward though, wasn't it?" Evan asked, trying to stop himself from smirking.

I nodded. "Big time."

"Too quick on the draw?" he asked.

I shook my head. "No, the sex was good. That part was fine. It was mostly the before and after. I mean, he was like a brother to me, I guess, so it just sorta felt off."

"Yeah, I could see how it would."

"That was the first and last time I ever got boned," I said, raising my hand to my face and miming a tear falling from my eye.

"When we get out of here, I got you, homie."

"I don't give up the chase that easily."

Evan smirked slightly and shook his head. "Well, if I have to spend the next 50 years being your bitch, I think I have time to chase."

"Touché."

"Have you ever been on a proper date?" he asked, pushing me back a little to look at me.

"Uh, no. Why?"

"I knew that answer was coming before I even asked. I really don't know why I bothered. Okay, anyway."

I looked him over trying to get a read for what he was thinking. "Anyway what?"

"Would *you*, Spencer Everett, go with *me*, Evan Fuller, on a date tonight?"

"You what? What do you mean a date?"

He sighed. "Go on a date with me, you soggy lampshade?"

"Can I get back to you on that?" I asked.

He shook his head. "Right now. Answer with your instinct."

I thought for a moment and then kissed him. I pulled away from him and smirked. "No."

"You're maddeningly confusing," he said, staring at me with a look of slight shock on his face.

"Well, where do you wanna take me?" I asked.

"Somewhere nice," he replied.

"And you know you're not getting any afterwards, right?"

He nodded. "Seeing you in a nice dress will be reward enough."

I sighed and groaned at the same time. "I have to dress nicely? I hate you. This is why I don't date."

He smiled at me and wrapped his arm over my shoulders. "So is that a yes?"

I scoffed at him. "Fine," I mumbled. "You can take me on a stupid date."

"I love how excited you are about it."

"You know, I don't think the cancer is gonna kill you," I said.

Evan looked at me with a puzzled expression. "You already sorta said that. You said you thought the treatment would work or whatever."

"No, I just meant 'cause I'm gonna kill you long before the cancer has any chance to do it."

"Why?" Evan whined.

"You're being sassy with me," I stated. "Being sassy is *my* thing."

He pulled me in close and kissed my forehead, which gave me all those stupid little butterflies. "Let's go reheat our hot chocolates, yeah?" Evan said, picking up our cups of hot cocoa from the ground.

"Totally forgot about those," I said, standing up with Evan.

Evan walked past me. "Nice ass, by the way."

Then it clicked in my head that I hadn't put pants on yet. A blush rose to my cheeks as I turned around. "Uh, yeah, thanks. I'm just gonna put pants on and I'll meet you out there."

He laughed as he turned and started walking away. "Just hurry up and try to keep that cute little blush on your face. It suits you," he called back.

I guess he *could* clearly see the embarrassed blushing on my face. At least he thinks by bum is nice, so that's kind of a win, right?

{Chapter: **Twenty-Four**}

I zipped up and buttoned my jeans and put my hair up in a messy bun, which didn't make it look any less messy than the ginger-coloured rat's nest I had on my head before. I walked out of the game store and over to the food court where Evan would be waiting for me. As I walked over, he came out of one of the kitchens with our cups.

"I just made fresh hot chocolate," he said as we both turned and headed towards a booth to sit at.

"Thanks, loser," I said, taking the cup from him as took a seat.

He scowled a little at me as he took a sip of his hot cocoa. "I'm burning your food later."

"That's fine," I said, winking. "Wait."

"What?" he asked.

"You're gonna ditch me for an hour and a half later. I'm gonna be all alone. No, I forbid you from doing that. I don't wanna be left all alone."

"So just go masturbate or something," Evan suggested. "I don't need to be with you all the time."

I smacked his arm. "You'd like that thought."

"It was just a suggestion," he said, shrugging.

"I'm fricking cold," I whined.

Evan nodded for me to come over to his side of the booth. "Come."

"Later," I said with a wink as I got up and waddled three feet around the table to his side of the booth. I slid into the booth as he slid over to make room for me.

"No, wait, get out for a second," he said quickly, scooting me back out.

I gave him a weird look as he slid out of the booth after me. "Why?"

"Just… wait here." He turned and jogged off towards the game store.

"Where are you going?" I yelled after him.

"Just wait there!" he shouted back, still jogging away from me.

I sighed and leaned on the table. This hoodie was doing nothing to keep me warm right now. I better not be getting sick or something. I hate getting sick. It's the worst thing.

I waited beside the booth for a minute and then saw Evan walking back over with a balled up blanket in his arms. "You got a blanket?" I asked as he came back over.

He nodded, walking past me and slipping into the booth. "You said you were cold."

"Right," I said, reaching for the blanket.

Evan pulled it away and gave me a sour look. "Come sit beside me, dumbass."

I groaned and slid into the booth like I just had a moment ago. "You're a dumbass," I grumbled at him.

"I know," he said, tossing the blanket around both of us. He wrapped the blanket all the way around me and then he pulled me closer to him as he leaned back slightly so I could lean on his shoulder and chest area.

"I take it back," I said, nuzzling myself closer to him. "I'm warm and comfy now. You're not a dumbass anymore." I scooted myself around, trying to get the blanket in a position where it would be warm but also let me reach my cup of hot cocoa.

I tried to reach for my cup and as I went to sit up, Evan's hand darted out and grabbed my cup for me.

"Here," he said, pulling it across the table.

"Why are you being so nice to me?" I asked, taking the cup from his hand.

He shrugged his opposite shoulder. "You deserve it."

"Are you trying to make me fall in love with you or something?"

He kissed my forehead again. "Not yet."

I sipped from my cup and tried to hide my blush. "Don't be doing that."

"Doing what?" he asked, kissing my forehead again.

"That," I grumbled. "You know good and well that forehead kisses make my knees weak and give me butterflies."

Evan smirked. "I didn't, but I do now, so thank you for that." He glanced at me and winked playfully.

"You knew. It is a well-documented fact that girls love forehead kisses."

"Everyone likes them. Well, everyone should. Forehead kisses are pretty great," Evan stated.

I put my hand on his cheek and turned his face so I could scoot up and kiss his forehead. "Did you like it?"

He nodded and smiled at me. "Yes, I did, Spencer."

"Nice," I said, nodding slowly.

"I need to give you a cute nickname."

"Please don't. I don't want another embarrassing nickname," I groaned.

"Another? Does Spencer have an embarrassing nickname she doesn't want me to know about?"

"No," I lied.

"Tell me."

"No."

"Tell me."

"Nah," I said. "I don't think I want you to know."

"Spencer, we both know that when we get out of here, we're still gonna hang out, which means that I'm eventually going to meet your friends, which means I will eventually figure out what this nickname is," Evan stated. "So it's either you tell me now and we move on from it or I find out the hard way and never let you live it down."

"Why is it always the names I hate that stick?" I muttered.

"Tell me. What's the name?"

I sighed. I groaned. I sighed again. "It's Dill Pickle."

"What?"

"Dill Pickle," I muttered under my breath.

"What?" Evan asked, getting a little louder this time.

"Dill Pickle. They call me Dill Pickle," I said begrudgingly.

"Tell me the story, come on," Evan said, poking at my ribs. "Are you wearing a bra?"

I shook my head. "No?"

"I was wondering why there was a lack of strap under your shoulder," he said. "Anyway, back to the nickname thing. Tell me your story."

"Random," I said. "Are you sure you wouldn't rather me just show you my boobs in exchange for you never asking me about this name or ever calling me by it?"

"Nope," Evan stated firmly. "You gotta tell me the story."

I groaned. "Fine. I was young and stupid and I ate a whole jar of pickles and drank all the juice, okay?"

"Dude, that's impressive," Evan said, raising his hand.

I sighed, high-fiving his hand. "It's embarrassing to me."

"I drink the juice too," Evan said, pulling me in close and kissing my forehead again.

I smiled. "You mean I'm not totally alone in my weirdness?"

"Of course not," Evan said. "You're *just* right."

"You're the real MVP."

"Want me to get you some pickle juice?" he asked.

I pouted at him. "Are you making fun of me?"

"Only a little," he admitted.

I sighed. "I hate you."

He mimed a tear. "I'm so hurt."

"Do you have any nicknames?" I asked him. I figured that he must have some kind of weird names or something. He has to. And he has to tell me his if he does, it's only fair. I told him about my stupid nickname. Sidebar, I hate my friends.

He shook his head. "I do not."

"Can I give you one?" I asked.

He was silent for a few seconds, thinking I presume. "What did you have in mind?" he asked.

"Something that refers to your penis size," I suggested.

"Oh, so something like Godzilla?" he joked.

I shook my head. "No, I was thinking more like Stuart Little or something like that."

"Low blow, Spencer."

"I told you that's just how I roll," I said, trying to sound slightly more thug than I had any right to be.

"You make my stomach do things."

"Random. What kind of things?" I asked.

"Like, nausea," Evan replied.

I smacked his chest. "Rude."

He smirked at me and kissed my forehead again. "I think they're butterflies. I don't know. I'm not used to it though, that's for sure."

I smacked his face lightly. "Cute." I smacked his face a few more times as I could see his face growing more and more annoyed with each soft thwack of my hand on his cheek.

"Stop smacking and punching and pushing me," Evan muttered, lowering my hand from his face.

"But—"

"No buts, Dill Pickle," Evan said sternly.

I scowled at him and stuck my tongue out at him. "So mad at you right now."

"Shut up," Evan said, giving me my cup of hot cocoa again. "Drink this and shut up."

I took the cup and started sipping the hot cocoa. I actually was really enjoying this though. This was such a nice way to start the day. I could get used to lying against Evan or being under a blanket with him or cuddling with him or just *him*.

We sat together under the blanket for a long time. We sat there so long that Evan had to go and make us more hot cocoa. It's not like we were in a rush to get anywhere. We were stuck in a fricking mall. So what if we spend all day drinking hot cocoa and cuddling in a booth seat.

And then I heard what sounded like a snore coming from Evan. "Evan," I whispered, looking up at him. I poked his cheek a few times and realized that he was fast asleep. "Why are you sleeping?" How could he even manage to fall asleep so fast?

I sighed and pushed him over a little so I could lie on his chest more. I took my sweater off and propped it between his head and the back of the booth so it would be comfy for him. I wrapped the blanket back around us and slipped his arm behind me as I laid myself on his chest. I could hear his heartbeat from where my head rested on his chest. It was so soothing and calming.

I listened closely to the steady beating of his heart in one ear as the other ear listened to his soft little snoring. I closed my eyes and let my hearing zero in on his heartbeat as I felt sleep nipping at my heels, metaphorically.

***

I rolled over and stretched out as I woke up from the nap I had taken on Evan, but I woke up in a bed, not in a booth or on a boy.

I sat up and rubbed my eyes as I started to look around. "Evan?" I called out in a croaky voice. There was no answer, just more silence.

I got out of bed, wrapping the blanket around me as I did. I don't usually nap during the day like that, but Evan just made me feel so comfortable and safe. Damn him and his warmth.

I walked back to the game store and then to the food court again resembling a walking human burrito. I waddled my way toward the food court, my sleepy bare feet hitting the cold tiles again. The cold of the tiles only really bothers me after I wake up from sleeping though. Weird. Also, where did Evan go?

I walked to the other side of the food court and saw Evan sitting at a table with what looked like a laptop. I waddled over to him and saw that he had a burrito in front of him too. "Hey," I called out to him. "Why didn't you wake me up?" I asked as he turned around. How neither of us noticed each other in the *same* food court. Well, that's just beyond me. We're both clearly very unobservant this morning.

"Oh, hey, sleepyhead," he said, pulling a chair out for me. "I didn't wake you up because you looked so cute while you were sleeping. When I woke up, you were asleep on me, so I just carried you to your bed so I wouldn't wake you up when I went to make food."

"Did you make me any?" I asked, sitting down at the chair next to him that he had pulled out for me.

"I did," he said, getting up. "Stay here. And try not fall asleep again."

"Okay," I said, smiling at him as he walked off. I turned to see what he had in front of him. It was a portable DVD player. I clicked play to see what he was watching and then *Madagascar* started playing on the grainy little screen.

"Hey, don't watch it without me," Evan said, walking back over with a Styrofoam container with my food in it.

"Sorry," I said. "You started it without me though."

"Just start it from the beginning," he said, sitting down.

I took the container from him. "Really?"

He nodded. "Yeah. If you want to watch it, I don't care." He reached for the DVD player and hit the skip back button until it was all the way at the start.

"Please like me back," I mouthed, half to myself and half to the ceiling, hoping Evan didn't hear/notice.

Evan turned and gave me a weird look. "What?"

Must have made some noises when I silently begged that. Oops. "I don't know. It's nothing. Thanks for the food, by the way."

He smiled and kissed my forehead. "As long as you don't get gassy later, you're welcome."

We sat and watched our movie and ate our burritos. I guess this would be considered part of the overall date experience, right? Meh.

After we ate, we shared a coffee and then we played Go Fish for a little while. We had another coffee and then Evan decided that it was time to leave and prepare.

"Don't leave me," I begged, jumping over and grabbing his leg as he went to walk out of the game store.

Evan turned around and picked me up from the ground and held me bridal style. He looked at me with a stern look on his face. "Dill Pickle, I will come back for you. We will meet in the food court in one hour and thirty minutes."

"Promise?"

"I promise."

"What am I supposed to do while I wait?"

"Go get a dress you like, do your makeup if you want to, and maybe do your hair. It's up to you. But you do have to wear a dress. We're conforming to social norms just this once," Evan stated.

"What are you gonna cook for us?" I asked.

He kissed my forehead and then set me down. "I'm gonna cook you stuff and things. You'll like it. Don't worry."

"I better," I said with a pout.

He smiled and stepped away from me slowly. "See you shortly, Dill Pickle."

"Stop calling me that," I muttered as he walked out of the store.

He smirked at me. "We both know that's not gonna happen." He turned on his heels and headed off to somewhere, leaving me all alone.

I waited a few minutes before wandering off to the dress shop. I pulled the metal gating up. Thank God it was unlocked. I walked into the store with my flashlight. I looked around for the light switches and clicked them on.

I went through a bunch of clothing racks, searching for a nice-looking dress. I finally settled on this one green dress with a wide strap that went over one shoulder. It was a pretty nice dress, and the shade of green contrasted my hair and complemented my eyes, so it was a good choice on my part.

I held it up to myself to see how long it would be on me, and it was about mid-thigh height on me. Perfect.

I swung it on my shoulder and walked off to find a store that had matching flats. Mama don't do heels.

After a few minutes of searching, I had my outfit together. I walked to one of the stores that had a shit ton of makeup in it so I could get my look together. I went with a simple and smoky-looking orange look. I was trying to keep with the theme of fire-breathing dragon. The eyeliner was black and the eye shadow was grey and or-ange to give the effect of burning and fire. 'Cause I'm hot. I am the girl on fire tonight.

I curled the ends of my hair and tied it off to the side that the dress strap would be on. It was a nice, wide strap, not that thin shit. I went back to the game store and went into the back to use their big-ass mirror.

I disrobed and then suited up. Well, kind of, I mean, it was a dress, not a suit. I slipped into my flats and fixed my hair and straightened the dress out.

I grabbed some scissors from a nearby table and cut off the price tags and shit. I finally took a deep breath and looked in the mirror. And I had to admit, I would have gone gay for myself. Is that even a thing? Selfsexual, perhaps?

I though Evan would be be mildly surprised at how good I looked because *I was* mildly surprised at how good I looked.

{Chapter: **Twenty-Five**}

I walked out of the game store and over to the food court. An hour and a half had passed since Evan left me alone. I only know that because of the timer I set in the game store before I went to go and get ready. I stood there, patiently waiting for him to walk up to me at any minute with a smirk on his face.

I waited some more. I waited so long that the author got sick of writing and hired a ghostwriter. Just kidding. It just felt like I was waiting so long because there was nothing for me to do *but* wait.

Evan appeared in the distance and walked towards me. As he got closer, I could see that he was wearing a tuxedo. His hair was swept off to the side slightly. He was even wearing dress shoes. And damn, the boy cleans up good.

I walked over to meet him. "So? What do you think?" I asked, doing a slight curtsey as I struck a pose.

Evan looked me over and raised his hand to cover up his mouth.

"What?" I asked, standing up straight. Why did he cover his mouth?

He lowered his hand and took mine in his, turning it over to expose the back of my hand. "My date is the most beautiful woman I've ever laid eyes on." He lifted my hand and kissed it. He was really pulling out all the clichés on this one.

"Thank you," I said, smiling like an idiot. There was no holding back the smiles or blushing. "You're looking pretty amazing yourself." I did a catcall whistle and winked at him.

"I'm still 20,000 leagues under you."

"Book reference, nice."

"I didn't think you'd get that reference," he stated.

I smiled up at him. "I'm smarter than you think."

"I think you're insanely smart. Actually, I know you are."

"Are we going for our date now?" I asked. I was starting to feel a wee bit peckish.

He nodded. "I'm just trying to get over how perfect you look right now."

"Watching me stuff my face with food might help."

"Nah," Evan said, lifting his arm up for me. "You'd just remind me of a cute little hamster or something."

I sighed as I linked arms with him. "Is everything I do just cute to you?"

"Pretty much," he said, leading me away from the food court.

"Where the hell are we going, by the way?"

"We're not getting dressed up to go on a date in the goddamn food court," Evan snapped at me.

"Don't get sassy," I barked back.

"I love feisty redheads," Evan said, nudging me.

I smiled. "I love us too. Anyway, how much farther?"

"It's just up here," Evan said. "Here." We stopped walking and he picked me up bridal style and started carrying me.

"Perks of being small, I guess."

"I could still lift you if you were taller and heavier. I'm not some weak-ass little boy, y'know."

"I'm sure," I teased.

He set me down. "Okay, wait, I can't carry you. I almost forgot something."

"Forgot what?"

"This," he said, pulling something from his pocket. "I want to surprise you."

"Is that a blindfold?"

Evan nodded. "It is."

"What the hell? I'm not into that. At least, I don't think I am."

"We can try it out sexually some other time, you idiot," he said, laughing slightly. He pulled me over to him and kissed my forehead. "Just trust me on this." He placed the blindfold over my face and pulled it down over my eyes.

"Please don't run me into things. Please."

"I won't," he muttered, sounding like I just offended his entire family or something.

Evan held my hand and guided me along for a few minutes. It would have been quicker if he just kept carrying me, but whatever. After a little while, we stopped and he let go of my hand. He went behind me and positioned his hands on my hips. He turned me a little to face the proper way and then lifted the blindfold from my face and tossed it away.

We were in the fancy restaurant. I looked around and then down to the table in front of me. It was candlelit and had two plates of pasta on it with a little plate of garlic bread in the middle. There was a boom box on the table next to ours.

I turned to Evan. "What's with the boom box?"

"It's for our music," he said, kissing my forehead before walking over to the boom box. He clicked the on button and some classical music started playing softly from it. "I figured, eh, we can't have a live band, but we can still have nice music."

"You're truly amazing," I said, looking over the pasta on the plates in front of us.

Evan pulled out a chair and motioned for me to sit down. "I try, y'know?"

I stepped over and sat down as he pushed in the chair. "This looks really good, by the way."

"It's in the sauce. Secret family recipe."

"Don't give me that shit," I said as he sat down.

He smirked. "It's not shit if it's true."

I grabbed a piece of garlic bread from the plate in the middle of the table. "At least this way you know I'm not a vampire, am I right?" I took a bite of the garlic bread.

Evan chuckled softly and smiled at me. "It's not my blood I'd want you to suck, so we're good."

"Ya nasty," I said, giving him a stank eye.

He smirked at me as he picked up a bottle of wine from seemingly nowhere. "Shall we have some wine, m'lady?"

I nodded. "Oh, so much wine, fine barkeep."

He poured some wine into two wine glasses that had been sitting on the table. I watched as he filled my glass and then his. I should have guessed that the glasses would be for wine of all things.

I took a bite of the pasta. "This is *really* good."

"Thank you." Evan smiled. "So, how was your day?" he asked.

I gave him a puzzled look. "You were with me pretty much all day."

"I'm trying to make small talk," Evan muttered to me.

"Oh." I nodded. "Right, well, okay, ask me again."

Evan sighed and shook his head at me. "You're an idiot," he said, regaining his proper composure. "So, how was your day?" He took another bite of pasta.

"It was good. I had a nap earlier. I don't usually nap, but it was nice," I replied. "How about you? How was your day?"

"My day was also good. I watched a movie and napped." And then there was an awkward silence.

"This is awkward," I told him after a few seconds of awkward silent eating.

"Yeah. Let's just go back to making fun of each other and you being a little nerd," Evan stated.

I stuck my tongue out at him. "Screw you."

"Why?"

"I'm not a nerd. You're a nerd, nerd."

Evan shook his head again. "You."

"You," I said, piling some pasta onto the garlic bread and biting.

"You look like a little chipmunk right now," Evan said, watching me try to chew half a piece of garlic bread with a bunch of pasta.

"Shut up," I mumbled through all the food in my mouth.

"I am so glad we're not in a public place."

I shrugged and swallowed my food. "I only eat like this in private and if I'm comfortable with the person or people. Really, you should take me eating like this as a compliment to our relationship."

"Just friends though."

I nodded. "Yeah, but a friendship is still a form of a relationship, idiot."

"The best form," Evan agreed.

"You got a little something on your face."

"Where?"

"All over it," I said.

He gave me a puzzled look. "What are you talking about? What's on my face? Tell me."

"A whole lot of cute," I said, winking and then taking another bite of pasta.

Evan sighed a little. "You're an idiot." He went back to eating.

"So, like, is there gonna be a dessert with this?" I asked, mumbling through some pasta. I took another bite of garlic bread while I waited for Evan to finish chewing his food to answer me.

He nodded. "Yeah. And I think you'll enjoy it."

"Is there more garlic bread?" I asked, grabbing another piece.

"There's not any more cooked garlic bread, but I can make more for you later if you want," Evan offered.

I nodded. "I would much want that. Thank you."

"You honestly look so beautiful though," Evan said, not going off topic at all. "Can't stop thinking about it."

I felt a slight blush rise to my cheeks and I smiled. "Thank you."

"So you agree?"

"What?"

"So you think you're pretty?"

I shook my head. "Don't start quoting *Mean Girls* at me."

"I do what I want," Evan said with a very slight pout.

"That's so fetch."

Evan perked up again. "Stop trying to make fetch happen."

I rolled my eyes at him. "Anyway, when do you think we're getting out of here?" I asked, taking another bite of pasta and realizing that, whoa, hey, I was almost finished.

He shrugged. "The real question is, do we even want to get out of here now? This is our home."

I nodded. "This is true. This has been a very great experience. I could get used to living in here. I'd probably go a little crazy, but that's mostly because of dealing with you."

"I think I would like it if more stores were left unlocked. How am I supposed to rob a jewellery store that's got a locked-up gate?" Evan asked. And hopefully he meant it in joking manner. I can't fall for no criminal.

I quickly finished the rest of the pasta and looked up at Evan with a mouth completely stuffed with food. "Finished," I mumbled.

"You're such a pig," he said, looking at me disapprovingly.

"You're cute," I mumbled through a lesser amount of food.

Evan hesitated for a moment. "I, uh, I wish I could say the same about you right now."

"Why can't you?"

He reached for a napkin and reached over and wiped my face. "You had sauce all down your face, so it was kind of ruining your cuteness." He pulled the napkin away and smiled. "Better."

"I made a mess on purpose," I lied. "I wanted to see if you were gonna keep up all the clichés or not."

"Well, you know I was going to," he stated. "You shouldn't be doubting me."

"I don't *doubt* you. I was just doubting your ability to stay in cliché mode," I told him, shrugging a shoulder.

Evan scoffed. "Just for that, I'm not giving you any dessert. It's all for me."

"I know where you sleep, buddy. You're giving me some dessert and you're gonna serve it with a smile," I growled at him.

He shook his head. "I might be your bitch, but I will still do what I want."

"Are you gonna eat that last garlic bread?" I asked, pointing to the last piece of the plate.

He shook his head with a small smile. "All yours, babe."

"Babe?" I questioned, reaching for the piece of garlic bread.

"Slip of the tongue," he said, winking as he took a bite of pasta.

I blushed slightly and tried to wash it away by taking the biggest bite I could out of the garlic bread. "I'm sure it was."

"You always talk with food in your mouth?"

"I'm trying to annoy you."

He smirked. "It's not working."

I swallowed and sighed. "Honestly, you're so hard to annoy."

"Yeah, that comes from being stuck in a school with super-annoying kids," Evan replied.

"I guess that makes sense," I said, shrugging. "So how 'bout that dessert though?"

Evan sighed. "Give us a minute to let our food settle and so I can finish it."

I groaned and pouted at him. "You're a frickin' jerk."

"Because I wanna finish eating?" he asked. "Or is it because I'm not a pig like you?"

"Shh, just finish."

"I'm trying," he said, taking a bite of his pasta. He didn't really have that much left of it, so I guess I could sit here and wait patiently.

I waited for Evan to finish eating and realized that he was just really slow at eating. "Hurry," I whined after about two minutes.

He took his last bite and scowled at me. "Hate you."

"I know you don't."

"I know I don't too," he said, lessening his scowl.

I smiled at him. "Is it dessert time yet?"

"In a minute," he replied.

"It's been a minute."

"It was a second. You're getting your time all mixed up," Evan stated. He stood up from the table. "But I'll go get us some dessert." He walked towards the kitchen and left me to wait.

I waited for a good three or so minutes until I saw Evan come back out of the kitchen. "What's the dessert?" I asked as he walked over with two plates of something.

"It's called a *dobos torte*," he replied.

"What the heck is that?"

"It's a cake thing. It's got chocolate buttercream and some vanilla and it's gonna be super great," he said, placing the plate in front of me.

I counted each layer of the cake. "It's a six-layer cake. Nice."

"It is," Evan said, sitting down in his seat.

I took a bite of it and let out a moan of absolute pleasure. The kind you only let out because of good food. You know the one. "This is so goddamn good."

"I know," Evan said, winking at me.

We sat and finished our dessert. And then we had another slice each, because why not? Someone's gotta eat it or it'll just go to waste. I had totally drowned out the fact that classical music had been playing this entire time that we were eating, by the way.

After we ate, we cleaned up the restaurant and then he held my hand all the way back to the game store, like a proper dork should.

"I guess this is where I leave you," he said, stopping us right outside the store.

I turned and looked up at him, cocking an eyebrow. "What do you mean?"

"Well, this is the end of our date. This is where your home is, at least for the last little while, so I figured I'd walk you home."

"Evan, this is your home too," I told him.

"You're ruining the moment," he said flatly. "I had a good time tonight."

"I did too," I said, smiling softly at him.

"I'll be sure to call you tomorrow."

I looked up at him, staying silent.

He looked down at me and stayed silent for a moment too. "Why are you being so quiet?"

"This is the part where you kiss me," I whispered to him.

"Oh," he mouthed quietly. "Right." His hand cupped my cheek and he planted a big ol' smooch on my lips. And once again, it was all fireworks from there.

{Chapter: **Twenty-Six**}

Evan came back to the game store after a few minutes, and in his hands were two cups of hot cocoa. I had forced him to go make us some because I was feeling the cravings for a warm, chocolaty beverage. Well, that and because I needed to change out of the dress and into some PJ pants and a baggy T-shirt. And also because I needed time to figure out how this *Minecraft* torch lamp worked. I wanted a nice dimly lit bed area for once. It felt more like home this way.

"Fresh hot chocolate, coming right up for my little gingersnap," Evan said, walking over to me.

I gave him a stink-eyed look. "Don't call me a gingersnap."

"Gingerbread?" he asked, handing me the cup.

"No," I said flatly, taking the cup from him.

He sat next to me on my bed. "That's not very cool of you. I think gingersnap is a cooler and cuter nickname than Dill Pickle."

"You do make a good point there."

"So you're gonna be my little gingersnap, okay?"

I sighed. "Yeah, sure, whatever."

"Thank you," he said, wrapping an arm over my shoulders and pulling me closer to him.

"This is so weird," I said. I think I said it absent-mindedly, to be honest.

"What is?" Evan asked.

"This," I said.

He gave me a puzzled look. "'Kay, so that doesn't help me at all."

"Like, doing this kinda thing. I'm not used to it."

"Oh, like, dating and being close and stuff?" he asked.

I nodded. "I'm more used to being alone and reading books and doing homework and watching Netflix and shit like that."

"I get that."

"You get none," I teased.

"Haven't gotten any in a while, but that's besides the point."

I laughed. "Don't you go to college parties and stuff?"

He shook his head. "Not really. I don't know. I just hang out with my friends. The best party I've been to all year was my friend's birthday party, so I mean, not exactly gonna bang his 14-year-old sister."

"That would make you a pedo," I said.

"Even if she was older, I still wouldn't. A bro's sister is off limits."

"Don't go ruining your image by spouting off douchey stuff from some Bro Code or whatever," I told him.

He stuck his tongue out at me. "I do what I want."

"Shh," I said, pressing my finger to his lips and sipping from my cup. It was a little too hot, but I wasn't about to let that stop me.

"Have *you* gone to any college parties?"

I shook my head. "Not even one."

"Why?"

"Well, a short, nerdy, ginger-haired girl isn't exactly a good fit for most of these parties."

"Why wouldn't you be?" Evan asked. "You'd be easy to lift up for keg stands."

"I guess that's kinda true." I paused and took a sip of my hot cocoa. "So are you gonna make me do a keg stand then?"

"I might," he said.

"Just the two of us with our close friends though," I told him.

Evan nodded. "I can agree to that."

"Maybe you can come with me if I go visit my friend Mindy in Toronto," I suggested, knowing that I would eventually go see her. I miss her already, to be honest.

"I've never been to Toronto, so I'm all for it," he replied.

I smiled and poked his cheek. "Nerd."

"Excuse me?" he asked, glancing at me.

"I don't know, I'm just super bored."

"Super bored because you're a super nerd." Evan poked me back. "Your cheek is so soft. Oh, my God." He cupped my cheeks with both of his hands and squished them together.

I tried my best to pout at him, but it just made him smile at me.

"Are you making a fishy face or a kissy face?" he asked.

I shrugged. "Both."

He leaned over and gave me a peck kiss. "Now blub for me."

"Blub, blub, blub," I mumbled through my squished cheeks.

Evan started laughing, which caused him to let go of my face. "You're the cutest thing I've ever seen."

"My fish impression is pretty spot on."

He nodded as he finally regained his composure. "It was pretty good."

"I had a lot of time to practise. Y'know, being a lonely little nerd."

"You don't have to be lonely anymore. I got you," Evan stated.

"I meant romantically lonely."

He smirked. "I know you did. And either way, it doesn't change what I just said. I like you a whole lot. You're the coolest and cutest girl in all the land."

"Liar," I said with a gasp. "The land is also totally empty."

He kissed my cheek. "I would never lie to you."

"How big is your dick?"

Evan's expression dropped and he narrowed his gave down on me. "Touché." He winked at me.

"You didn't technically lie though. You just said touché. I guess avoiding lies is not lying, so you're technically still not lying to me," I stated. "You might be a little too clever for your own good."

"I might be," he said, shrugging.

"So… you really wanna be romantically involved with me?"

"Yeah," he said. "But we're just friends for now."

"Right, yeah, we're just friends who make out and have sex and go on dates and do things together a lot."

"Excuse me? We'll be official after at least one more date. Maybe even two. We're just friends, but we go on dates," Evan stated.

"You know I was just being sarcastic right?"

Evan nodded. "You have your set of morals. I have mine. I don't think either of us wanna bang on the first date."

"Eww. I can't believe I'm technically dating you now," I lied. It was a great feeling because Evan was a great guy. I needed someone good in my life, finally.

"Shut up, gingersnap."

"You shut up," I barked back at him.

He scowled at me. "You're mean."

"You're nice."

"Meh."

I poked at his cheek again. "Hey. Hey, you. You should give me that back massage now."

"Why would I do that?" he asked.

"Well, you like me a whole lot and you also knocked me over in the mall the other day, so I think I deserve a massage," I told him.

He sighed. "Goddammit, you make a good point there. I owe you a booty rub."

"A good point? You're just saying that to shut me up, right?"

He nodded. "Yeah, kinda."

"So will you do it?" I asked.

"Only if you're okay with laying down topless."

"You have to look away then," I stated. "I'm self-conscious about my nipples, okay?"

"That's fine," Evan said. "Is it because they've got freckles on them too?"

I smacked his chest with my free arm. "Well, now you're never seeing them."

"Well, get your top off and lie down behind me on the bed and I will get to masseusing you," Evan said, looking away and using his hand to cover his eyes.

I sighed, set down my cup, and climbed behind him on the bed. I swiftly whipped my shirt off and unhooked my bra. I put a pillow under me and plopped down on my stomach and groaned. "Okay, we're good."

Evan fiddled with the lamp to make it a little brighter. "You have so many freckles all over your shoulders and back."

"Thanks, bruh," I said.

"At least you finally get that it's a compliment," Evan said with a soft chuckle.

I shrugged. "I figured I might as well stop fighting it."

"Lotion or no lotion?" he asked.

"Use the lotion, but try to make it not so cold," I said. "Like, don't just squirt it on my back. Keep it between your hands a little and make it warmer."

"I can do that," Evan said, reaching over for the bottle of lotion and then climbing onto my back and basically on my butt.

"You're so fat," I groaned.

He moved my hair off my back. "You're just too small and frail, clearly."

"I am not!"

"You are," he said. "Now this might still be a little cold."

"Hoe, don't do it."

He poured some lotion onto my back directly from the bottle. "Sorry. You didn't pre-warm my lotion."

"Oh, my God," I yelped out as I tensed up from the cold lotion.

Evan laughed a little as he started rubbing the lotion in. "Sorry, but I had to get you back for when you did it to me."

"I hate you," I mumbled. "I asked you so nicely to not do that. I know I did that, but that's because *I'm* a jerk."

"I can be a jerk sometimes."

"Barely," I said, scoffing slightly at him.

He started working his hands across my back, which was good because the lotion would finally not be just sitting like a pile of ice on my back. "So I was thinking how this isn't even fair."

"How is it not fair?" I asked.

"Well," he said, "I've been so good to you ever since we've been in here and then you try lording the fact that I knocked you over, um, over me. Yeah."

"You're the best at words," I said, laughing softly at him. "Dummy."

"I know I am," he said.

I groaned a little from how good this massage felt on my back. "I really needed this fricking massage though."

"Yeah?"

I nodded. "I did. My back has been knotted up for so long."

"I'm thinking we should do this every once and a while."

"Do what?"

"Like, massage each other. Nobody likes having their back get all out of whack," Evan stated.

"Nice rhyme, but I agree. You massage me once a week and I'll do it once a month."

"Deal."

"Really?" I asked. I can't believe how easy that was.

"Yeah. Why not," Evan shrugged, or at least it felt like he did. I wasn't really looking at him. "I figure that's the best offer I'd get out of you anyway."

"Beggars can't be choosers, am I right?"

"You are correct," he said, pushing a little harder into the knots of my shoulders. "Okay, you really needed this. Your shoulders are so knotted up and tense. Why you so stiff for?"

"Backpacks," I replied.

"Goddamn backpacks," Evan said with a slight scoff.

"What, like you don't wear backpacks?"

"Touché."

I let out another small groan of pleasure. "Seriously, quit business and go into a massage school. You'll pass for sure, and I'll even let you practise on me. It'll be win-win situation. I promise."

"Yeah, I'll get right on that, gingersnap."

"Evan," I groaned.

"Don't whine my name."

"Why not?"

"I don't know," he said. "It sounds weird and naggy. I don't like it. Sounds too nasally."

"Why don't you wanna go to massage school for me? I, uh, I mean for you."

He sighed softly. "I don't even think I wanna finish doing the schooling I'm already in. What's the point in studying for a life I might not get to live?"

"Whoa, hey, don't be thinking like that. You're gonna be fine. Believe me on that, okay, bud?"

"Spencer, I have to look at facts here. If I only have, like, five years left, why would I spent the next two or three in school?" he asked.

I went to reply, but I was out of a comeback. He made a point, and I didn't personally know how bad it was. The only person who knows how bad it is would be Evan, and his doctors too. All I knew was that he had it, but I didn't know how much or where or how aggressive it was. I knew next to nothing.

"Tell me more," I said.

"About the cancer?" he questioned.

I nodded. "Yes."

"There's a buttload of it."

"Is it all in your butt?"

He laughed a little, the kind of laugh you make when you're sad but still find the joke funny. The kind of laugh that says that you haven't fully lost hope yet. "All over my butt," he said.

"Gross," I said in a childish way.

"You're gross," he whined back at me.

I scoffed. "I'm the least gross person I know."

"Did you want some pickle juice with that lie?"

"Yes."

"Touché," he said with a small laugh.

"Hey, can I shoot you a riddle?" I asked.

He paused for a minute, letting out a soft groan. "Fine. Okay. What's the riddle?"

"How is a raven like a writing desk?" I asked him. Of course, the riddle doesn't actually have a proper answer. It was never intended to have an answer. I just wanted to see what his response would be.

He paused for another moment before answering. "Love, love, love, do not worry. It's just a raven and a writing desk."

"What does that even mean?" I asked.

"Well, people got so worked up over the riddle, but it's just a raven and a writing desk. The two things are so minor."

"Huh. I guess you make a good point," I said.

"Yeah, it's like a reminder to not be so worried about little things. Y'know? I think. That's how I've always taken it."

"I guess I do now."

He hopped off my back and laid himself down beside me. "My hands are hurting, sorry."

"It's okay. You can be done," I told him. "For now at least."

"Oh." He sat up and sighed. "Okay, put your shirt back on."

"I'm only putting the shirt on. Screw a bra," I said, reaching beside him to the floor where my shirt had been just chilling. I pulled it up to me and slipped it over my head and back onto me.

"Alright. I guess this means that it's bedtime?" Evan asked.

I made a gagging sound. "I hate bedtime."

"Why?"

"Sleeping alone sucks."

"I'll get you a teddy bear," Evan said as he stood up.

I watched him move back to his bed as I tried to muster up some courage to just ask him.

"You can turn the lamp off whenever you're ready," he stated. I'm just gonna conk out now." He plopped onto his bed.

I fought myself to blurt it out already. I could feel my hands getting clammy. And then I just went for it. "Evan."

"Yes, Spencer?" he asked, rolling over to look at me.

"Do you maybe wanna...?" I asked motioning for him to come join me in my bed.

"Are you asking if I want to sleep with you or if I want to *sleep* with you?"

"The first one?" I said with a puzzled look on my face.

He nodded and grabbed his pillow as he stood up. He walked over to my bed and made me scoot over. I made some room for him to get in.

"Don't think this means that you're gonna get any. I just need the cuddles and warmth."

He nodded. "I totally get it. Everybody likes cuddles and warmth when they're going to sleep."

"Get in."

"I'm getting." He sits on the edge of the mattress and looks over at me. "You're so pretty."

"Shut up and lay down," I whined, pushing him over so I could lay myself down on him properly.

"You are really cranky when you're tired."

"Shh. I'm sleeping," I said, resting my hand over his mouth.

He licked the inside of my hand and then laughed when I pulled it away to wipe it on our blankets.

I pouted at him. "You nasty."

"Yeah, yeah," he said, stretching back and turning the lamp off. "Goodnight, gingersnap."

"Goodnight, Evansnap."

{Chapter: **Twenty-Seven**}

I rolled over and only got about halfway to the edge of my bed before Evan's sleeping body obstructed my movement. I had completely forgotten that he had slept in my bed with me. I lifted my hand to his face and poked at his face a little.

"Psst." I kept poking his cheek a few more times. "Are you awake?"

He shook his head slightly. "Nope," he mumbled.

"Liar," I muttered to him.

"Stop poking me." He raised his hand and pushed mine away. Poor little Evan didn't even open his eyes or anything. He was still basically asleep.

"Wake up," I whined.

Evan sighed. "I don't really want to wake up. I'd rather stay sleeping with you by my side. Thanks."

"Too bad. It's time to wake up."

"Go to sleep, gingersnap."

"No. I refuse," I said with a pout, not that he could see right now.

"Spencer," he whined.

I poked his face some more. "Just wake up. I'll make coffee."

He lolled his head over to face me and he just pouted at me. "I'm comfy."

"Stop being so damn lazy."

"I like sleep," he stated. "Sue me."

"I will. Don't tempt me."

"Okay, what grounds do you possibly have to take legal action?"

I paused for a moment to think. "Well, for one, your arm is not around me anymore."

"Here," he groaned, lifting me up and sliding his arm back under and around me.

"And secondly," I started off, nuzzling myself into him a little, "you're not kissing me right now."

He leaned over and planted a sleepy kiss on my forehead, and then he worked his way to my lips, leaving soft little kisses as he went.

"Evan," I whined.

"That's what you wanted. Right?"

"Well, yeah, but no."

He sighed. "Can I just go back to sleep? I'm not feeling today."

"But today is the day."

"What day might that be?" he asked.

"The day you make us waffles," I replied.

Evan sighed. "No."

"Why?"

"Spencer, I'm tired. I just wanna lay here for another two days."

"But, Evan," I whined, shaking him slightly. "I want some waffles. And I know you can make them the best."

"I'll waffle your face."

"What does that even mean?"

He shrugged. "I don't know. I'm still half asleep. Get off my ass."

"I'm on your chest," I said, correcting him.

He poked my cheek a little. "Shut up."

I pouted at him. "Rude."

He smirked and then pulled my face up so he could kiss me.

"Less rude, but still rude," I said after I nuzzled my face back down into his chest. "I just wanted some damn waffles, man."

"I will make you waffles in a bit," Evan said. "I just want to sleep or at least just lay here for a little bit, okay? I'm frickin' tired."

"Promise?"

"I promise. I'll make my little gingersnap a nice stack of waffles. And I'll even get some nice maple syrup for you."

"You da best," I said, poking his cheek again. "You also need to shave. You gettin' a little too scruffy there, bud."

"Shut up," Evan muttered, swatting my hand away from his face.

I pouted at him again, raising my hand back up to rub his face. "I like it though. It's all scratchy and stuff."

"Shush. I'll shave it later."

"I just said I liked it. It feels nice."

He sighed. "You feel nice."

"Question mark?"

"You're warm," he said, shaking his head slightly. He flipped me over in the bed and curled up into my back.

"Maybe I wanted to be big spoon," I grumbled as his arm snaked over my body.

"There's no way you're ever being big spoon. I'm sorry, you're just way too small for that."

I scoffed. "I could say the same for your dick. Rude."

"Ouch, that hurt," he snapped back sarcastically.

"I'm just kidding," I said, wrapping my face in some blankets. "I'm so frickin' warm right now. I'm like a little ginger burrito."

"You're cute," Evan said, kissing my neck.

I elbowed him sharply in the ribs. "None of that!" I shouted.

He groaned in pain. "What?"

"No neck kissing! You know that's a recipe for disaster."

"Disaster?"

"Neck kissing is such a turn on, you don't even know," I said, wriggling myself around halfway to I could turn my face and look at him. I put my finger on his nose and looked at him sternly. "So no kissing my neck. I will jump your bones."

"Is that something you should be telling me?"

"Probably not, but I trust that you won't use this information for evil," I said, rolling back over.

"Well, not yet anyway."

"Evan!" I groaned.

"Well, I mean, like, if we start dating or something, I'm clearly going to use this against you."

"Well, I'd probably be okay with it then," I told him. "We're just friends right now though, so it'd be weird."

"But you laying here with no pants on and me with no shirt on and our bodies as close as they pretty much can be is normal, just-friends stuff?" he asked.

I nodded. "Of course. I spoon with all my friends."

"I don't doubt that."

"My friend Mindy is smaller than me," I said. "So I get to be big spoon with her. So there! I do get to be big spoon sometimes."

"When I said that you couldn't be big spoon, I meant with me."

"No, I knew that," I said. "I just wanted to let you know that I've been big spoon before. So deal with it."

"Do you think heaven has waffles?"

"Random question, but yeah. I would assume they would have waffles, Evan."

"Sorry, I was just thinking about waffles and death and stuff."

I cocked an eyebrow out of reflex. "That's a little bit, um, weird. What made you think about those two things?"

"Well, I was thinking about food and wondering what my last meal would be, and because you want waffles so bad, I was thinking about waffles and death and stuff," he replied.

"Evan, you're not gonna die for a long time. We've been over it."

"Spencer, you know good and well that I might die tomorrow. Life is fickle. I could die right now. Maybe I'm having a heart attack right this very second," he stated.

"No, wait, you can't die," I pleaded.

"Why not?"

"You haven't made me waffles yet," I said flatly.

"You're such a jerk."

I smiled to myself. "Yeah. But I'm a loveable jerk, so I would say that it evens out."

"You're not that loveable," he said.

"I'm cute, warm, and cuddly. I'm basically a kitten. I'm loveable," I argued.

He sighed and then stayed quiet. I guess that means I won. And then, after a few minutes of silent spooning, I heard some soft snoring from behind me. He really was pretty tired.

I sighed and decided not to bother him. I just nestled myself into him and closed my eyes to let myself fall back to sleep. I might as well just sleep while I can. It was warm and comfy. And I don't think I'll ever be this perfectly cozy ever again in my life, which is weird, because I'm on a mattress in the middle of a game store in the middle of a shopping mall.

After a while of lying here awkwardly trying to sleep, I gave up. I just decided that being here with Evan would just have to do. I was too rested to go back to sleep, and Evan was just a sleepaholic.

I listened to Evan's soft snoring as I scanned over the game store. It was slightly lit up from the light coming from outside of the store, you know, from the skylight.

I closed my eyes again, trying to force myself back to sleep, but my body was having none of it. Usually, I'd be able to sleep all day, but now I'm just having no luck with that. It was probably all the hungries from my stomach. I really wanted food, but I didn't wanna wake Evan up again.

I watched the walls for a good 30 more minutes or so before Evan curled up closer around me. Finally, he's up!

"Morning, gingersnap," he mumbled in a voice that was heavy with sleep.

I rolled over to face him. "You're a jerk. You fell asleep and I didn't wanna wake you up, so I just spent the past 45 minutes listening to you snore softly in my ear."

"You're the best," he said, eyes still closed. He nudged my head up and kissed me right on the lips. "Sorry for falling asleep again though."

"The last five seconds just made up for it."

"You're cute."

"Shh, no."

"Stop disagreeing with me or I will burn your waffles."

I smiled widely and widened my eyes. "You're gonna make me waffles?"

He nudged my head back up and kissed me while nodding softly. "You taste like nerdiness."

"Shh," I said, pushing away from him. "I need to put pants on and you need a shirt and we need to go cook waffles."

Evan quickly wrapped an arm back around me and pulled me back. "No. You're my warmth."

"Evan, I'm hungry," I whined.

"But I'm too comfy to move," he whined back.

I rolled back to face him properly and kissed his cheek. "Love you and all, but I'm getting out of bed now." I wiggled my way from under the blankets and into the cold air of the game store. Well, it wasn't that it was cold in here. It's just the contrast of going from the heat of the blankets to the not-as-hot heat of the game store.

"I hate you," Evan groaned, sitting up in the bed. He yawned and then started rubbing his eyes. "We better have cinnamon waffles. I've got a craving for them."

"Ooh, yeah. Cinnamon waffles and maple syrup. Yum."

"That's my thoughts exactly," he said, reaching for his shirt.

"Toss me my pants."

"I probably should. Your legs are so pale."

I scoffed. "It's winter. I can't tan in the winter."

"Or in the summer."

"Okay, you're a jerk. Give me back those kisses," I demanded.

Evan shook his head and sighed softly as he stood up. "You're such a little dork. It's so cute." He stretched out and walked over to his shoes and put them back on.

"I'm not a dork."

"You are. You're also very slow. You hurry up and get your pants on. I'm gonna go start cooking us some waffles."

"Okay," I said. "Have fun." I watched him leave and then fell back on the bed. I waited a minute or two to make sure Evan was gone.

I tidied myself up and changed my drool-stained shirt. I got some nice, warm, comfy pants on, y'know, instead of jeans or something. I sprayed myself with some perfume I had found earlier. I threw my hair into a messy bun and walked out of the game store and over to the food court.

I walked over to where I knew Evan would be. "There you is."

"There you are, finally," he said, glancing over at me. He was busy plating waffles and pouring coffees.

"Sorry. I'm slow."

"Well, come and eat." He walked over and handed me a plate with some waffles on it. "You're looking peppy today."

I smirked. "Yeah. I had a lot of sleep."

"Here's a coffee too," he said, handing me a cup of coffee.

I took it from him and smiled. "Thank you, kind sir. It smells of the most divine heavens."

"Stop," Evan said flatly.

"Sorry," I said, turning on my heels and heading towards the nearest booth seat I could find.

Evan walked behind me with his plate of waffles and coffee. "It's fine. You're just a little bit weird is all."

"We should go up to the roof after we eat. I need some fresh air," I suggested as I started cutting up my first waffle.

Evan nodded. "Take your time though. We're not in any rush. I just woke up. I don't wanna do too much moving right now."

"I feel you," I said, shovelling a good half of a waffle into my face. I could feel the maple syrup dripping down my chin.

Evan sighed, grabbed a napkin, and wiped it off for me. "You're such a mess."

"A hot mess," I mumbled, barely managing to keep the waffle in my mouth.

"No," he said. "You're just a mess."

I shrugged and then nodded. "You make a good point."

We sat and ate. And then ate a little more because I'm a fatass and I love me some waffles. And then we made another cup of coffee and headed up towards the roof.

"Carry me," I said as we got to the stairs that led up to the roof.

Evan looked up at the stairs. "Nah. There's way too many steps."

"Dude," I whined. "Just carry me. The roof is right there."

"You can walk it," Evan said, walking in front of me and starting up the stairs. "Like you said, the roof is right here."

"Just go," I whined, pushing him up the stairs as I followed close behind him.

"I'm trying," he said, smacking my arms away from his back.

I scoffed and followed him up to the door. "Ladies first," I said, walking past him and walking outside. The air was a nice out here. Cold and brisk.

"Bye now," Evan said from behind me.

I swung around to see the door had been closed. I started banging on it. "Evan, you asshole. You can't do that. This isn't funny, man. My coat isn't warm enough to spend that long up here. Come on. Don't be a douche."

"Shoulda brought a warmer coat!" Evan shouted back through the door.

I sighed and gave up. "Whatever," I grumbled. I walked over to the barrier wall and looked over at the sea of snow that had covered the parking lot. I noticed something new about the parking lot today though.

Snowplows. Four of them.

"Evan!" I called out, running back to the door. "Evan! There's snowplows down there! We're gonna get rescued!" I shouted to him.

The door budged open slowly and he peeked around it. "You're just lying so I'll come out."

"No, seriously, come look," I said, grabbing him.

Evan jolted out of the door and quickly lunged back, grabbing it before it could close back over. "You idiot!" he shouted. "Don't just pull me out the door. We need to prop it fucking open first. I don't think you wanna be stuck on the roof," he whined, getting up and fixing the door so it wouldn't close.

"It doesn't even matter," I said walking back over to the barrier wall. "There's other people." I started jumping up and down and waving my arms to try to get them to notice me up here.

"What are you doing?" he asked, walking over. He looked over and frowned.

"Why are you frowning?" I asked as I stopped jumping around like an idiot.

Evan sighed. "This means our adventure is almost over. It means we have to go back home now."

"Shit. Yeah. I guess you're right," I said, pouting slightly now that I realized our adventure was indeed over.

I wish he hadn't mentioned that because that made the rescue a little bit bittersweet. He was right though. If we get rescued now, things won't be the same. Real life would have to commence again. And our adventure would be over.

"But after tonight when we get home, things won't be like they were before we got trapped in here. I don't want to forget you or lose you from my life, okay?"

"Right. Now, can we get their attention? I have turkey leftovers from Christmas Eve that are most likely sitting in the fridge waiting to be eaten by me."

"After you," he said, smirking.

I nodded, turned back to the parking lot, and started shouting to the horizon so that the snow removal team would hear me.

{Chapter: **Twenty-Eight**}

We shouted for a few minutes, jumping up and down as we did. We were basically doing jumping jacks while we tried to get the attention of the people working the snowplows.

"I think they see us," Evan said as we stopped jumping.

I watched as the one of the people in the group of them pointed up at us. "They see us!" I shouted in happiness. I jumped toward Evan and hugged him. "We're saved."

We watched as they got in the trucks and drove them closer over towards the mall.

"Hey!" Evan called down as the trucks pulled to a stop.

One of the drivers got out at looked up at us. "Hello!" he yelled up at us. He looked pretty shocked to see us. If I had been in his shoes, I would be pretty shocked too though.

"Hi. Hey. We're stuck kind of stuck in here," Evan yelled back down to him.

"I can see that," the worker yelled back up. "We'll dig you out the front exit in a few."

"Okay. We'll come down and meet you there!" Evan shouted.

"Alright!" The worker nodded and got back in his truck. We watched as they drove around the mall.

Evan sighed. "It's gonna take them a while to get us out."

"Why didn't we dig ourselves out? Actually though. We could have just dug ourselves out. Like, we had an entire hardware store. Why didn't we just do that?"

"Well, we're lazy and we wanted to explore the mall," Evan stated. "Don't say you regret it."

I shrugged. "Fair enough. We'll go and get rescued now," I said, turning and walking towards the door.

Evan followed behind me as I opened the door and walked back inside. "Still so sad. We were having such a great time in here." Evan let out a soft sigh as he shut the door behind us.

"I know," I groaned, following Evan as he started down the stairs. "But now we get to have a great time out there in the great wide world."

"Oh, I swear to God, if I have to shovel when I get home."

"You're good at shovelling though."

He sighed. "But I don't want to shovel anymore. My back is gonna break and I'm gonna fall over and die. Do you want that to happen, Spencer?"

I pushed him into hallways of the third floor. "Maybe."

"Rude," he said, turning to lead the way back to the game store.

I followed him closely. The halls were all dimly lit. Not a whole lot of light anywhere in the mall, just faint yellow lights from the emergency lights that I guess were hooked up to the back-up generator. I wondered if we could have just charged our phones and gotten out of here sooner.

We reached the game store, having not made much conversation since the stairs. I guess we were both taking one last look at the empty mall. Well, I know that's what I was doing.

"We should go make a slushie real quick," Evan suggested.

"Do you want to?" I asked.

He nodded. "We have time. They're gonna take a while to get us out. There's so much goddamn snow out there."

"Can you go make me one? I'm gonna fold up my clothes and tidy up all of our things."

"I'm too nice to you," he said, sighing slightly.

I smiled at him. "I know, but that's not a bad thing."

"Well, obviously not for you." Evan shook his head and sighed.

"Shh, go get us some nice, cold ice slush."

"Don't be bossy with me," Evan snapped at me.

I scowled at him. "Go," I growled.

"Fine," Evan whined. He walked out of the game store.

I knew that the store that had the slushie machines was on the other side of the mall, so I knew I had a fair bit of time. I jumped onto the mattress and plopped out on my stomach. I stayed on the mattress with my face down for quite some time. I was so drained today for some reason.

I rolled over and watched the doorway for Evan. I probably should have gotten my stuff together, but I mean, it's all in a plastic bag and my phone's in the pocket of the jeans I had worn when I got stuck in here. So it's mostly Evan's shit that needs to be packed up, not mine. I'm all good.

I finally saw Evan walking back over with two big slushies. The one he was sipping from was red and blue, mixing in the middle so it was slightly purple. The other one was all yellow and green. "What flavours did you get me?" I asked as he walked in.

"Banana and green apple," Evan replied, handing me the yellow and green slushie as I sat up on my bed.

"Those flavours aren't gonna work together, are they?"

"They shouldn't, but they do," he replied.

I took a sip from the slushie and got overwhelmed by the taste of banana. "The banana's good though."

"Well, yeah, that's 'cause it's banana," Evan stated. "Everything tastes good in banana flavour."

"Would people taste good with banana?" I asked.

Evan sat down on his bed across from me. "You're weird."

"Says you."

"Yeah, says me."

"Pfft." I ignored him and went back to slowly sipping my slushie. I wanted to sip it slowly enough so that I wouldn't get brain freeze.

"You didn't tidy anything up, did you?" Evan asked, looking around.

I shook my head. "I literally just plopped onto the bed and that was it. I just laid down and waited for you to come back."

"Smart idea. You ready to go home?" he asked.

I sighed and shook my head. "Not really. I mean, yeah, a part of me is stoked to go back home and watch Netflix, but another part of me wishes I could just stay in here with you and enjoy this simple existence."

"Come on." He nodded toward the exit.

"You're a dork," I said, sipping more of the slushie.

He nodded again. "I'm familiar with this theory of me being a dork. You don't let me forget."

"Good," I barked.

"Shh, gingersnap. You're being sassy."

I cocked an eyebrow at him. "Duh."

"I hate you sometimes," Evan said with a sigh.

"Oh, shut up."

He stood up and let out a sigh. "We should probably get over to the main entrance and wait for them."

"Yup," I said, standing up to join him in the land of stand.

Evan set his slushie down while he gathered up the clothes he had worn over the last few days. "Let's go," he said, picking up the plastic bag of his stuff.

I nodded and grabbed the plastic bag with my stuff in the other bag. I kept my sweater on, because comfy. "Are you taking home the gifts I got you?"

"I don't think we should. It's bad enough we're taking the clothes," Evan said, letting out a small chuckle.

"Makes sense."

"How about at the start of the New Year, we go out and get belated Christmas presents for each other? Real ones that we actually paid for."

"I like that idea," I stated. "But I'm still keeping your gifts." I lifted my bag to show him the slippers and book he had gotten me.

He pointed to his. "I'm keeping yours too."

I looked up to see he was now wearing one of the beanies I had picked out for him. "We're such thieves," I said, nearly snickering about it.

"Yeah, we are!" Evan said, raising his hand out for a high five.

I leapt off the ground as high as I could to reach his hand and I smacked it with a good high five. "You're still a dork though," I said upon landing. I took another sip from my slushie, thank God I didn't spill it all over him when I jumped up just then.

"Let's go," he said, walking over and turning off the lights of the game store.

I sighed and followed him out of the store. "I'll miss it," I said, blowing a kiss to the game store.

"You're a weirdo," Evan stated, turning and walking in the direction of the main entrance. "Keep up."

"I can't help it," I whined. "I have little legs."

"Well, make them longer," Evan joked back.

"Oh, yeah, because I can just make my legs longer. I'm sorry genetics, I don't care much for your plans about my height, I'm gonna just go ahead and make my legs longer because screw you."

Evan nodded. "Sounds about right."

"I'm not doing that bone lengthening surgery either," I stated. "That shit looks uncomfortable and it seems like it's more trouble than it's worth."

"What if I made myself shorter?" Evan asked.

"That would be nice of you."

He scoffed. "Nah. I like being taller than you."

"Then slow the hell down a little, damn," I whined.

Evan slowed down his pace and let me catch up to him. "Better?" he asked as he adjusted to my pace of walking.

"Much."

"It looks like they still have a ways to dig out," Evan said as we walked up to the main entrance. All the glass doors in the front were completely covered up by all the snow. "Let's just take a seat and wait."

I walked over to a bench and sat down, placing my bag beside me. "I wonder how long it's gonna take."

"Probably a half hour or so. There can't be *that* much snow out there," Evan stated.

I sighed. "I'm bored. Let's go make waffles."

"I just made you some waffles."

"I want more."

He rested his arm over my shoulder and sighed. "Later, gingersnap. Later."

"Promise?"

"What's with you and your waffle kick today?"

I shrugged. "Waffles is like my family."

"You're weird."

I nodded. "I know this."

"Hey."

I turned to look at him. "Yeah?"

"I lost my phone number, can I have yours?"

I sighed and shook my head. "You're the lamest person I've ever met."

He smiled and handed me a pen. "I still need your number so I can call you tomorrow."

"Right," I said, taking the pen from him. "Do you have a piece of paper?"

He handed me a brown napkin, the kind that looks like it was made from recycled papers. "This is more cliché."

"You're a dork," I stated, scribbling my phone number down onto the napkin. "Try to call after eight."

"I'll call when I call and you'll be pleased about it," he said, taking the napkin and putting it in his pocket.

"No, you won't."

"Why?"

"I'll be more likely to be in a place where I can talk to you past eight. My family doesn't do activities at night."

"Okay. I'll call you at eight."

I smiled softly at him. "You know what, you're the bestest friend in the whole wide world."

"I know," he said, winking at me. "I wish I had made some burritos for the ride home."

"Stop. You're gonna make me hungry again."

"I'm already hungry," Evan said. "I want you to suffer with me."

"Well," I nudged his ribs with my elbow, "you could always eat some gingersnaps. Eh, Evan? Some gingersnaps?"

"Serve me," he said, pushing my nudging arm away from him.

I smirked. "I'm saving it for your dessert."

"I'm actually really hungry though. Those waffles were not very filling," Evan groaned. "I hope there's frozen pizzas at home."

"I hope there's waffles."

"Enough with your waffles."

"I love waffles," I said, pushing Evan. "Oh, hey, look." I nodded toward the entrance. The snowplow people had finally managed to get almost all the way through in the time we spent bickering on this bench here.

"In other news, my slushie has melted quite a bit," Evan said, holding up a rather disappointing excuse for a frozen beverage.

I looked over to my slushie and noticed that it had melted too. "Whatever. The banana flavour was a bit much for me."

"Wasteful."

"Shut up," I barked at him. I grabbed my bag and stood up as the workers came into view. They work pretty quickly.

Evan got up and walked with me over to the doors. We waited for a few more minutes as they cleared the rest of the path. The workers unlocked the doors and came inside to us.

"Hello, hello," a somewhat elderly man in a police uniform said. I'm guessing he was the chief. "You two are okay, yes?"

We nodded together. "Yeah," we replied.

"That's good. I'm glad neither of you are hurt. Is there any damages we should know about?"

Evan nodded slowly. "Yeah, we had a paint fight in the hardware store on the other end of the mall."

"Did you break anything serious?"

"I crowbarred a lock on one of those metal gates," I said, pointing to one of the stores that still had a gate closed over it.

The man nodded and pulled out a small notebook and scribbled something onto one of the pages. "We can write those things off as a dire situation."

"I'll come by and help clean up the paint though. I mean, it was my idea," Evan said.

The man nodded and scribbled something else down. "Can you write your name, number, and address down for me?"

Evan nodded as he was handed the small notebook and a pen.

"Should I do the same?" I asked.

The man shrugged. "I can't see why not." The man took the notebook and pen from Evan and handed it to me. "The mall most likely won't be open until the New Year sets in, so we'll have time to call you for the clean-up around the fifth or so."

"That works perfectly. We don't go back for classes until after then," Evan stated.

I nodded. "And it gives us some time to enjoy the holidays."

"I'm sure you two had quite the romantic getaway though."

Evan laughed softly and shook his head. "No, no. We're just friends. We were actually strangers until she rescued me from the boiler room on Christmas Eve there."

"Well, how about we get you two back home?" the man asked.

We both nodded.

"I could use a proper bath," I grumbled.

"You'll be riding in the back of a police cruiser," the man said, opening the door for us. "Try not to feel too badass about it."

"Ooh, I'll be a convict," Evan joked as we walked outside.

The path from the door out was like a field of view. The snow looked as if it had been cut straight and removed. The wind was pretty cold, but we didn't care. We were finally free and on our way back home. We kept following the man over to where a few cruisers were parked.

I turned to Evan as we reached the two cruisers that were on. "So, I guess this is it. This is goodbye."

"It's not goodbye," Evan replied. "I'll see you again."

"That is a goodbye," I said.

Evan shook his head. "If you don't say goodbye, you can never be gone. You just won't be here right now."

I shake my head at him. "It's gonna be weird seeing you in the great, big, open world."

He nodded. "Yeah, you're probably right, but now we can go on to have bigger and better adventures."

I smiled. "Text me later though, okay?"

Evan nodded. "Will do, gingersnaps."

I smiled and pulled Evan into a hug. He lifted me up, leaving my feet to dangle in the air. He hugged me super tightly. I'm pretty sure my back cracked 117 times.

He set me down and wasted zero seconds in cupping my face and planting a firm but sensual kiss onto my lips. And I wasted zero seconds in kissing him back. And after at least four-zero seconds, I pushed him off of me because I realized we were making a scene.

"Okay, we need to get home, Evan. We can do this later," I whispered to him.

He nodded. "Right."

"Right. Just friends," the chief teased from behind us.

"Just friends," Evan replied to him, winking his general direction.

"Until next time," I said with a smile.

Evan nodded. "Get home safe." He turned and got into one of the cruisers.

I turned and an officer was waiting with the back door open for me. I hopped in and off we went. Back home and away from the mall, away from Evan, away from my surreal getaway.

{Chapter: **Twenty-Nine**}

I gripped my plastic bag of things a little tighter in my hands as the cruiser pulled into my driveway. I don't remember the last time I was this nervous about going home. The officer parked the car, got out, and then let me out of the back seat.

"Thanks for the ride," I said, getting out of the car.

"No problem," the officer, Jamie, said. "This might be one of my last public service rides. You should feel a little lucky about that."

"Oh? Are you quitting the force or something? You must not have aged in 40 years if that's the case," I said.

He chuckled. "Nope, I'm being promoted to the special operations team down in Toronto."

"That sounds dangerous."

He shrugged. "It probably will be."

"In that case, do me a favour," I said.

"What's the favour?"

"Go kick some criminal ass."

Jamie chuckled again. "Will do. Anyway, you should get going. You've kept your family waiting long enough. Take care."

I walked up to my front door. I turned and waved as he pulled off. I hope he stays safe. He seems like a really cool dude based on the brief car ride I just had with him. I watched him drive off down the snow-coated road. I took a deep breath and turned back to the front door. I walked up to it and opened it.

"Hello?" I yelled out to the empty house.

From upstairs I heard some loud smashing and banging sounds, and then my mom popped into view and tore down the stairs at me.

"We were worried sick," she said, launching herself towards me and hugging me tightly.

"Well, stop worrying, okay? I'm fine. I'm okay," I said, hugging her back. "I'm home."

"What happened to you?" she asked, pulling out of the hug.

"The mall," I replied flatly.

She cocked an eyebrow. "The mall?"

"Yeah. I got stuck in the mall," I said.

"How?"

"I fell asleep in the fitting room."

My mom shook her head at me. "At least you're okay."

"Where is everyone else?"

"They're out shopping for groceries two towns over," my mom replied.

"Why so far?"

"All the other ones are still snowed in. It was the only one that's open and we were running out of food. Did you eat? Come sit down and we'll figure something out for lunch." My mom was all jittery right now. She rushed me into the kitchen so I could take a seat at our table and watch her panic around the kitchen for something to make.

"Mom, relax. I had waffles not too long ago. Food doesn't have to be a thing right away."

She turned to me and sighed. "Are you sure?"

I nodded. "It's fine. Just relax."

"I'll be right back. I'm gonna go call your dad and let him know you're home," my mom said, walking over to me. She kissed my forehead and walked off to the front door and stepped outside to make the phone call.

I hopped out of my seat and started going through the fridge for something to drink. I might not be insanely hungry, but I was pretty thirsty. I grabbed the first can of root beer I saw and cracked it open.

I siphoned down the first half of the can within 2.2 seconds as I walked back to my chair at the table. I was beyond thirsty, so the fizzy bubbles felt super intense this time.

I let out a loud, satisfied sigh of content as I plopped back down to my seat. I set the can down on the table and waited for my mom to come back from her phone call. I sipped my root beer for a few more moments until I heard the door pop back open.

My mom walked into the kitchen and looked over to me. "Good news," she said, setting her phone on the counter. "They're on their way back home."

"Good. I missed y'all, you know."

"We missed you too," my mom said, sitting down next to me at the table. "We called your phone a whole bunch of times and never got through. We called all your friends, thinking that maybe you had stayed there because of the storm. So obviously, after all of them had said you weren't there, we got insanely worried."

"Did Mindy leave already?" I asked.

"She did." My mom nodded. "But she's been calling every, like, two hours or so to ask if we found you yet."

"I should probably call her," I said, reaching for our home phone that was on the table.

My mom shook her head. "She got a new phone from her girl-friend, so she has a new number now."

"Dammit."

"I'm sure she'll call pretty soon," my mom told me. "It's been a while since she called earlier."

"I miss her already," I said with a slight sigh. "I wanna go visit."

"I'm not stopping you." My mom got up and walked over to the counter and clicked the kettle on. "But I am going to ask you not to run off for at least a few days."

"Well, I'm not about to jet off to Toronto anytime soon," I said. I had a date to make with Evan. It was a friendly date, a date just for friends, because we were just friends.

And then the phone started ringing. "That's probably Mindy," my mom said.

I grabbed the phone from the table and stood up. "I'm just gonna take this to the other room."

"Okay, I'll just hang out here."

I nodded and went upstairs to my room, taking my plastic bag of stuff with me. I clicked the button to answer the phone and put it to my ear. "Hello, hello."

"You're alive!" Mindy's voice screeched. "I thought you had gotten kidnapped or something. Or maybe you froze to death in that snowstorm. Why didn't you text me?"

"My phone was dead," I replied, walking into my room. God, it had been a while since I had been in here.

"I don't even care. I'm still mad at you for going AWOL. I was worried."

"Sounds like you were more than just worried," I joked. "My mom said you called every two hours or so."

"Well, yeah, I care about you. When I heard that you never made it home, I got super worried that you might have gotten stuck out in the snowstorm."

"Actually, I got stuck in the mall, so I was okay the whole time."

"Just lonely, right?" Mindy asked.

"Actually," I said, sitting on my bed, "I was stuck in there with this guy."

"This guy? Was he cute?"

"He was. He was very cute," I replied, remembering Evan's laugh and smile. "I kinda miss him already."

"Tell me more."

I sighed. "I don't think I want to. I'm so tired and sore and I feel dirty and I just wanna lay in my bed and not think for a while, or at least until he calls or texts me."

Mindy sighed back. "Fine. But you do owe me some details at some point."

"That's a given," I stated. "I'll even come visit you in the New Year at some point, and then maybe you can just meet him for yourself."

"That sounds like a plan."

"Do you have cool friends out there?" I asked.

"Yes, but this phone call isn't about me," Mindy barked quickly. "It's about you and how it's nice to finally hear from you."

"Have you talked to Charlotte?" I asked.

"I've called her a few times. Yeah," Mindy replied.

I plopped back onto my bed and let out a small sigh of comfort. "And?"

"And nothing. She was worried like the rest of us. I'm gonna call her right after we get off the phone to let her know you're okay," Mindy stated. "So if she comes over in an hour or so, that's my fault."

"Do me a favour," I said.

"What's that?"

"Don't."

"Why?" Mindy asked. "She's worried about you."

"I'm gonna get bombarded when my dad and sisters get home," I told her. "The last thing I need is for a convoy of my friends to show up and harass me even more."

"I guess that makes sense. What should I tell her?"

"I don't know, just tell her that you haven't heard from me yet," I replied. "I just want to have a quiet night later."

"Yeah, Charlotte probably would keep you up for a while. Fine. I won't tell her anything," Mindy said.

I let out a sigh and stared up at my ceiling, listening to the TV that Mindy had on in the background. "What are you watching?" I asked.

"I'm not," she replied. "My girlfriend's watching *Family Guy* or something."

"Tell her I say hi," I said.

"Haley, Spencer says hi."

"Hi," Haley's voice said back.

"She says hi," Mindy said, making sure I heard.

I laughed softly. "You sound pretty happy out there."

"Well, I know my friend is safe and home and I'm here with my loser girlfriend and my other good friend."

"Is it that Emily girl I met that one time back in, like, May?"

"Mm-hmm, she was the one who introduced me to Haley."

I heard the front door open and close. "Hey, I'm gonna go now. I'm pretty sure my dad and sisters are pulling in."

"Call me when you can. I'll text you tomorrow or maybe later on tonight," Mindy said.

"Okay, love ya. Bye," I said, sitting upright in my bed.

"Love ya too. Bye," Mindy said. She hung up the phone and I heard the dial tones beeping in my ear. I clicked the end button and put the phone on my nightstand.

I stood up and stretched out a little. I lifted the sweater over my head and tossed it onto my bed. I quickly put on a loose-fitting shirt and then headed downstairs. I walked into the kitchen to see my dad and mom standing there talking. No doubt talking about my dumb ass falling asleep in the fitting room.

My dad turned around and smiled at me. "There she is!" He rushed over and hugged me, picking me up a little as he did.

"Here I am," I said, wrapping my arms around him.

"You changed?" my mom questioned.

I nodded as my dad let go of me. "It's warm in here. A sweater was a bit of overkill."

"Makes sense," my mom said.

"So tell me the story," my dad said as he sat down at the table. "What happened?"

"Well," I said, walking over and sitting in my usual spot at the table, "I went to the mall and I fell asleep in a fitting room and then I woke up to an empty mall."

"How did you manage that?"

I sighed softly. "I was tired okay?"

"Get your sleep schedule together, okay?"

I scoffed at him. "I don't have school till next week or whatever. Let me enjoy my haphazard sleeping pattern."

"Must have been lonely," my dad said. "I'd have gone crazy."

"Well, yeah, but I wasn't alone."

"You weren't?" my mom asked, sipping from her cup of tea.

I shook my head. "No. There was this guy who had gotten stuck in the boiler room. I found him when I was looking around the mall," I explained. "I saved someone's life. You guys should be proud of me."

"You were snowed in with some stranger?"

"Was he at least your age?" my dad asked.

I nodded. "He was a stranger and he was also of my age. He goes to my college. I just never see him because he's in a different program than me."

"Did Spencer make a new friend?" my older sister, Taylor, teased. She was standing in the doorway. I hadn't even noticed her standing there.

"I did," I said, turning my chair slightly to face all three of my family members a little better. "Also, is it just me, or does your hair keep getting redder every time I see you?"

"Just you," Taylor replied, walking over and hopping onto the counter. "I have been thinking of dyeing it a deeper red though."

"The Everett curse of ginger hair," my mom said, ruffling my sister's hair to annoy her.

Taylor swatted our mom's hands away and scowled at her. "You're lucky I don't have anywhere to be today, jerk."

My mom scoffed at her as she walked over and sat next to my dad at the table. "It's not like you look good anyway." Mom winks at her and shares a laugh with Dad.

"Where's Jordan?" I asked.

"Oh, we dropped her at her friend's house," Taylor told me. "She didn't wanna go shopping with us."

"Typical," I said, sighing softly. "I'll just see her later."

"Are you going to see Charlotte later?" my dad asked.

"Nah," I replied. "I want to have a quiet night while I readjust to normal life again. The mall, man, it changes you."

"You're so weird. How are we even related?" Taylor joked.

"We're not. You're adopted."

"I think our hair is proof that we're related," Taylor said, laughing slightly. It was true though. We did have the same fiery ginger hair. Minus dad. Poor outlier.

"Make me a hot cocoa, please," I said, motioning to the kettle behind Taylor.

She turned and groaned. "Fine," she said, hopping down from the counter.

"Thanks, you're the best," I said. As I watched my sister pour water into a cup of hot cocoa mix, I started thinking about Evan. I couldn't help but wonder what he's up to now and if he got home okay and if he was wondering about me too.

"You should grab a shower soon," my dad said, standing up. "I'll start cooking the turkey."

"You guys didn't cook it on Christmas Day?" I asked.

"We were waiting for you to get home first," my mom replied.

I smiled a little. "You guys are the real MVPs."

"We try," Taylor said, walking over and handing me a cup of hot cocoa.

"Thanks," I said, taking it from her hands. "I'm gonna go get my stuff together and take a shower now. I will see y'all later."

I stood up and walked back up to my room. I put my phone on the charger and opened my laptop. After checking all my social media accounts and sipping all my hot cocoa, I went off for a shower. I tossed the sweater into the dryer so it would be somewhat clean and warm for when I got out of my shower.

And, damn, it felt so goddamn good to have hot, flowing water cover my body instead of having to sit in a hot tub or a fricking mall fountain. I was probably showering for over 30 minutes. Easily over 30 minutes.

I finally got out, dried off, and got back into my sweater. It felt like putting on a sweater made of all the world's best things. I threw my damp hair into a messy bun and went back to my room and got my Netflix set up.

It felt so good to be back in my own house and my own room doing nothing but watching good shows and movies on Netflix. I mean, yeah, I missed hanging out with Evan, but he'll call me tomorrow and I'll get to see him then, so I'm not too worried about that. Tonight is just for me to be alone and try to mentally readjust.

{Chapter: **Thirty**}

I woke up and stretched out in my bed. I had forgotten how comfy my bed actually was. I think spending a few nights in a mall on a mattress on the floor of a game store really made me appreciate my bed just that much more.

I rolled over and grabbed my phone. I turned it on and checked for texts. After a few seconds, a message from Evan popped up. I saved his number and texted him back immediately.

He texted me back and quipped about my late reply. I guess I did sleep in a little later than I usually do. It's not like I'm in a rush to be anywhere today.

I spent a half an hour talking to him before getting out of bed. I took my phone with me as I left my room. I walked downstairs to the kitchen to get breakfast, which at this time would be more like lunch.

My mom turned to me as I walked in. "There you are."

I smiled sleepily, rubbing some sleep from my eyes. "Turkey really puts your girl to sleep." I walked over and sat at the table, letting out a long, satisfying yawn.

"Yeah, I'm sure it was the turkey," Charlotte's voice said from somewhere just behind me.

I jolted my head over to see her standing there in a coat and snow-covered hat, holding a tray with three cups of coffee on it.

"I missed you," I said, standing up and walking over to her. I grabbed a cup of coffee from the tray. "Oh, sweet coffee."

"You're a dick," Charlotte said with a slight laugh, pushing me lightly.

"Yes, but I'm a dick that you love," I said, realizing how weird that was only after I had said it aloud.

Charlotte winked at me and handed the third coffee to my mom. "I figured you might need this since Spencer is back."

"You've no idea," my mom joked. "Thanks, hon."

"No problem," Charlotte said, tossing away the tray. "So, Spencer, you've got quite a bit to fill me in on here."

"I'll leave you two alone," my mom said, turning and walking out of the kitchen.

I groaned. "Dammit, Charlotte, now I have to make my own food. If you had just waited to show up for, like, ten more minutes, I'd be basking in the warmth of a half pound of bacon."

"Fatass."

"I'm not fat," I barked. "Yet."

"Anyway, this whole you being stuck in a mall and being stuck there with a cute boy, what up?" she asked. "Yes, Mindy called me last night at almost midnight to tell me."

"She really couldn't keep her mouth shut for a few hours?"

"No, she could not."

I sighed. "Okay, well, what happened was that—"

"No, I know how you got stuck in there. I want details," she demanded.

"We hooked up so many times, like, whoa. He was so hung and he just ruined my body. I still can't walk straight," I rambled sardonically.

Charlotte gave me a seriously unamused look. "Don't be a dick."

"Sorry." I peeled the tab of my coffee back and sighed. "He made me a lot of coffee and food."

"Did you guys become friends or anything?"

"Yeah." I nodded. "But we're *just* friends," I added quickly.

"The manner in which you just said that leads me to conclude that you like this mystery boy," Charlotte said, narrowing her eyes slightly at me. "Do you have a crush, Spencer?"

"No," I lied. "He doesn't like me like that either."

"Something makes me not want to believe you."

"He's not even that cute," I lied again.

Charlotte nodded, playing along. "Okay, whatever you say. So what did you guys do?"

"We had a paint fight in the hardware store," I told her.

Charlotte cocked an eyebrow. "Oh?"

"We made a pretty big mess."

"What else? Tell me more."

"We used a hot tub, so that was cool."

"In the mall? What?"

I nodded and sipped some coffee. "Yeah. It was nice. I kinda think my life's been missing a hot tub lately."

"You and him should get one together, eh? Eh? Eh?"

"Stop," I snapped. "We also played some hockey, some Go Fish, we had a little boxing match, and we also went skating on the roof."

"You did what?"

"Skating on the roof?" I questioned, figuring that it was the weirdest of the activities mentioned.

"How did you manage that?"

"With skates," I replied.

"Don't get smart with me," Charlotte snapped back.

"The roof door was unlocked and we went up there a few times a day to hang out, and then one night we just went up and decided to go skating on a frozen pond of water."

"Did you guys kiss?"

I cocked an eyebrow. "Did we class?"

"Kiss," Charlotte said, giving me a look like she already knew the answer to her question.

"Kids? Kids isn't a verb, Charlotte," I said, feeling a slight blush rising to my cheeks. I got caught.

"You guys did!" she shouted, smacking my arm lightly. "You two better not be just friends. Come on, he likes you. Don't mess it up."

"He's a dork," I said with a sigh.

Charlotte peeled her coffee lid open and took a drink. "Well, he's a perfect fit for you, because, if you haven't noticed, you're kind of a dork too."

"Oh, I've noticed," I said.

"So what's the draw? Why are you saying you two are just friends?"

I shrugged. "Relationships are dumb. We had a fun few days playing pretend, and now that it's back to the real world, why keep up that act?"

"Because maybe it wasn't an act. You two weren't in there long enough to develop anything beyond minor mall fever."

"Is that the urban version of cabin fever?" I asked.

Charlotte nodded. "At least go on a proper date with him if he asks you. And then, and only then, can you make a proper decision on whether or not you two are gonna stay friends or become a beautiful relationship flower, blooming like the spring."

"Creative writing class has turned you into a douche," I chirped her. She's just trying to help, I know.

"You're a douche."

"I'm not the one trying to make poetry out of everything!"

"I bet if he made poetry out of everything, you'd just kiss him and call him a dork."

"Yeah, but he's cute, and you're, well, you're *you*," I stated.

"I bring you a coffee and this is how you repay me?"

I shrugged. "Yeah, I mean, you know I love you though, so it's okay."

She started to pretend to cry with happiness and fanning herself with her hand. "Spencer Everett, you make me the happiest girl in the world. I love you too."

"Okay, Mindy," I teased.

Charlotte stuck her middle finger up at me and went back to sipping her coffee. "Anyway, did you get this guy's number or what?"

I nodded. "Sorta. I gave him mine, but he did text me earlier, so I technically also got his number."

"Didn't even wait the 72 hours? I don't know about this one."

"That rule is stupid, for one, and for two, I told him to text me today. I wanted it."

Charlotte nodded softly in acknowledgment. "I still can't believe you made Mindy wait to tell me."

I rolled my eyes at her. "Dude."

"No, dude, you suck. I'm your best friend too," Charlotte snapped. "When your mom called me asking if you had stayed at my house the previous night, I got really upset and worried, because I knew you wouldn't have gone home with anyone else."

"I'm sorry," I groaned.

"I didn't even sleep the first night. I thought you were freakin' dead or something."

"Well, hey, here I am," I joked, trying to lighten her mood.

She scowled at me. "Seriously, Spencer. Even a text would have been nice."

"I'm sorry. I just wanted to minimize the amount of people that would be asking me about it all in one day," I explained. "Plus, I wanted the night to spend with my family and myself."

"You owe me," she whined.

"There's leftover turkey in the fridge," I muttered. "You can have some if you want."

Charlotte cracked a small smile. "You just get me, you know?"

I sighed and rolled my eyes a little. "Yeah, whatever. Just make me a turkey sammich too."

"Ah, ah, ah. Where are your manners?"

"In a deep, dark grave somewhere in Indiana," I replied. "But seriously, please make me a sandwich. Okay, much thanks."

"I'm doing it, I'm doing it," she grumbled.

My phone started buzzing on the table. I looked over and saw that it was Evan calling me. My eyes sorta widened in a mixture of happiness and fear.

"Are you gonna answer it or not?" Charlotte asked, looking over at me from the fridge.

"Right, yeah," I said, picking it up and answering the call. "Hello, hi, hey, bad time."

"Are you too busy for me, gingersnap?" Evan's voice teased.

"No, it's not that," I replied. "It's just a bad time. I'm with a friend."

"Are you guys *just* friends too?"

"Oh, shut up."

Evan probably smirked at this point. "Make me."

"I will. Tomorrow."

"Is that when we're going on a date?" he asked.

"If you want to."

He hesitated. "Where do you live?"

"Why?" I asked.

"So I can come pick you up tomorrow," Evan stated flatly. "Wow, you really don't know how to date, do you?"

"Right. How about I text it to you later?"

"Is it awkward because your friend is there?" he asked. "Is she gonna make fun of you?"

"Yes," I replied. "To both of those."

"Fine." Evan let out a sigh. "Just for that, you're only getting a small popcorn if we go to a movie."

"But—"

"No buts!" Evan snapped, cutting me off. "You're a nerd."

"No, you," I muttered.

Charlotte walked over with my sandwich. "Food's up. Get off the phone."

I hushed her as she walked back to make her sandwich. "I have to go now, okay? I'll drop you a text later."

"Fine," Evan grumbled. "Leave me to wallow in my sadness."

"I'll talk to you later."

"Goodbye, *mon cheri*," he said.

I hung up the phone and put it down on the table. "This sandwich looks good. You should be a chef."

"So was that your secret boyfriend?"

"He's not my boyfriend," I whined at her. "We're just friends."

"Right," Charlotte said, walking over to the table with her sandwich. "That's like telling me this turkey is actually chicken."

"Maybe it is," I said, lifting the sandwich up to take a bite.

She shot me a vacant look. "Spencer."

"What?" I whined, holding the sandwich a few inches from my face as we stared at each other.

"You deserve a nice guy, and he clearly likes you," Charlotte stated. "So why not just try?"

I shook my head. "It was just mall fever."

"Spencer," she growled. "You gotta stop trying to find reasons for things to not work out for you."

"But being alone is nice," I said, putting my sandwich back to my plate. "You can't get hurt that way."

"Not every guy is gonna hurt you, Spencer," Charlotte said, frowning slightly. "You can't give up all hope."

"Look, we had a good few days while we were stuck in a mall. I just don't see us going any further than that."

"You're just scared of anything that's real, huh?"

I shook my head. "It's not that."

"Then what could it possibly be?" Charlotte asked. "Because I'm not seeing any reason for you to not at least *try*."

I hesitated to think for a minute. "Got it. I'm too busy. I have school and work and homework and I have other friends. I wouldn't have time for him."

"You'd make time," Charlotte chided at me.

"How do you know?"

"You make time to read and watch Netflix and go out for coffees," she stated. "You'd make time for him too."

"But what if he loses interest?"

Charlotte pouted slightly. "Well… that's just a risk you're gonna have to take. But you're never gonna know if you keep playing *what if* with yourself."

"I just don't wanna end up all messed up again."

Charlotte rested a hand on mine. "You won't. You're gonna be fine. I just think you should listen to your heart for once."

"When does that ever work out?"

"Mindy is a prime example of it."

I cocked an eyebrow. "How?"

"She had a 16-hour drive separating her from Haley and they stuck it out. She listened to her heart and look how happy she is right now," Charlotte explained.

I sighed. "Yeah. You have a point. But I'm me."

"And you're pretty awesome. This guy would be lucky to have a girl like you," Charlotte said, pulling me over and hugging me. "You gotta stop letting the past haunt your future, okay?"

"Okay," I mumbled into her neck.

"Now eat up," she said, pushing me back toward my chair.

I groaned. "I might just save this for later."

Charlotte stared at me with an annoyed look. "Why did I even make you a sandwich if you're not gonna eat it?"

"I said I was gonna save it for later," I barked. "I'm just not hungry at this point in time anymore. You soiled my appetite."

"Did you get anything cool for Christmas, by the way?"

"Oh, yeah. Clothes and gift cards and stuff. The usual."

My family had also not opened any presents until last night. They waited to have their holidays with me. I wonder how long they would have waited before thinking I was really dead.

Charlotte smiled. "Did you open mine?"

"Yes," I mumbled.

"Did you like it?" she asked, nudging my leg with her foot.

I shook my head. She had gotten me a jar of pickles and a stuffed pickle. It was a pickle plushie. I don't even know where she got it. I don't even know why they rip on me for that pickle thing. It's not even that weird, but I guess they need to rip on me for something.

"Why do you hate me?" she whined.

"I don't. You hate me."

Charlotte sighed and went on with eating her sandwich.

"We should go do something today."

Charlotte glanced over to me, mouth full of food, and asked, "What did you have in mind?"

I shrugged. "Let's shovel driveways."

"Are you on crack?" Charlotte asked. "It's freezing outside and there's way too much snow per driveway to finish shovelling even one."

I sighed. "We could go watch Netflix all day," I suggested. I figured that would keep her mostly quiet while I think about how much I missed Evan right now.

{Chapter: **Thirty-One**}

I woke up to my sister Jordan tugging on my arm. I tried to roll back over, but she was a persistent one. I mumbled something to her. I don't even know what I said. And then she said that there was someone at the door for me.

I rolled over and looked at Jordan. "What do you mean, someone's at the door for me?"

"This guy," Jordan said. "He's kinda cute. You should keep him around if he's that mystery guy Charlotte was talking about."

"I don't know. You might try to steal him away from me," I said, ruffling her hair.

"Nah. You're the pretty one. And you're the smart one. And you're the artistic one," Jordan stated. "It's not fair that you got all the good qualities."

"You haven't finished growing up and developing your qualities yet," I said.

"Neither have you," she teased. "Now get up, he's waiting."

"I'm not even dressed," I groaned, sitting up sluggishly.

"I'll send him here if you want," Jordan said with a wink. "I won't tell Mom or Dad."

"Jordan!" I shouted, smacking her in the arm. "He's a friend, you little shit."

Jordan winked. "I'm sure he is. Either way, he's waiting for you. Get dressed." She turned and walked out, closing the door with her.

I grumbled and walked over to my dresser and started pulling out shirt after shirt. I finally settled on a button-up plaid shirt with a white tee underneath. I grabbed a pair of jeans and pulled them on.

I quickly brushed my hair and put it up in a ponytail. I was too lazy to bother with fixing it properly. I grabbed my phone and house key and wallet, just in case, and then headed out of my room. I shut the door and walked downstairs.

Evan whistled at me as I came down. "Looking good, ginger-snap."

"Shut up," I said, blushing slightly. I reached the bottom of the stairs and hugged him. "Missed you."

He hugged me back and lifted me up in the air. "It was only, like, 36 hours."

"Thirty-six hours of suck," I muttered to him.

"Aww, little Spencer missed me."

"Yeah," I said with a sigh. "Just a little bit."

"It's okay," he said. "I missed you too."

I smiled. "Good to hear."

"You look really cute with your hair up, y'know."

"Really?" I asked as he let me down.

He nodded. "You look like a cute country girl. My uncle has a tractor if you wanna go feel more at home? Maybe we get you out there shucking some corn?"

I smacked his arm. "Shut up. I'm not a country girl."

"You have an attitude problem."

"I do not!" I snapped back.

He cocked an eyebrow and held a hand out to motion to me. "See what I mean? Attitude."

I laughed a little and shook my head. "Well, are you gonna take me for coffees now?"

He frowned slightly and shrugged. "Nah. I think I'm gonna just go home."

"Can I come?" I asked.

"Let's go for coffees," he said, smiling softly as he turned and opened the door.

"I'll see you later," I yelled into the living room. "Going out for coffees. Text me if you need me." I walked out the door and shut it behind me.

"Wanna go get stuck in a mall?" Evan asked jokingly as we walked to the street.

"Nah, I think I'm good on the whole mall thing." I followed him across the street to a dark orange SUV. "Is this your car?"

He turned to me and cocked an eyebrow. "Is that a problem?"

"No," I said. "I just picture you having an old two-door coupe from the '90s that's all beat up and falling apart."

"I think this would be a better choice," Evan said. "At least this one won't kill you if it goes more than 40 klicks."

"I guess this is a better option than a clunker," I stated, walking over to the passenger side. I hopped in and buckled myself in. Safety first, kids.

Evan started the car up and then we were off. We drove off to a coffee shop because, as college kids, we couldn't realistically afford too much more than that. We went to some coffee shop on the edge of town. It was nice and quiet out this way, so it was a good place for a "date."

"Here we are," Evan said, shutting off the car. "The world's best coffee shop."

"This isn't my normal coffee place," I said questioningly.

Evan smirked and pulled me over to him. He kissed my forehead and smiled at me. "That's because this place is better."

"Lies."

Evan popped open his door. "Come on, then. I'll prove it to you."

I got out of the car and followed Evan to the front door. He opened it and we went inside. It definitely did look nice. It felt rather cozy and calming in this coffee shop, as opposed to busy and rushed like chain stores.

"It certainly looks nice," I said, looking around.

Evan smiled and nodded. "Yeah, I know. And the coffee is even better."

"I don't know about that."

"You'll change your mind," Evan said. "Go get us a table, I'm gonna go get us some coffee."

I sighed. "Fine. Make it snappy." I turned and walked through the coffee shop to find a nice place to sit. I settled on the table in the corner. The whole corner was a set of windows, so we got a nice view of the outside world.

Evan walked over a few minutes later with our coffees and a small bag. "Got us doughnuts," he said, sitting down across from me.

"Did you get me a sour cream glazed?" I asked.

He nodded. "But don't you dare touch my maple dip."

"I won't," I said, pulling my doughnut from bag. I grabbed a napkin from the thing on the table and put my doughnut on it. "And now time for the real test. It's time to see how good this coffee is." I cracked the tab back and took a sip.

Evan cocked an eyebrow at me and waited. "So... how is it?"

I nodded. "It's good, it's good," I told him. "However, I do not think it's better than my other place."

"What?" His face was one of shock. "I don't know if we can be just friends anymore."

"Sorry, I don't date dorks," I said, shrugging while I ripped a piece of the doughnut off.

"But I didn't say I wanted to date you."

"But you're not gonna cut me out of your life, are you?"

He hesitated and sighed. "Okay, yeah, you got me on that one."

"So..."

Evan pouted a little. "This is weird. It's weird not being in a mall with you. I just feel out of place."

"Right," I said. "Just drive me home and we'll never talk to each other ever again."

And that was it. He drove me home and we never spoke again. I did see him once more in a supermarket. We made small talk about the weather. It was raining. He had grown a full beard and had a young daughter. She was only four or five at the time.

I'm just kidding. Imagine if that was the ending to this story. Wouldn't you just be a little bit pissed? Imagine if I had made you read that whole thing about being stuck in a mall just to have them end it like this.

Evan waved his hand in front of my face. "Hello? Earth to Spencer."

"Sorry," I said, "zoned out for a second."

"I can tell." A small smile stretched along his lips.

I sighed. "Just a lot of stress came back since getting out of the mall. The mall was like our escape."

"Like?"

"Like school and family. Life in general."

"I feel you. I'm not ready to go back to school. Please save me, Spencer. Please."

"Hell no. If I have to go back and suffer, you better believe you're going back to suffer too," I stated.

Evan groaned and then sipped his coffee.

I watched him as he fiddled with the corner of the doughnut bag, ripping it slightly and flicked the torn part between his thumb and index finger. "You're nervous about something," I finally said, breaking the silence that had settled between us.

"What?"

"You're fiddling. What are you nervous about?"

"Holy shit, you're good."

I smiled at him and winked. "I am. Now tell me what's got you all nerved up, nerd."

"It's nothing."

"Is it something to do with me?" I asked.

He didn't reply. He just fiddled with the torn corner of the bag some more.

"So it is me," I said. I'm so good at sleuthing.

"Yes," he grumbled. "But that's all I'm admitting to."

"Why am I making you nervous?" I asked. "We've kissed. We've slept together while we were half naked and in the same bed. You shouldn't be nervous around me."

"It's not that I'm nervous because of you exactly," he replied.

I cocked an eyebrow. "What do you mean?"

"It's not important," he said, quickly raising his coffee to his lips and taking a long, slurping sip.

I sighed. "Is it something that involves just the two of us?"

He nodded as he continued to take small sips from his coffee.

"Then just tell me," I whined. "Come on, man. The suspense is killing me. I just wanna know what's going on with you."

He shook his head. "It's not important."

"You're really nervous about this," I said. "Hmm, what could it be then?"

He shrugged. "I don't know."

"Hey, is that the beanie I picked out for you?" I asked, noticing the beanie on his head.

"Yeah. It's my favourite one because you picked it out for me," he replied.

I smiled a little. "That's kinda cute."

"You're kinda cute," he muttered back.

"Okay, so I've been thinking about something," I said.

"What's up?"

I sighed. "Okay. You know how we agreed to be just friends or whatever?"

"I do remember this, yes."

"Is that what you really want?"

He hesitated and sipped his coffee some more. "No."

"No?"

"No," he reaffirmed for me.

"Okay, then what does that mean for us?"

"It means I want you to be my friend comma girl," he said.

I cocked an eyebrow. "I, uh, I don't follow."

"You do, you just want me to spell it out for you."

I nodded. "You're a smart one. You can spell."

He took a deep breath. "Okay, so I don't want to be just your friend. I want to be more than that because you're the most beautiful and amazing girl I've ever met in my entire life. I don't wanna lose out on the opportunity to make you happy every day that I can," he explained. "So... what do you say, date me, you dork?"

"Nope," I said, getting up and walking away from him.

"Spencer," he groaned.

I walked back over to him and kissed him on his face and lips. "I would love to be your girlfriend." I sat back down across from him at my seat. "But you have to promise me that this is what you want. I don't want to lose you next week. You know? This has to be something you want for real."

"You're what I want. Yes."

"Really?" I asked, cracking a small smile. I could feel my heart finally start picking up.

He nodded. "Like I said, you're the most beautiful and amazing girl I've ever met."

"This means you have to massage me," I said, leaning over the table to whisper in his ear. "Every. Single. Night."

"I'm okay with that," he replied as I sat back down properly. "I wanna make you happy. If you could see how adorable your smile is, trust me, you'd want to make you happy all the time too."

"You're already winning boyfriend points."

He winked. "All I do is win."

"You just lost some," I said flatly.

"Can you let me play connect the dots with your freckles?"

I shrugged. "Maybe someday."

"Dammit," Evan said suddenly.

"What is it?"

"I should have asked you to be my girlfriend by asking if we could be Facebook official. I missed that opportunity."

I scoffed. "You're an idiot," I told him. "At least you're a cute idiot though."

"Babe."

I felt a slight fluttering of butterflies in my stomach. Something about him calling me "babe" really just got me feeling some type of way.

"Yeah?" I responded.

"Tomorrow is New Year's Eve."

"And?"

He shrugged. "Do you have any plans for it?"

"I do," I replied. "Some friends are coming over for a small get together at my house."

"Sounds like a fun time."

I took a sip of coffee and waited for him to say something else, but he didn't say anything. I sighed softly. "Do you want to come over?"

"Me?" he asked. "What if your friends don't like me?"

"They'll like you because I like you," I said. "If you make me happy, they'll like you. And lucky for you, you do make me happy."

"That's really all I want out of life," he said with a small smile.

"So you're coming tomorrow?"

He nodded. "I'll make an appearance. I don't have any plans."

"Nice. Be at my house for eight."

"Do I have to sneak in my own booze?" he asked.

"Nah, I have a bottle of whisky in my room," I told him. "I stole it from my friend's bar a month or so ago for New Year's Eve. I was gonna drink it with my friend Charlotte, but now I figure I could share it with you."

"Aww, that's so nice of you."

I ripped off another piece of the doughnut and threw it at Evan's face. "You were supposed to catch that in your mouth."

"You didn't tell me to catch it," he stated, picking up the piece of doughnut. "You catch it." He threw the piece of doughnut right back at me.

I smacked it away. "I don't wanna."

"Boo, you're a buzzkill."

I smiled at him. "I know."

"Tomorrow is the start of a new year," Evan said, fiddling with his coffee cup. "It feels like just yesterday was the start of this year. It's crazy how time just passes by."

"Stop, you're gonna give me an existential crisis," I said, taking a sip of my coffee.

He shrugged. "It's just weird to think that a year ago my life was so crazy different, but now it feels like last year was last week or something."

I nodded in agreement. "Wanna go do something?" I asked.

He shrugged. "I don't know. I like sitting here talking to you."

"I do too. I just, I don't know," I said with a sigh.

"You wanna go for a drive?"

I nodded. "Yeah. That'd be nice."

Evan smiled and stood up. "My girlfriend wants to go for a drive, so let's go for a drive."

"I like the sound of that," I said. "*My girlfriend.*"

{Chapter: **Thirty-Two**}

Tonight was the big night. It was the end of the year and the start of a new one. I was pretty excited about New Year's for once. Maybe it was because for the first time in forever, I would have someone to kiss at midnight. Hopefully. Maybe it was because I had family and friends to hang out with this year, but there was no Mindy, so that was a little saddening.

I brushed my damp hair vigorously. This is what I get for waiting until seven to shower. People are gonna be here and I don't wanna look like a lazy bum when they get here.

I tried to perfect my eyeliner at least fifty times before finally settling on "good enough." I even threw on a little lipstick. I never go for anything too bright or poppy, I just stick with a light pink that accentuates my natural lip tone. Is that how you describe? I don't know. I'm just tryna bring my A game to this get-together.

"Hey, Spencer," Jordan said, opening my door and walking into my room. "Are you planning to get clothes on before everyone shows up? This isn't a bra party?"

I turned around and put my makeup down. "I'd like to start a new trend. It's a cute bra though, right?"

"Yeah, sure. Mom just wanted to let you know that they're gonna be heading out soon," Jordan said.

"Right. I forgot that they were going to that party tonight," I said with a wink.

"My ass. You've probably had it marked in your calendar so you could have your annual sleepover."

"Aww, see, look at you. You're getting smart," I said, teasing her.

Jordan scowled at me. "You're not getting all dressed up for a guy are you?"

"Pfft, what? No," I lied. I could feel my face getting heated. Goddamn, I'm such a bad liar.

"It's that guy from yesterday, isn't it?"

I sighed and nodded. "Yeah. I invited him over for the night."

"Remember, Spencer, no sex until marriage," Jordan said, trying to sound as parental as she could.

"I'm not gonna sleep with him on the first night we spend together," I said, which even if we did do anything tonight, I wouldn't even *technically* be lying.

"Right, okay." Jordan winked at me.

I threw one of my seven hairbrushes at her. "Get outta here."

"Okay, jeez, rude," she said, picking up the brush and tossing it back at me. "But seriously, get some clothes on. You're too pale to be without proper clothing."

"It's not my fault that I'm so pale," I groaned. "And I'll be down in fifteen minutes or so."

"Okay, okay," Jordan said, walking out and closing my door behind her.

I turned back around and finished getting ready. After that was the harder part, do I go for casual clothes or more formal clothes? I could wear a dress, but I could also wear a tee and jeans. Decisions, decisions.

After a few minutes of debating my options, I went for a button-up shirt and jeans options. I mean, he likes me in plaid anyway. And it's not like this is a black-tie event, it's a New Year's Eve "party."

I walked downstairs to meet with my family, even though my parents were long gone by now. I sat in the living room next to Taylor.

"Your friends are mature enough to be around mine, right?" Taylor asked me.

I shrugged. "Are yours even mature?"

"Touché," she replied. "You wanna take the basement and I'll take the living room and dining room area?"

"What about me?" Jordan asked from behind us.

"You're only having, like, three people over," Taylor stated. "You can just have them in your room. It's not that big of a deal."

"Whatever," Jordan said, rolling her eyes slightly. "You guys better not drink and eat everything though."

"I will do as I please," I told her. "As the head of this goddamn household—"

"Whoa, who said you were in charge?" Taylor butted in.

"Well, I'm the oldest one of the three of us that actually *lives* here," I stated. "So that means I win the election for house president."

"Whatever," Jordan said. "Just send them up to my room when they get here."

"Will do," Taylor said.

"She grows up so fast," I said. "I didn't start to get bossy until last year."

Taylor chuckled softly. "Yeah, I remember when you were that age though."

"I was nerdy and ugly at her age."

"Mm, I guess that hasn't changed, then," Taylor joked, winking at me.

Then the doorbell rang, so I stood up. "I got it," I said, checking the time on my phone as I walked over. It was 7:52. Could this be Evan? I opened the door and was greeted by Charlotte.

"Hello, gov'na," she said, walking in.

"No, no, just make yourself at home."

Charlotte took off her sunglasses, and then she clicked her tongue and winked at me as she walked into the living room. "Where is everyone?"

"Not here yet," Taylor replied. "We sent the invitations to the important people for eight. All the loser people are gonna be here for nine."

"So is Evan gonna be here within the next dozen minutes?" Charlotte asked, turning to me.

I shrugged. "I told him eight. It's his deal if he shows up late or not."

"I'm so excited," Charlotte said. "I haven't met any guys that Spencer had a thing with since, well, you know."

"Yeah, so let's not mention to him how shitty I really am," I told Taylor and Charlotte. "I think I'd like to keep this one around for a while. Well, I guess for as long as he'd have me around. We haven't really discussed where we're going in terms of a proper relationship and stuff. But my point still remains a valid one."

Taylor smirked at me. "Little Spencer has a big ol' crush, doesn't she?"

"Shut up," I barked. I got up and walked over to the door and looked outside. Where the hell was this guy? I pulled my phone out. It was only 7:55. He has five more minutes to show up or I'm gonna beat him up for being technically late to the party.

I waited by the door like a loser for the next few minutes and then finally turned back to go to the living room. As I entered the living room, the doorbell dinged.

"I got it!" I shouted, spinning on my heels and heading back to the door. I never thought I'd ever be this excited and nervous to see someone in my life. But it was Evan, my boyfriend... my *boyfriend*. I don't think I'm gonna get tired of saying that.

I swung the door open and saw Evan waiting. When he saw me, his face lit up a little. His eyes brightened a little and he had an ever-so-slight smile tugging at the corners of his lips.

"Hey," he said, pulling me into a hug. "Missed you."

"You saw me yesterday," I said, hugging him back.

"Yeah, but you know how much I like being around you."

I pulled back and stuck my tongue out at him. "You're a minute late, y'know. You need to learn how to be punctual, mister. You had me worried there for a second."

He smirked and lifted his phone up and showed me the time. "It says here that I'm right on time."

I groaned. "Fine. You got lucky." I went to walk inside, but I was pulled back around by Evan. "What do you want?"

He shook his head and kissed me. "It's been over 24 hours since I last kissed you, so..."

"Right," I said, hiding the blush on my face. "Anyway, let's go so you can meet my sister and my partner in crime."

"Oh, shit, I wasn't nervous until you just reminded me of that," he said.

"You're not actually nervous, are you?"

He shrugged. "It's always nerve-racking to meet your girlfriend's friends and family."

I smirked. "Ha, nerd, you said I was your girlfriend."

"Well, you are my girlfriend."

"Yeah, but still."

"Okay, well, let's go so I can meet my *girlfriend's* friends and family," he stated.

"You givin' me the bubblies in my tummies."

"Sorry," he said, kissing my forehead and stepping inside. "Shoes off or shoes on?"

"Shoes off," I stated. "What kind of animal wears their shoes in the house?"

"It was a joke," he said, taking his coat off. "Nobody in Canada leaves their shoes on in the house, especially not in the winter. Wet carpets just aren't fun."

"Gimme the coat. I'll go run it upstairs and you just wait here and try not to die or get kidnapped before I get back. Can you manage that?" I took his coat and ran off upstairs and threw it on my bed. I ran back downstairs and walked back over to him, albeit slightly out of breath.

"Shall we get to it?" he asked.

I nodded. "Might as well."

I led him into the living room and introduced him to Charlotte and Taylor. We all sat around and talked. They seemed to love him, which was good news for him and me. Jordan even came down to say hello too.

This is when I found how gentlemanly and/or proper Evan could actually be. Of course, neither of us mentioned that we were doing whole dating thing yet. I had texted him about that earlier. I just didn't want that being the focus of things. It's okay if they all think I have a crush on him or whatever, but people hound other people about relationships too often.

Eventually, nine rolled around and everybody started piling in. My friends and I were all piled into the basement and Taylor's friends had taken over the main floor and Jordan's friends had taken over her room.

At least neither Jordan nor me had to worry about people leaving. They knew what was up. They're out of here by 1:30, well, most of them had to be. There wasn't enough room for *everyone* to crash here. Taylor was the police for that job.

Which was good, because when 11:45 rolled around, I pulled Evan off to the side and rushed him upstairs, leaving a group of slightly drunk people in my basement.

"Why are you kidnapping me?" Evan asked as I pushed him into my room. "You specifically told me earlier not to get kidnapped."

I shut the door and locked it. "I hate parties, dude."

"Why did you lock the door?"

"Privacy." I shrugged.

"Please don't murder me," Evan joked.

I smirked at him. "Well, the night's not over yet." I winked at him as I walked over and moved his coat from my bed. I hung it up in my closet so it was out of the way.

"So... why did you bring me up here?" he asked, looking around my room.

"So we could have some privacy and because I hate parties," I said. "Were you even listening?"

He shrugged. "I tend to zone out sometimes."

"Come," I said as I jumped onto my bed. "I require cuddles."

"You have a pretty nice room," he said as I clicked on my lamp.

"Turn off the lights first," I said, pointing over to the switch beside my door.

He groaned and turned the lights off and then he walked back over to me. I lifted the covers up for him and he plopped down next to me. I scooted over a little to make more room for him.

"You're a cutie," I said as he laid himself down next to me.

"Do you have any food?"

"I do," I said. I reached my arm back to my other pillow and pulled out a bag of sour gummy worms. "I kept these babies for just such an occasion."

"Me being in your bed?" he asked, taking the bag from me.

I shook my head. "No, being in bed and wanting food. Why would I want to *leave* my bed to get food?"

Evan stuffed four of the gummy worms in his mouth. "These are good."

"Good thing I have two more bags," I said, taking one from the bag and eating it.

"This is a nice way to spend New Year's Eve, don't you think?"

I shrugged with my one shoulder that wasn't pinned to the mattress. "I suppose it is."

"Do you have any resolutions for the New Year?" he asked.

"Get fit, eat healthy," I replied. "Just the usual stuff that people say but never do."

"For real, is there anything you wanna do or improve on?"

"I guess I could learn to get over things in the past," I said flatly. "Or maybe learn the guitar. Yeah, let's go with that."

"I'll help," he said, sticking another two gummy worms into his mouth.

"Do you have any resolutions to make?"

He shrugged. "I mean, I guess I could make the resolution to not switch chemo drugs."

"Why's that?" I asked, cocking an eyebrow at him.

"This drug doesn't make me lose my hair," he said, taking off his beanie and rustling his hair. "See? No hair loss." He laid down his beanie on my nightstand and popped another worm into his mouth.

"I guess that's a kind of good one. I just meant more along the lines of something you have to do yourself."

"Kick cancer's ass," he said. "I don't really know what you want me to tell you. I'm pretty content with the way my life is right now. I got nothing to change, nothing to do, nothing to learn. I just like taking things as they come."

"Lame," I grumbled, putting two gummy worms in my mouth. "These aren't as sour as I want them to be."

"That's because all their sour is in your attitude," Evan stated.

I dropped my jaw and scoffed softly. "Rude." I couldn't even be mad at him if I tried, and I think he knew that, considering all he did was smirk back at me.

"Is there any last-minute wishes you wanna make before the year ends?" he asked.

"I wish for you to stop hogging all the blue-and-pink worms," I said, pushing around the gummy worms to find one of the last blue-and-pink ones in the bag.

"I'm sorry. They're the best kind," Evan said.

"I know," I said, putting a gummy worm in my mouth. "That's why I wanted them, ya jerk."

"Here," he said, putting a gummy worm between my lips. "You need more sugar in you."

"I need more you in me," I said, winking. "Psych! Nerd."

"You're a nerd."

"I know I'm a nerd. I've been a nerd for a long time. You're just mad because I'm gonna get a kick-ass job, and you're gonna be stuck in an entry-level accountant job, okay?"

"That's so cold, but it's also so true at the same time."

I winked at him. "You know that I got your back financially though."

"Do you though?"

"Yeah," I said. "Like, there's two possibilities with us dating. It's either we're staying together for life or we're gonna break up. And until we either die or break up, I totally got your back, it's a 50-50 split."

"That's kinda sad, eh?"

"What is?" I asked.

"That we're either gonna be together until one of us dies or that we're gonna break up at some point."

"Well, when you put it like that."

"Yeah, but all well. I think that's the beauty of it. It's a gamble," Evan stated. "It's either we do or we don't, and I guess that's just life."

"What about you?" I asked, looking over at my 24-hour clock. It was now 23:59. One minute left until midnight. "Any *last-minute* wishes?"

He shook his head. "I've got all that I want and need right in this bed with me: a working body and a beautiful girl."

"Touching," I said with a wink.

"You want your midnight kiss?" he asked.

I nodded and he pulled my face closer for a kiss. And it felt like time had frozen for the moment. There was no tomorrow, no yesterday, just this moment. I was frozen here. And then, before it even began, it was over.

He pulled away and went to open his mouth, "I love y—"

And then the clock struck midnight.

About the **Author**

D. I. Richardson is, at the time of writing this, a student at Durham College. He enjoys writing, napping, gaming, drinking coffee, staying up late, and learning things.

When it comes to writing D. likes to write about teen fiction, teen romance, young adult fiction, general fiction, fantasy, crime, and really anything he feels up for. He finds the most challenging part of writing to be getting the motivation to keep going when you're already halfway through a novel.

When he gets older, he hopes to still be writing and creating things in every facet of media and art that he can. His advice for writers, young and old, is to just keep writing. Even when it feels like you're completely tapped out of words, keep trying to get something written. Every word is one step closer to a finished product.

Made in the USA
Middletown, DE
11 September 2020